Eureka Man

A NOVEL

Patrick Middleton

Acer Hill Publishing Company
2014

Published in the United States by Acer Hill Publishing Company

LIBRARY OF CONGRESS CATALOGING--
--IN-PUBLICATION DATA

Eureka Man: a novel
p. cm.
Summary: "The story of a young man's journey through America's prison system and the irreversible choices he makes to survive"—Provided by publisher
ISBN-10: 1494224208
EBook ISBN-13: 978-1494224202
Library of Congress Control Number: 2013921953
CreateSpace Independent Publishing Platform,
North Charleston, South Carolina

1. Prison culture—Fiction. 2. Criminal justice system—Fiction.
3. Prison education—Fiction. 4. Hope—Fiction.
5. Pittsburgh (PA)— Fiction. I. Title.

FIRST EDITION

In memory of Michael and Huck

"Come, let's away to prison,
We two alone will sing like birds i' the' cage.
When thou dost ask me blessing, I'll kneel down
And ask of thee forgiveness. So we'll live,
And pray, and sing, and tell old tales, and laugh
At gilded butterflies, and hear poor rogues
Talk of court news; and we'll talk with them too:
Who loses and who wins, who's in, who's out;
And take upon the mystery of things,
As if we were God's spies; and we'll wear out,
In a wall'd prison, packs and sects of great ones
That ebb and flow by th' moon."

King Lear

Eureka Man

1976

chapter one

OUT OF SIGHT of the judge, Oliver sighed and then trembled. Not so the deputy sheriffs flanking him could notice, but enough so his knees started to buckle halfway up the steps of the Valley Forge Training School for Boys. When he paused and glanced down at his shackles, both deputies held on to his elbows and told him to take his time. For the rest of the way up the steps he listened to the metallic clicking of the chains and there were no more outward signs of trembling.

Nor when he entered the receiving room and saw thirteen pairs of eyes staring at him. While one deputy handed his commitment papers to the female clerk, the other removed his handcuffs and shackles, and Oliver shook the stiffness out of his wrists as he sized up the other boys. One wearing a blue knit watch-cap pulled down over his eyebrows glared at him and Oliver glared back. The clerk looked up from her paperwork and frowned at him. "Hey, you. Tall guy. Take a seat on the bench," she said, cracking her chewing gum like a pro.

Oliver licked his lips and shoved his hands down in the pockets of his blue jeans before he wedged himself between two boys who were sitting at the far end of the bench. Immediately he started pushing buttons inside his head until he found the one marked countenance. *You fellows better leave me the hell alone! Don't start any trouble and there won't be any! I'm not afraid of you punks!*

For the next two hours he and the other new arrivals moved in and out of the barber's chair, the medical examiner's room, and the psychologist's office. When it was his turn, the psychologist asked him if he knew where he was, and Oliver said, "Yes, sir. Reform school. What kind of question is that?"

"What day is this?"

"Hey, man. I'm not crazy."

"Just answer the question, please."

"January 23rd, 1976."

The man nodded and in a pleasant, conversational tone, said, "Thank you. Now tell me what brought you here."

Oliver shifted his weight in the chair. "Robbery."

"Let me hear about it."

"Well, I was a long way from home and I needed gas money so I robbed this little country store. That's all there was to it."

"Did you have a gun?"

"No, sir. I poked my finger out from inside my jacket like this." He made a fist and then stuck out his index finger.

"I see. You said you were a long way from home. Where's home?"

"Southern Maryland. Know where that is?"

"I'll ask the questions. What were you doing in Pennsylvania?"

"Hell, I didn't even know I was in this damn state until a cop pulled me over."

"Watch your language, young man." His admonition was clipped off by the slam of a door down the hall. "It says here you assaulted your stepfather hours before you were picked up on this robbery. You want to talk about that?"

Oliver sat bolt upright, stiff. "Assault? That's a lie, man! He was the one doing the assaulting. He had my mother tied up and bent over the dumbwaiter in our dining room when I came in the door. And he had a handful of her hair wrapped around his goddamn fist! All I did was help her get away. I was defending her. Would you let a man do that to your mother?"

"Again. I'll ask the questions. So what'd you do to him? Your stepfather."

"I broke a wicker chair over his back."

"I see. Now tell me. What was the last grade you completed in school?"

2

"I'm *in* the twelfth grade. I'm supposed to graduate this spring, and the Mother Superior where I go to school said my SAT scores are high enough to get me into the college of my choice. I've got three scholarship offers already."

"Well, that's quite impressive. Have you thought about a career choice?"

"Yes, I have. My Aunt Florence, she's an amateur genealogist, and she spent years tracing our family tree all the way back to the early 1800s. My ancestors have been cobblers, bricklayers, merchants, engineers, blacksmiths, nuns and you name it. Except for doctors. I'm going to be the first person in my family to become a doctor. I haven't decided what kind yet. I might be a heart surgeon or a pathologist, or maybe even a college professor."

"Well, it's good that you have such high ambitions. While you're here you can study for the high school equivalency examination. Do you have any questions?"

"Yes, sir. When can I call my mother?"

"In thirty days. Any other questions?"

"No, sir."

"Okay. Tell the next boy to come in. And good luck to you, son."

After the last boy saw the doctor, Oliver counted thirteen heads in front of him as they marched out the back door of the administration building and onto the main grounds of the training school. The January wind stung his freshly shaved head during the long march across a parade field that was flanked by a row of white cottages three stories high on either side. When they stopped at the last cottage on the right, Oliver read the words on the brass plaque over the door: Welcome to DoRight Cottage. He followed the line to the basement where each boy was issued a set of bed linens, two towels and a washcloth, three pairs of khaki trousers and three shirts, socks, underwear, a cap, a pair of dress shoes and work boots, a navy pea coat, a toothbrush, a bar of soap, five postage stamps, four Buckhorns, and a small comb.

While the boys were stowing their belongings in their assigned lockers, a short, squat white woman appeared at the foot of the basement steps. She wore an oversized lime green dress, her hair was

3

sparse and unruly and there was a mole on her chin the size of a lima bean. In her left hand she carried a black cane and when all but a few boys were staring at her, she rapped it against one of the wall lockers. Her face was void of friendliness. "Listen up, boys!" the woman bellowed. "I'm Mrs. Ronnie John, your cottage mom. During your stay in my cottage you will conduct yourselves like gentlemen at all times. That means no horse playing, no bullying and no fighting. If you misbehave you will not see the light of day for the rest of the time you are in my care. Any questions?"

Later that night the door to Room 34 slammed shut and the trembling moved from Oliver's legs up through his chest. He sat on the edge of the bed and stared at the heavy black screen covering the window and then at the furnishings in the room. A toilet, sink, bed, desk and chair. He stood again and paced the length of the room several times before he stopped and stretched his arms out to measure the width of the room. Not even six feet. The revelation that the room was a prison cell stirred the butterflies in his stomach and when the trembling got worse, he laid on the bunk, covered his eyes with his arm and recalled something he had memorized in his eleventh grade logic class. A passage from the Red Queen's lecture to *Alice*: "Down here we got our act clean yesterday and we plan to start getting our act clean tomorrow. But we never clean up our act today." The Red Queen's logic was all the inspiration he needed to clean up his own act right then and there. When he told himself they couldn't keep him past his eighteenth birthday and that day was only nine months and three days away, he sighed, then smiled, and there were no signs of trembling at all.

With the bell at dawn he and the other thirteen new arrivals awoke to the feel of wool rags and wooden floor brushes, the smell of orange paste wax, and the sound of Mrs. Ronnie John's bellowing voice. "All right! Listen up, everybody! I said listen up! Don't make me have to say it again! You're going to need every bit of energy you can muster up this morning, so I would advise you to eat every morsel of food on your tray!"

All morning, every morning for six weeks they paste waxed and polished the burnt-red cement floors until their knees opened like tomatoes. Mrs. Ronnie John walked behind them checking their work as they pushed and pulled the gray shine rags and wooden floor brushes over every inch of floor in DoRight Cottage. Oliver worked between two boys named Philly Dog and Funky Melvin, but not one spoke to the other while they worked. Their body language said it all: "Missed a spot; I got it." "I need a break; can you help me?" "Heads up, here she comes."

Sitting side by side and rubbing the scabs on their knees one evening, Philly Dog said, "What you in for, Priddy?"

Oliver glanced sideways and said, "A stupid ass robbery, man."

"Hey, I know that accent! You talk just like my cousins from Newport News, Virginia. You ain't from around here, are you?"

"Nope. Other side of Baltimore. Southern Maryland." He said it with pride. "Never been in Pennsylvania before in my life. I should have kept my ass below the Mason-Dixon Line."

"You got that right, my man."

"Why do you say that?"

"Cause you don't know one motherfucker in this joint, do you?"

"Nope. But what's that got to do with anything?"

"Well, no offense, but you look like you should be in prep school instead of reform school."

"That's funny. That's real funny. I *was* in a prep school. Our Lady Star of the Sea. And guess what? Once the Mother Superior told me I should be in a reform school instead of a prep school."

"You're shitting me."

"No I'm not."

"That *is* funny, man."

"Yeah, but why did you say I should be in a prep school?"

"Cause you look too fresh and clean to be in this place. Somebody's bound to try you."

SIX WEEKS and they were off their knees and on their way to another cottage on the rolling green hill. The frailest went to Mary Cullen Cottage, named after the widow of the late founder of the place. The most illiterate were sent to Woodcock Cottage where they received remedial instruction six hours a day. Oliver and his floor-shine companions were escorted straight to the Cottage of Hard Knocks. The night they arrived Oliver stood at a urinal conjuring up images of running water when a fight broke out behind him.

"You ain't tough, nigger!"

"Lemme show you!"

In midstream Oliver heard the punches but didn't turn around to see them. *Hey, fellows! I don't mean to rain on your parade but I gotta piss!* He shook off the last drops and turned around just in time to see blood spatter against the wall. No one saw the pool ball until it rolled across the floor smeared with the blood of the boy who said lemme show you. The boy was on the floor looking up at the culprit. Six-four, two-forty, with a hairy face molded in a scowl, the culprit looked more like a member of the training school staff than a juvenile delinquent. Oliver had been around bullies before but this fellow they called Jimmy Six took the grand prize. The victim, a black boy who didn't weigh a buck forty, was the one who should have rightfully had the pool ball. He had a gash over his left eye and the blood pouring from it ran right down into his eye.

That night the Man came and interviewed each boy one at a time and each said he didn't see a thing. At the breakfast table the next morning, Mrs. Viola Plenty, the cottage mom, said, "Okay! Since none of you saw what happened to Ron-Ron last night you can all see the inside of this cottage for the next thirty days! No movies, no canteen, and no playing ball! And during your free time you can all strip, wax and shine every inch of floor in this place! Any questions? Anybody want to hit *me* in the head with a pool ball?"

They called her the crazy bitch with the cock-teasing hug. One minute Mrs. Viola Plenty was consoling a boy so close their groins kissed and the next she was beating him into submission. Those who had known her closeness also knew her finest feature, her chocolate-brown skin. Even those who had known her wrath were wild about her smooth-as-velvet chocolate-brown skin and her black corkscrews for hair and her thick, round hips. What kept them at bay was her smile. More than flawless teeth, it was an admonition, uninviting and unamused.

Oliver listened to the stories the other boys told about her and waited for confirmation of his own that she was stone crazy. The proof came one Sunday afternoon when P-Rat smacked Little Andy on the backside with a dishtowel. Mrs. Viola Plenty dropped the number-ten can of green beans she was retrieving from the pantry and smacked P-Rat across the back of his thighs with a wiffleball bat.

"Do you want to be incorrigible forever?" she said in outrage. "If you do you'd better find somewhere else to practice!" She grabbed Little Andy by the scruff of the neck and swung the bat at his ass as if she was hitting curve balls. *Wham!* "Repeat after me!" *Wham!* "I will not horseplay when I'm supposed to be drying dishes!" *Wham!*

After that Oliver took his time and got every black mark and speck of food off every pot and pan put in front of him. He would neither talk nor look at the other boys while he worked. His scrutiny was solely for the grease and grime on the pots and pans. So he was astonished when she slid up beside him in his third week at the kitchen sink and said, "Priddy, come with me!"

He followed her up two flights of steps to her third floor apartment and on the way he wondered if she was going to molest him or knock him into the next day for mistaking a speck of food for a stain. But when they got inside her apartment it wasn't like that. He surveyed the dirty laundry sleeping on the lampshades and end tables, in the dusty corners and on the backs of the sofa and love seat; the cups and saucers and crusty plates that looked like abstract art strewn about the coffee table. He was amazed by the filth and stench in the room but he knew better than to show it.

"Priddy, I need someone to clean this place up," she said matter-of-factly. "Someone I can depend on. Can I depend on you?"

"Yes, you can, Mrs. Plenty. I'm very dependable, ma'am."

"Good. You can start in the kitchen. Take your time and do a good job. You don't have to clean everything up in one afternoon. Save some for tomorrow. Here's a pack of cigarettes and a book of matches. You'll have to return what you don't smoke before you go downstairs for supper. I can't have anyone accusing me of playing favorites. You understand, don't you, Priddy?"

"Yes, ma'am, I do."

"All right. Now there are sodas in the refrigerator when you want one, but don't drink them all. Any questions?"

"No ma'am, I'll just get started."

"Good. I'll be around to check on you later."

When she was gone he opened the Kools and took out five. He lit one and carefully stashed the other four down his sock, making sure they were parallel to his leg so they didn't snap in half. Though he had never smoked a cigarette a day in his life before he arrived at the Valley Forge Training School for Boys, he knew how to look cool doing it. He let the cigarette hang from his mouth the way he'd seen James Cagney do it so many times on the silver screen, turning his head sideways to keep the smoke from getting in his eyes.

He opened the refrigerator door and took out a grape Nehi. After gulping it down he washed every last dish in the sink and on the counter tops. Then he gathered two stacks of cups and saucers and plates from all over the living room and washed them too. Later he cleaned the refrigerator and stove and drank another grape Nehi. When it was time to leave, Mrs. Viola Plenty revealed her perfect white teeth when she smiled and said, "Very decent job, Priddy. I'll see you tomorrow."

The next day he cleaned the living room and helped her change the sheets on her queen-size bed. He stood on one side and pulled down the sheet, making a neat hospital corner the way his mother June had shown him when he had been old enough to make his own bed. Mrs. Viola Plenty did the same on her side and when she leaned over, he saw the curves of her chocolate-brown breasts. Just before he stood and turned sideways to hide his erection, she leaned against the dresser, shifted her weight and stood on one foot scratching the back of her velvet calf with her painted red toenail. It was a quiet and sensuous gesture that filled him with excitement and gratitude. "How would you like to work for me every day, Priddy?" she asked.

"That would be fine, Mrs. Plenty."

"Good. From now on you'll be my helper. I want you to report to work up here every morning after breakfast."

"Yes, ma'am! I'll be here on time too. I guess I'll clean the bathroom now if that's all right."

"Just be careful with my ceramic gee-gaws over the toilet. My late husband Joe won those for me in Atlantic City. Ever been to Atlantic City, Priddy?"

"No, ma'am, but I've been to Ocean City, Maryland many times."

"You have? Ever eat salt water taffy?"

"Yes, ma'am."

"You like?"

"Yes, indeed, ma'am."

"Well, I have three different flavors and maybe I'll give you some after you clean the bathroom."

"I'd really appreciate that, Mrs. Plenty."

Inside her bathroom, Oliver closed the door, squeezed his groin and looked around the room for things that were familiar to him. A box of Kotex. A jar of Pond's skin cream. A bra and matching panties hanging in the shower. Lavender panties that aroused him and made him recall the budding girls he had kissed and fondled behind the school auditorium stage, in the aisles of the public library and the back corners of the movie theater. He took the lavender panties off the line and ran the bath water so she wouldn't hear him. Then he placed the panties against his lips, closed his eyes and pictured what he had just seen of Mrs. Viola Plenty's chocolate-brown breasts. He was through before he breathed her scent and when he ejaculated, he leaned against the door, excited to giddiness, and muffled a grateful sigh.

Even though there was no rabbit's foot in his pocket, he felt lucky every morning he walked into her apartment and straightened out a knickknack or a doily. Scooping orange marmalade right out of the jar with his fingers. Smuggling candy bars, sodas and cigarettes downstairs to trade for other loot. Listening to his favorite Sam Cooke records on her hi-fi. Not a bad way to work off punishment. The sheer joy of smelling her perfume and other feminine things made it all easy for him. And though she didn't waste a lot of words because she didn't have many, there was much small talk. About her dead husband Joe whose picture was on every wall of her apartment, how wonderful he

9

had been and how he had died after having his throat slit in a Friday night crap game. Also she told him about her twin sister who had died at birth so that Mrs. Viola Plenty could live. Also she showed him photographs of poor black children that made him homesick for some of his childhood playmates. Also she taught him how to sew buttons on his shirt and iron a stiff crease in his trousers.

The day he broke the cottage record for scoring the highest on the high school equivalency examination, she rewarded him with a phone call to his mother and a dozen lemon cupcakes. He had been trying to reach his mother for three months and this time she was home when he called. "It's about time we heard from you!" his mother June said, pretending to be sarcastic. "How are you getting along, son? When are you coming home?" He was fine he told her, and he would be there in a few months. The last thing she said before she said goodbye was, "Remember what you promised me in that courtroom, Oliver. Take whatever you have coming to you on the chin, son. Don't lose your temper."

When he hung up the phone, Mrs. Viola Plenty said, "Tell me about your parents, Oliver." He started off by bragging that his mother was a horticulturist and the hippest woman in the world. She used to have a drinking problem, but not anymore. Now she devoted her time to the local historical society designing flower gardens and leading tours around the estate of Dr. Samuel Mudd, the man who had set the broken leg of the man who had assassinated President Abraham Lincoln. "And you should see her dance, Mrs. Plenty. She can sing and dance like you wouldn't believe. As for my real father, his name was Ernie Boy and he left us when I was five. Then we had a no-good stepfather whose name was Ernie Boy also, so we called him Ernie Boy the Second. We, meaning my older brother Skip and my older sister Anna. Anyway, to make a long story short, Ernie Boy the Second liked to argue and fight all the time. I could be sucking on a fireball and he would swear it was a cherry bomb."

"I read in your file that you assaulted him," she said. "Is that true?"

"Yes, well, I was protecting my mother, Mrs. Plenty. See, things had been awfully bad at home for quite some time, so my brother

Skip and I were living with our grandfather at the time. One afternoon I stopped in to check on my mother and Ernie Boy the Second was there. He had her tied up in the dining room with her clothes ripped off. He was lying on her back when I broke a chair over his back. I swear I would have killed that sucker if I had a gun, Mrs. Plenty." As he was telling her these things she let her fingers fall on the back of his neck and so light was the touch that he let his head rest on her shoulder. He kept it there until she told him he'd have to be going downstairs soon and she had more work planned for him the next day.

If walking out of her apartment at four o'clock every afternoon was like coming off the lam, the rowdy boys in the basement lavatory were like the hounds that tracked him down. Every evening when he went there to shower or relieve himself, he thought the crisscross of tips and advice he heard sounded like a bunch of handicappers at a racetrack. Soap and water removed the ink marks from used postage stamps so you could use them again and a dab of toothpaste worked as well as a drop of glue for securing the stamp to another envelope. Covering glass with masking tape during a midnight burglary stopped the glass from shattering and cut down on the noise. Pressing a double-edge razor blade into the heated end of a toothbrush made a fine-ass weapon.

And spit worked as well as grease when there wasn't any grease. The same boy Oliver saw bawling his eyes out the day the barber plowed off his dreadlocks he saw on the shower floor one night giving pleasure to the biggest boy in the cottage. Oliver walked across the shower room as if the scene was something he'd seen a hundred times before. He took the corner shower and watched out of the corner of his eye as Jimmy Six spit into the palm of his hand, stroked himself with it and then lay on the boy's back. Oliver had heard stories about boys being sodomized, but he had never witnessed the act before. As he watched Jimmy Six thrust himself into the boy, he squeezed his own anus tighter than a vise. For a split second the two exchanged glares and Jimmy's cold grey eyes and feral grunts reminded Oliver of a junkyard dog he'd once fought off with a tire iron.

MRS. VIOLA PLENTY CONCEDED nothing but seemed uneasy at the choice of leaving her sofa where it was or going downstairs to find help moving it. When she said let's try one more time, Oliver was all nods and conciliatory grunts. The sofa weighed a ton and this time when she couldn't lift her end she went downstairs to find someone to help them. Minutes later she returned with Jimmy Six who was smiling like a mental patient. He picked up his end like he was picking up a sock.

"Over here against the wall, boys. Not too close. Don't scuff the paint."

"How's that, Miss Plenty?" Jimmy Six asked.

"Okay, I guess. Now I'll have to figure out what to do about those circles on the carpet."

"They'll go away in no time, Miss," Jimmy Six said. "I used to work for a moving company. Have Priddy here go over them with the vacuum cleaner a few times and they'll disappear before you know it."

"You think so, Jimmy?"

"I know so, Miss Plenty."

"All right. Would you like a couple of cigarettes for helping us?"

Jimmy Six blinked at the offer but didn't comment. He merely thanked her when she extended the two Kools to him.

"That's it, boys. Thanks a lot."

Jimmy Six ambled silently behind Oliver all the way to the basement locker room. "Man, that was really something, Priddy."

"What's that?"

"You know. Seeing how the other half lives around here."

"Huh?"

"You know what I'm talking about. You got it made, don't you?"

Oliver made his voice pleasant, but he knew something was developing. "How do you figure?"

"Come on, you're up there all day with that crazy bitch and I know she gives you all kinds of fringe benefits. The way I see it you're either hand washing her nasty drawers or you've got your hands inside them. Which is it, Priddy? You tapping that?"

"Are you kidding me?"

"Do I sound like I'm kidding?"

"That's real funny. First, she's not my type. Second, she's too old for me and third, she's crazy."

"Not your type or not your gender?"

"What?"

"Maybe you don't like women. You walk on the wild side, Priddy?"

"Very funny."

"Why aren't you laughing then?"

"Cut the shit, Jimmy."

"OK, let's talk business."

Oliver opened his locker and took out his soap dish, washcloth and towel. "What's on your mind?"

"What's on my mind is I want a piece of the action."

"What action?"

Jimmy Six sighed as if his patience was being tried. "You think I'm stupid, Priddy? I see you passing off cigarettes to that nigger Philly Dog almost every day and I know he trades them off for cupcakes and postage stamps and all kinds of other shit for you. I know everything that goes on around here. You're pretty fucking slick. I've got to give you that. But dig this. I've got a real bad nicotine Jones, and four Buckhorns a day ain't getting it. You're gonna cut me in on your little racket and that's all there is to it."

Oliver smiled and so did Jimmy Six. "Wait a minute, I get a few extra cigarettes and you think I'm supposed to cut you in, is that it?"

"Not exactly. See, it ain't what I think, it's what I want, and what I want is four Kools every day starting tomorrow."

Oliver slung the towel over his shoulder. "I'm not giving you shit, Jimmy."

"Listen, Priddy, you're a real smooth dude, and you're probably real tough, I don't know. But I want to show you something. Come here for a minute."

"Look, I'm going to wash up, man." He was decisive, too, and he was proud of the arrogance in his voice.

"No, no, you have to see this now. It won't take a minute." Oliver sighed and followed Jimmy Six to his locker. Jimmy opened the door and pointed. "Look at that."

13

In what seemed to him like a nonchalant and slow motion, Oliver looked inside Jimmy Six's locker and saw a men's magazine sitting on top of a bag of Oreos. *Black Amazons.* "OK, so what? You've got a smut magazine. Congratulations."

Jimmy Six smirked. "Look at the address label, dumb ass."

After Oliver had time to read Joe Plenty's name, Jimmy Six lowered his voice. "Now if you don't want that magazine to wind up in your black mammy's hands you'll do what I tell you. Starting with four cigarettes a day." Jimmy Six slammed his locker. "And I already know that you stole more than just this one cause I saw your nigger buddy with two other ones last night when he rented this one to me. You're slick, Priddy. Real goddamn slick. I'm looking forward to being your partner."

Oliver smiled but he was not amused. "Are you kidding? I'm not going to be your fucking partner. No goddamn way. Go ahead and show her the magazine. That's the same as being a rat, Jimmy. If you want to be labeled a rat, go ahead and give it to her. I don't give a fuck."

"Who you calling a rat?"

"You're standing here trying to blackmail me, Jimmy. That's some jive shit. I'll take an ass whipping before I let somebody blackmail me."

Oliver sensed the blow was coming a split second too late. Just as he was backing up, Jimmy Six punched him in the center of his chest and knocked him to the floor. He got up quickly and backed up to give himself more room. The ebony handle of the knife glittered in his hand.

Jimmy Six laughed when he saw it. "Well, I'll be goddamn! There's only one place you could have gotten a switchblade in this joint. First you stole Mr. Plenty's woman, then you stole his smut magazines, and now you've stolen his knife. I like you, Priddy, I really do. You've got balls, kid."

Oliver smiled. "That's right, Jimmy. And if you put your hands on me again, I'm gonna cut your fucking throat."

The other boys were forming a circle around them now. Jimmy Six pulled his sweatshirt off and wrapped it around his left fist while the boys jeered and shouted.

"It's on now!"

"Give 'em room to swing!"

"Stick him! Stick him, Priddy. Stick that big motherfucker!"

The shouts provided enough curiosity for the Man to push through the circle and interrupt what was about to get good.

"All right, all right! That's enough of this."

Oliver put the knife away as fast as he'd brought it out.

"You two boys cool it. We're not going to have any fighting in here. Priddy, you go in the television room. Six, you stay in here."

Everywhere he went for the next three days, Oliver listened to the two/two beat of his own footsteps while he gripped the switchblade inside the front pocket of his pants. Each time he and Jimmy Six crossed paths, he held his finger on the button and waited. On the fourth day, when there were no more signs of hostility in Jimmy's demeanor, Oliver returned the switchblade to the back of Mrs. Viola Plenty's utensil drawer where he had found it. Confident for having stood up to the biggest bully he had ever known and won, and sixty-two days away from gaining his freedom, he stepped into the shower room and was immediately blindsided by a haymaker that knocked him to the floor and almost into a coma. He tried to call out who was the coward cocksucker, but the only syllable he could utter was cow. Dazed and dizzy, he swiveled his head in Jimmy Six's direction, squinting through watery eyes and white sparks as he attempted to push himself up.

"Where's that blade now, Priddy boy? You were gonna stick me the other day, weren't you? Weren't you, punk?"

Jimmy Six banged Oliver's head off the concrete floor twice and then turned him over on his stomach and yanked off his boxers. Oliver tried again to get on his feet, but Jimmy kicked him in the ribs and then slammed his boot into the side of Oliver's head. With the last blow he lost consciousness.

What came to him when he came to a couple of minutes later, what rose above the bells and flashing sparks in his head, were vials of battery acid, switchblades and baseball bats. Slowly, gradually, he sat up, his arms around his knees, staring through the slits of his swollen eyes as though he were in a movie. His lip was split in three places and he thought his cheekbone was broken, and though both his hands were soaked with the blood pouring from his nose, a little still trickled down.

He got to his feet and staggered along the wall until he reached the corner shower. After he retched and vomited up nothing, he turned on the nozzle, lifted his hands to shield his eyes from the sting and saw rivulets of shit and blood flowing over his ankles, turning into mud. He squatted in the muddy water, peed in it. He waited and he killed. The vandals who had stolen the Welcome to Pennsylvania sign; the judge who had sent him there; and Ernie Boy the Second for what he had done to his mother. After he washed himself a hundred times, he walked out of the room, still panting. Four of Jimmy Six's boys were standing in the hall staring at his nakedness as he walked past them and into the equipment room at the end of the hall. Their eyes were wide but noncommittal when he walked back out of the room with a Louisville Slugger leaning against his shoulder. A tear was trapped in the corner of one eye as he walked past the four boys and through the door. Jimmy Six was reaching for the baby powder in the back of his locker when Oliver raised the bat over his head. He did not ponder the force or angle of the blow, but merely followed in its wake.

HE FELT THE NIGHT watchman's long, cold fingers thrust between his shirt and his belt. Beneath his feet he could feel the winding steel of the staircase to the basement of the solitary confinement cottage, could smell the moldy, stale air. At the threshold of the cell door, he placed his hand on his chest and turned slowly to the night watchman, his face a pious oval in the shadows. The night watchman's mouth was open and he closed it before saying, in a voice made paternal by experience, "Let me give you some advice, young man. When you get to the penitentiary, keep your head up and lose that fear in your eyes." The man gently placed one of his large hands on Oliver's shoulder. "Step in, son," he added softly.

The door slammed behind Oliver and his chest rose and fell, rose and fell under his hand.

1977

chapter two

RIVERVIEW PENITENTIARY'S FIRST annual Memorial Day fast-pitch softball game between the Vanguard Jaycees and the Pennsylvania Lifers Association had been brazenly advertised as the "Mother of All Softball Games." This was because it was known that the Lifers Association's new pitcher, Calvin Africa, had once pitched a one-hit shutout against the internationally famous King and His Traveling All-stars. According to the bold print on the bulletin board flyers, Calvin would pitch to every Vanguard batter from behind second base while wearing a blindfold.

The game drew a bigger crowd than the donkey softball exhibition between the guards and the Jaycees had two years earlier. Packed in the bleachers on the first base side of the infield was a mural of black and white faces belonging to the prisoners from Homewood, the Hill District and other ethnically mixed Pittsburgh neighborhoods. On the third base side was the entire entourage of North Philly prisoners who had shown up on the breeziest, sunniest day of 1977 just to keep an eye on their downtown rivals who were sitting in the shade fifty feet away down the left-field sideline. After eyeing their foes back, the South Philly gang seemed convinced that the sky-blue hue of the sky would keep the blood-red red of the Norris Street, Oxford Street and Diamond Street boys content for at least a day. Pigeons that had escaped the city streets and pebbled sidewalks agreed and found refuge on the rooftops of the hundred year old clapboard buildings beyond the outfield fence--the prison chapel, the Young Guns Boxing

Gym, and the Free Yourself Law Library. Even the thirty or forty red-necks and born-agains sitting behind home plate felt safe enough to cheer for their team, the all-white Vanguard Jaycees, and wave their homemade banners while the sandwich peddlers, clothing merchants and queens walked by.

Early Greer, the head orderly and only horticulturist inside Riverview Penitentiary, was sitting in the top row of the Pittsburgh bleachers reading the *Post Gazette* and socializing with his friends, Peabo, Oyster and Bell. Early tapped his index finger against the front page and said, "Another niggah's on his way to jail. This guy caught his wife fucking a dog and shot her three times."

Peabo didn't take his eyes off the batter, but said, "That's a crime of passion if ever there was one."

"What about the dog?" Oyster asked. "He kill the dog too?"

"We betting or what, Peabo?" Early said.

"Read the details first."

Early straightened out the paper and read the story. "'Forty-six year old Maurice Wiley from Bruston Hill in Homewood was arrested yesterday morning for killing his wife in their home at 461 Mayview Street. According to police, Wiley discovered his wife, forty-two year old Mabel Joyce Wiley, engaged in a sexual act with Wiley's American Bull Terrier and shot her once in the head and twice in the chest. Wiley is being held without bail in the Allegheny County Jail.'"

When it was apparent that Early was through, Peabo said, "That's a simple crime of passion."

"Nah," said Early. "Three shots was overkill, man. I say he gets life."

"Life!" said Oyster. "For a crime of passion? Shouldn't no man get life for a crime of passion. That's what those crackers did to me."

Bell looked at Oyster when Oyster uttered the word cracker.

"Okay, Early. Let's bet. How much?"

"The usual," Early said. "Loser buys ice cream for a week."

"You're on."

"What about the dog?"

"What about the damn dog, Oyster?" said Early. "You're not making one bit of sense. It wasn't the dog's fault. A dog ain't got no sense."

"Well, it'd have to go just the same. I wouldn't want no dog hanging around my house after it's been with my woman."

Early pulled out a stack of three by five index cards from his shirt pocket and wrote Maurice Wiley's name on one and then recorded the bet Early and Peabo had just made. Ever since they had made a game out of betting on new arrestees, Early had been keeping stats on each one: name, age, race, type of crime and location, amount of bail, name of the judge, and any other relevant facts he could glean from the newspaper or the six o'clock news. Before laying down a bet, he usually studied his facts like a statistician, unless the bet was a sure thing. Maurice Wiley was a sure thing. Maurice Wiley had committed premeditated murder and Early was certain the man would receive nothing less than a life sentence.

A band of young bucks walking by the bleachers transfixed them for several seconds, as did Tommy Lovechild, a born-again pedophile who was sitting on the bottom bleacher handing out Jesus Saves tracts. "Give yourselves to Jesus, brothers, and you can enter the kingdom of heaven." Two of the young bucks stared at Tommy, not sure if they wanted Jesus' kingdom or to knock the smirk off Tommy Lovechild's pitted white face. Tommy stared back and said, "You can curse me out, brothers, and you can beat me black and blue, but I'll love you just the same." The taller of the two young bucks smacked Tommy's hat off his head and told him to shut the fuck up.

"That man's out!" cried Bell. The runner on third base tagged up and scored on a shallow fly ball to left-center. "He's out, ump!" Bell's protest was drowned out by the B&O railroad cars rattling along the banks of the Ohio River just beyond the prison wall.

"Bell, you know damn well you can't see that good," said Oyster.

Bell, who had lost his left eye somewhere along the Ho Chi Minh Trail, said, "I can see better than that umpire. That man was out!"

Early, Oyster and Peabo joked with Bell, but never argued with him. Not because they feared the five-one, hundred and twenty pound white man, but, rather because of where he had been. "*La rue sans joie,*" the Street Without Joy. Shortly after arriving at Riverview four years ago, Bell had stood up at his first lifers meeting to tell the members something about himself and ended up taking them to the Phong Dien district of South Vietnam, 1970, where his Third Battalion of the 187 Infantry had gone to support a pacification program. *La rue sans joie* was where Bell had lost his left eye while rescuing a seven-year-old girl from a burning hamlet. When he described with piercing poignancy how he had passed the little girl's body to the medic while her skin remained in the crook of his arms and how, seconds later, a mortar exploded five feet from where he stood on *La rue sans joie*, Early knew by the way Bell had uttered those four French words, *La rue sans joie,* that Bell was permanently astonished and in need of a friend. That was four years ago and since then, Bell had been spending every spring and summer evening watching softball games and eating ice cream sandwiches with Early, Oyster, and Peabo on the top row of the first base bleachers.

Bell stood and stretched between innings and said, "This game reminds me of 'Casey at the Bat.'"

"Casey? Who the hell's Casey?" Oyster asked.

"You never heard the poem, 'Casey at the Bat'? It's famous. It's about a baseball team that was losing a big game just like these guys are. 'The outlook wasn't brilliant for the Mudville Nine that day.'"

"We don't read no poems where I come from, Bell," Oyster said.

The Lifers had the bases loaded for the second time in the inning. Peabo bit into the fried onions on the corner of his sandwich and nudged Bell who was already sniggering. Oyster spit out a popcorn kernel and hollered for the umpire to invoke the mercy rule. Early laid the newspaper in his lap to stare at a prisoner who was standing near the right field fence. Early couldn't see his face. All he could see was a tall lanky fellow, wide at the shoulders, standing with his back to the game and apparently gazing at Early's flowerbeds on the other side of the fence. When he finally turned around, what Early saw was a young man whose beauty bloomed along with the sweet Williams, morning glories and chrysanthemums. "That's him," Early said. "Remember that boy we read about who killed a boy in reform school last summer?"

"Used a baseball bat, didn't he?" said Peabo.

"Yeah. We didn't want to bet on the outcome because he was just a kid."

"Don't say *we*!" Oyster said. "I wanted to bet. He was a white boy and I said right from the start he'd get off light because he was white."

"Yeah, well, you were wrong," Early said. "They gave him life. I read about him in my neighbor's hometown paper. That's him standing over there by the fence." Early pointed toward the first base foul line.

"He don't look like no killer to me," said Peabo.

"Looks more like a choir boy," said Oyster.

"Reminds me of *Billy Budd*," said Early.

"Billy Budd? Who the hell's Billy Budd? He in a poem too?"

"How do you know that's him?" asked Peabo.

"Cause they put him in a cell right up the tier from me when they brought him in two days ago. Read his door tag. His name's Priddy—Oliver Priddy."

"And lookie there!" said Oyster. "The booty bandit's on him already!"

"If he only knew what we knew."

"Yeah. He'd leave that Louisville slugger alone."

"You ain't never lied, Early."

"Kill the umpire!" Bell yelled. "That man was safe by a mile!"

No sooner did Bell protest another close call at home plate then the controversy died and two hundred and fifty pairs of eyes shifted to the new prisoner, Oliver Priddy. A passerby stopped dead in his tracks to sing about what they were looking at. "A fight! A fight! A nigger and a white! Look at that nigger beat that white!"

Early flexed the newspaper in his fist while he watched Winfield "Fat Daddy" Petaway knock Oliver to the ground, then stroll away before the guard in the number one tower could figure out what the commotion was all about. When Oliver got to his feet, he headed behind the backstop and paused right in front of the born-agains who were reciting Bible verses out loud. Early and the others watched Tommy Lovechild ease up to Oliver. "Do you know Jesus?" he asked. "Would you like to come and pray?"

The other born-agains gathered in a tight knot of seven on the bleachers and then separated into two lines of three with Deacon Bob up front. Then they jumped down and circled Oliver like a lynch mob.

Oliver reached for the hand that pressed into his shoulder. "Heal in the name of Jesus!" Tommy Lovechild prayed. But before he could say it again, Oliver grabbed his hand and bent it back until it folded like a hinge.

"Let go! Oh, God! Ple-e-e-ease let go!" Tommy cried before he fainted. It was only then that Oliver let go.

But the born-agains wouldn't leave well enough alone. The one called Swanee concentrated on Oliver's long sinewy arms while Deacon Bob tried to restrain him in a full Nelson. In one quick motion Oliver freed himself and found Bob's throat. It took several minutes for Swanee and the others to wrestle him to the ground where they laid hands on his prostrate body and began praying in tongues. Oliver struggled to get to his feet just as the goon squad turned the corner of the icehouse and trotted across the ball diamond.

"You men get back!" the fat sergeant shouted, waddling his tub of guts while he whirled a black baton over his head. "Get off that man!"

As quickly as the sergeant commanded, the born-agains dispersed and the guards beat down Oliver's flailing arms, handcuffed him and snatched him off the ground in one violent jerk. Even though the excitement was over, every prisoner on the yard watched in silence as the guards jacked Oliver up and carried him away to the redbrick Home Block.

The procession came down the first base line and Oliver swiveled his head toward the bleachers, apparently oblivious to the drip and slide of blood from his nose. "Hey, what the hell'd I do?" he asked. His voice was laden with incredulity.

NEAR THE REAR GATE, where the coal trucks, ambulance drivers and delivery vans rolled in, there was a two-story redbrick building with thick black screens and bars covering the windows. This building did not recede into its background of stonewall, nor harmonize with the white clapboard buildings in front of it—the Young Guns Boxing

24

Gym, the Free Yourself Law Library and the prison chapel. Rather, it imposed itself on the eye of every passerby in a manner that was both irritating and depressing. Official visitors who toured the prison every spring and summer—doctors, judges, law students, clergymen and juvenile delinquents on a scared straight tour—wondered aloud why the building hadn't been torn down. Over the years different interest groups had come to use different euphemisms when referring to this dilapidation. The prison administrators referred to it as the Behavioral Adjustment Unit, whereas the local chapter of the Pennsylvania Society for the Prevention of Cruelty to Prisoners called it the Solitary Confinement building. The guards and prisoners called it something else. They called it the Home Block. So named because it was home to the most incorrigible prisoners in Riverview Penitentiary. Home, also, to the sociopaths who turned the keys.

When Oliver was told to place his nose against the vestibule wall of the Home Block, he moved his head from side to side to think about it. The guards closed in before he made up his mind and a blue-eyed lieutenant slammed the end of his flashlight into Oliver's left kidney, causing his knees to buckle.

"You like to fight, boy? Stand up!"

Oliver stood as tall as his six three frame would let him. "That's the third time I've been knocked down today. What the hell'd I do?"

"Shut up, boy! Speak when you're told to speak! Now get naked, turn around and bend over."

Oliver followed orders. When he bent over, gas broke from his bowels and the stink knocked the guards back on their heels. The mean-ass lieutenant with the blue eyes held his breath and tried to grab Oliver by his elbow, but Oliver stood tall and spun around to face the man. Just as he did a guard drove his flashlight into Oliver's stomach, and made him lean forward. He took a couple of deep breaths and stood tall again. "I've had enough of this shit!" he said, and struck the lieutenant in the jaw with a left hook.

But it was the only punch he got in. After that it was as if all the bars and bricks and razor wire in the building came down on him, the way they lit into him. Two held him down while the blue eyed lieutenant punched him in the ribs. Then the guards circled and kicked him until he spit blood and mucous at them.

"I thought you liked to fight, boy! Why aren't you fighting?"

"Fuck you, man!" Oliver cried.

Under the gallery gate a sewer rat moved its tail and whiskers as it waited to taste the blood that flowed from Oliver's nose for the third time that day.

"Who am I, boy? Who am I!" the lieutenant demanded. Oliver tried to get to his feet but the lieutenant shoved him back down so hard his right arm snapped. When he tried to get up again, Lieutenant Blue Eyes planted his boot between Oliver's bare buttocks and held him down. "I'm the Man, you young punk! That's who I am!"

WHEN HE OPENED his eyes two days later, he was propped up in a bed in the prison hospital, his right arm sealed in Plaster of Paris. Before him on a tray was another tray divided into four compartments. In one compartment was a slice of ham, in another, black eyed peas, in another sweet potatoes, and in the smallest one, tapioca. Oliver stared at the soft colors. As he reached for the spoon, he winced at the pain in his arm.

"Use your other arm."

Cautious and wide-eyed, Oliver turned his head a little to the left and saw a brown-skinned man dressed in an apple green uniform standing there. The man's silver, wooly hair was parted high on the left side.

"We're not going to have any trouble today, are we, Priddy?"

Oliver looked up and down the man's uniform and then at the janitor who was pouring Lysol into a bucket in the middle of the ward. He could smell the strong antiseptic just before the stench of vomit from a patient two beds over became a reeking fog. He laid his head back on the pillow and tried not to breathe through his nose while he stared at the man in the apple green uniform.

"I'm not a doctor if that's what you're thinking," the man said. "The name's Early Greer and I'm a convict just like you. I hope you're not going to give me a hard time like you did yesterday. Because if you do, I'm telling you right now you're in for an ass-whipping."

Oliver looked confused. "What the hell did I do?"

"You don't remember? You overturned the breakfast tray and then you tried to knock me into the hall."

"Somebody kicked the shit out of me, man."

"That was three days ago."

"I thought I was dead."

"You're not dead."

Sweat slid from Oliver's armpits and down his sides. With extreme care Early lifted Oliver's broken arm and wiped the sweat away with a sponge. Then he picked up the spoon and placed it in Oliver's good hand. He hadn't eaten in two days and his appetite was ferocious even with the malodorous emanations in the room. As he fed himself with the large spoon, he concentrated on the pink and green of the ham, the dead eyes of the black-eyed peas, the orange ovals of the sweet potatoes and the creamy lumps of tapioca until they were all consumed.

"Those guards kicked the shit out of me, man." He wiped his mouth with the back of his hand.

"What did you do to piss them off?"

"Hell, they started it. The tall lieutenant with the blue eyes. Know who I'm talking about?"

"I know him well. Lieutenant Blue Eyes. He's a real bastard."

"Well, he pushed me into the wall and then shoved his flashlight into my back. Then he started yelling like a goddamn maniac. 'You think you're tough? You think you're tough? This is my jail, boy!' I didn't say a word. Not one goddamn word, Mr. Greyer."

"Greer. Early Greer. And you better learn something quick."

"Like what?"

"You can't beat them, son. They'll win every time. I know cause I used to fight them all the time."

"Yeah, but a guy's got to defend himself, doesn't he? I wasn't doing anything but minding my business. First this goddamn freak asked me if I wanted to be his friend. I told him to go find someone else to play with and he sucker-punched me. Then this other weirdo started touching me and asking me if I wanted to pray with him. All I did was make him take his hand off me. Then all his buddies jumped me. What was I supposed to do?"

"I've got two things to say to you, young buck. You've got a lot of time to do—"

"Hey, how do you know that?"

"Read about you in the newspaper. You killed a boy in reform school. So the paper said."

Oliver's face was knocked clean of meanness when he looked Early in the eyes. "The judge gave me life, Mr. Early. I can't imagine staying in here the rest of my life."

"You won't be here the rest of your life. Not unless you screw up some more."

"What do you mean? The judge gave me life."

"You can get out in fifteen. All you have to do is stay out of trouble and do something with your time. Go to school, learn a trade."

Oliver sat up, excited. "I might take up boxing."

"What? A clean-cut kid like you? You don't look like a boxer. Go to school and learn something."

"Wait a minute. You said you can get out in fifteen years. How long have you been in this place?"

Early hesitated. "Listen. There's three things you don't ask another con. How long he's been down, what he's in for, and how much time he's doing. I've been here seventeen years if you really want to know. I'm still here because that fifteen years I mentioned is the average a lifer does before he gets a pardon. But averages don't apply to every-one. Now right now I've got to go check on the patients in the next room. I'll stop in and see you again tomorrow."

As Early was turning to leave, Oliver said, "Hey, what's the other thing you wanted to say?"

"What?"

"You said a little while ago there were two things you wanted to tell me. What's the other thing?"

"You know that convict who wanted to be your friend?"

"Yeah. What about him?"

"His name is Winfield Petaway. They call him Fat Daddy. He's a notorious asshole bandit. He only messes with pretty white boys like you and he usually gets the ones he goes after. You should stay as far away from him as you can."

"Hell, I'm not afraid!" Oliver said it as if Early was the culprit. "I killed one guy for trying that shit! I can do it again if I have to!" Oliver clutched the bed sheet in the fist of his good hand and laid back trembling. The tendons in his neck rippled.

Early waited patiently and then he said, "A man's got to do what he's got to do. All I'm telling you is watch your back. Now I'll see you later. I've got to go do my job."

When Early was gone, Oliver laid his head back on the pillow and sighed heavily under the weight of memory and dread.

1978

chapter three

THE TWO CELL BLOCKS at 100 Ohio River Boulevard were light years away from being those bastions of oppression they once were. Long gone from the hundred year old cells were the once standard Gideon Bibles and natural light only. Gone, too, was the mandatory dead silence. In the official records these blocks were named North and South, but for the past forty years the residents had called them by another name: Little St. Regis and Big St. Regis, respectively, so named, according to local folklore, after the sleazy but still popular St. Regis Hotel located two blocks up the street from the prison in Pittsburgh's Manchester section. Both of these cell blocks were five stories high and a little longer than a football field. The cells in the big St. Regis, however, were significantly larger than those in the little St. Regis, hence the name big St. Regis.

For a long time counselors and other administrators fought the movement to rename these cell blocks. They simply refused to answer any correspondence that referred to big or little St. Regis. Who did these convicts think they were, trying to personalize the names of the buildings in which they were assigned to live? But eventually, some warden or assistant warden rightly decided that the euphemisms were harmless and the names big and little St. Regis became a part of every-one's lexicon.

To keep track of the residents' whereabouts, officials had long ago assigned letters to the tiers and numbers on the doors. In the little St. Regis the five tiers that looked out over the Ohio River were labeled

A through E from bottom to top; on the courtyard side, they were labeled F through J, top to bottom. On the big St. Regis the tiers on the courtyard side were labeled K through O, bottom to top, and on the riverside P through T, top to bottom.

The cells in these blocks called by any other name were still cells, so where was the harm in calling them a "hut" or a "house" or a "room" and changing the dècor? A cardboard box cut and assembled to specifications and painted candy-apple red or two-tone blue became a nifty medicine cabinet for the wall over the sink. Multicolored throw rugs sewn together made a cozy quilt; a bed frame raised vertically and draped with cloth made a convenient privacy panel; and a mattress rolled up in a ball and covered with a homemade afghan became a perfect couch (or love seat). Photos and calendars, posters and murals, on freshly painted walls softened the look and feel even more. A clothesline here, a makeshift hamper there. A plastic flowerpot or collection of rocks on the shelf. Bright lights when you needed them, shades when you didn't. Each morning you could smell the coffee brewing along the tiers and the stench of vomit in the back of them. If you could afford it, there were tailors for hire and cleaning service, too. On the riverside of both blocks the view through the curtains of glass was spectacular in the summer: speedboats and skiers bumping up and down the strong currents all day long; red and rust-brown coal barges moseying along five deep; scantily clad sunbathers sprawled out on the banks and always willing to flash their goods. At night the magnificent Gateway Clipper, lit up like a Christmas tree, with a live band playing Three Dog Night songs on the upper deck, floated down the river and back two or three times a night.

The St. Regises had their own parties, too, year round. Shooting galleries and prayer meetings, card parlors and crap houses. You could smell perfume at one door and Jade East at the next one. If you were hungry you could find a sandwich shop or a grocery store that gave credit. It was all there. And the noise. The cacophony of sounds. Televisions blasting. Pimps and tricks fighting over prices. Dope addicts nodding to the wailing horn section of Tower of Power or the guitar riffs of Van Halen. Men crying, others laughing. Some crying and laughing at the same time. Razor blades were free, as were sheets to tie around your neck and if you were in a hurry, a dive off the fifth tier was only a few flights of stairs away. Like any sleazy hotel, the St. Regises had their share of crime, too: robbery, rape, homicides and insults. It was all there, beating like a pulse. If you paid attention to the way it breathed it wouldn't hurt you, but you had to remain circumspect and try to figure out everyone's angles long before they did, because anywhere you went in the St. Regises you could find trouble or be it. You could fight till you couldn't fight anymore and you could laugh out loud when you dodged the knife and die when you didn't.

FREE AT LAST from the redbrick Home Block, stronger and smarter than he was a hundred and eighty days ago, still afraid in a dangerous way, Oliver welcomed cell B-49, to get away from the sewer rats that scurried brazenly in broad daylight, not to mention the dark, then to get on with his life. When he walked into the cell, the first thing he did was pull the piece of cracked porcelain away from the base of the toilet and retrieve the ten-penny nail he had found in an alley on his first day at Riverview. Then he knocked on his neighbor's door and asked him if by any chance he had seen the louse who had fished his rugs from his cell. The neighbor, courteous and friendly, introduced himself and told Oliver he hadn't seen anyone lurking in the area. Then he offered Oliver two rugs of his own that were as good as new. The neighbor succeeded in befriending him.

His name was Albert DiNapoli, and having lived through twenty-two years of being called Parrot Nose, he had learned to kill the momentum by introducing himself that way. The self-deprecation worked every time. Apart from that one physical flaw, Albert was a handsome young man. He enjoyed being around Oliver and Oliver appreciated the older boy's friendship. Oliver wanted to know about the stacks of books in Albert's room and where he disappeared to every afternoon and evening. Albert wanted to know what reform school had been like and how he had just managed to spend six months in solitary confinement without losing his mind. They exchanged information like pickpocketing partners. Once, though, Albert asked Oliver why he had to kill that boy. Oliver didn't flinch, but told him matter-of-factly that the boy had crossed him something terrible, and left it at that. Albert said the boy surely must have because Oliver was a real decent fellow. Oliver nodded, pleased with the serious word Albert had used.

Having a pyramid of friends and connections, Albert called up a pretty girl named Penelope to visit Oliver. He showed Oliver how to smuggle contraband, and then had his connections supply Penelope with the contraband to bring him. Quaaludes and marijuana. Albert sold the pills and let Oliver keep some of the reefer. Later he vouched for Oliver before the Holy Name Society board, that seldom admitted new members. Now Oliver and Penelope had four conjugal visits a year on the bathroom floor of the chapel. Oliver had been an altar boy in his youth so he agreed to do his part and serve the four "family masses" the Society held each year. After the priest gave his blessing and disappeared into his office to watch Steelers' football, the prisoners and their guests had the run of the chapel. Two bathrooms and a storage room behind the altar were made sparkling clean on Saturday so they could be used as conjugal visiting rooms on Sunday.

Oliver almost put himself in the soup at his very first family mass when he and Penelope stayed in the room longer than their allotted time. The next man in line was a fellow who looked like James Dean but thought he was Sonny Corleone. He had a hair trigger temper and was known to end fights quickly. He got in Oliver's face and told him if he wasn't going to be a team player maybe he should think about joining the Protestants. Oliver apologized three times, and Albert intervened. After Albert offered the man some of his own time everything between them was smooth sailing.

To help him pass the time Albert gave Oliver a stack of books to read and after reading them, Oliver talked about Jay Gatsby as though he knew him personally. Then he went all over the prison looking for someone who reminded him of a character named Raskolnikov. Even more impressive to him was a book called *The Mind and Its Control*; he fell in love with words like serendipity, existentialism and osmosis.

One morning Albert brought him to the education department and Oliver ended up showing the most dangerous criminal in the state how to solve an algebraic equation. Before he even got to the school, though, he was mesmerized by the street that led them there. Turk's Street, named after the sergeant who directed traffic there every week-day morning and afternoon, was a planet away from being just a drive-thru on the prison's campus. Two lanes wide and a city block long, it beat to life every day from seven in the morning until eight forty-five at night. With brick buildings two stories high on both sides of the street, delivery vans and trucks coming and going all day long, along with secretaries, teachers, college professors and their students; the sweet smell of diesel fumes, fruit, potatoes and hind quarters of beef; conversations, friendly and otherwise, between prisoners making their way to the ice house, butcher shop, food storeroom, dry cleaners, clothing exchange, arts and crafts shop, barber school, license plate factory, paint-electric-plumbing-and-carpenter shops and the education building, there were no signs of restraint—no barbed wire, no gun towers, and no thirty-foot wall—on this street.

When Oliver strolled down Turk's Street for the first time, he knew his burden had just been lightened and there was good reason for rising in the morning. As he waited for Albert to square it with the guard so he could enter the building without a pass, he memorized the words on a wooden plaque over the entrance to the stairway: Free Knowledge—Bring Your Own Container. At the top of the stairs a lobby that opened up and shot the length of the academic section was bustling with business. Some prisoners were holding forms and stand-ing in line, others stood around talking with young ladies and men dressed in Ivy League suits. Albert picked up a set of forms from a table and got in line. While Oliver waited for him beside the bulletin board, a round, rosy-cheeked man asked him if he was there to regis-ter for college. The man wore a name-tag attached to the lapel of his tweed jacket. Dr. Fiore Puglia, *University of Pittsburgh*. The doctor smiled at Oliver when Oliver told him he was just waiting for a friend. Oliver appreciated the man's kindness. As he continued observing the friendly atmosphere in the place, he noticed the mural of Rodin's *The Thinker* on one of the walls above his head. Oliver was in awe of the pose.

As he stood there taking it all in, a second man walked up to him and asked him if he was there to apply for the janitor's job and just like that, Oliver said yes. The man told him to wait in classroom number one and he would be with him shortly. Oliver backtracked until he found the room. A black prisoner and a white prisoner were working on a math problem when he entered and took a seat in the back. The black prisoner wore a black satin jacket with the words Pittsburgh Boxing Team inscribed in big gold letters on the back. When he looked over his shoulder at Oliver, he reminded Oliver of Joe Frazier. The other prisoner wrote a problem on the board. *4x -3 =9.* Joe Frazier said, "Go slow, man. I've got to write this shit down."

"All right, Champ. Let's add three to the minus three and three to the nine, now we have 4x=12. Remember. Adding the three to the minus three cancels it out, and adding three to the nine gives us twelve. Now you just ask what number times four gives you twelve."

Champ sighed. "Come on, man. Three. What's so hard about that?"

"That's all there is to it," said the tutor.

After he noted Joe Frazier's other name was Champ, Oliver said, "'Scuse me," and he said it like he was apologizing. "I don't mean to butt in, but if you're going to learn algebra, you don't want to start off on the wrong foot. It gets harder as you go along. You've got to know the right way to solve for any unknown. That last step he gave you was wrong, big man."

"What are you talking about? Four times three is twelve, dummy," said Champ.

"Right. But it's the way you got to the three that's going to screw you up later."

"Show me, white boy."

Oliver hesitated until the tutor waved the piece of chalk in the air. "Yeah, show us please," he said. "I just started tutoring and math's not my forte."

Oliver walked to the board and took the piece of chalk. "Okay. Four *x* equals twelve, you're good up to there. Four *x* means four times *x*, right? Now we want to get rid of the four so we have to do the opposite of the sign. Always do the opposite of the sign. The opposite of multiplication is division. Divide four by four and that gets rid of the four, leaving only x. What you do to one side of the equation you have to do to the other side too, right? Twelve divided by four equals three. So $x=3$."

"Damn! You know your shit, white boy. I got that! You going to be my new math tutor. You work up here?"

"Not yet. I'm hoping to get hired as a janitor."

"A janitor? You don't want to be no janitor. Tell that man you want to be a tutor."

"Okay, I will."

There were no tutor positions available but he got the janitor's job and met the head janitor Melvin who wore a baby Afro, had one eye and used the word Jim in almost every sentence. Oliver liked Melvin from the start. His attitude and the hitch in his giddy-up reminded Oliver of his old reform school friend, Philly Dog.

"Ever done any janitorial work before, Jim?"

"Yeah. And I once took a class on maintaining tile, terrazzo and wood floors."

"That's real funny, Jim."

Oliver was serious.

"All right. Check this out. I clean the classrooms and offices. You got the stairwell and the main corridor and hall, and the rest rooms. You set your own hours and you can come and go as you please. Just make sure your areas are good and clean every morning." He grabbed a pack of Pall Malls that were pushing out of his shirt pocket and lit one. "You smoke, Jim?"

"No, thanks. I'm getting ready to go into training."

Melvin stared at Oliver as if this was another joke, and then he went on. "Now dig this. There's all kinds of advantages to working up here. You can hang out all day, come up at night and find an empty room, write letters or listen to your radio, and there's always some fine-looking bitches walking around up here from the university, too. But dig this. There can be disadvantages, too, if you step on my toes. Don't make no wine up here. It brings too much heat. And stay away from Gloria. She's the secretary. If you stash a shank or any drugs around here, make sure the shit's in a good spot so the search boys don't find them. We don't need no heat up here, Jim. You got any questions?"

"I can't think of any right now, Melvin, but I'm sure I might once I get started."

"Dig. Just holler when you need to know something, Jim. Now I'm out of here."

THE SAME DAY Oliver started his life as a janitor in the halls of higher learning, he walked into the Young Guns Boxing Gym, a whitewashed clapboard building that leaned fifty feet in front of the Home Block, and told the civilian trainer he wanted to join the team. Moose Godfrey scratched his beard and chewed on a raggedy cigar while he studied Oliver up and down, apparently looking for a sign that he was just kidding around or on medication, or both.

"You do? A clean-cut kid like you? You ever been in a fight before?"

"Yeah. Lots of them."

"You don't look like you have. Can you fight?"

"I'm pretty good."

"Oh yeah? Well, white boys don't usually last long in my gym, but you're welcome to stay and work out with the team and we'll go from there. What's your name?"

"Priddy. Oliver Priddy."

"Wait here, Priddy."

Oliver looked the place over while he waited. A ring in the center of the room and an office and shower room in the back were all there was to it. The fractured walls were stained with blood, sweat and nicotine. One old hurricane fan leaning in the corner rattled in rhythm with the jump ropers. The room was as hot as the inside of a Pittsburgh steel mill.

Two boxers were stepping into the ring to spar when the head trainer shuffled out of the office with another old man in tow. "This here's Mr. Palmer," Moose Godfrey said, snatching the red-plaid porkpie hat off his large wooly head. "He'll be your trainer. What'd you say your name was?"

"Oliver Priddy. P-r-i-d-d-y."

"He's all yours, Luther."

The old trainer led Oliver to the side of the gym and got him ready to work out on the heavy bag. When his turn came he threw jabs, right crosses and hooks nonstop up and down the bag for five minutes. Luther told him that was enough for the first day; he had seen what he wanted to see and told Oliver he had natural punching ability. They moved to the speed bag and after Luther demonstrated the proper technique, it only took Oliver a few minutes to get his timing down and a steady rhythm going. When he finished jumping rope, Luther told him to go to the mat in the corner and do two hundred and fifty sit-ups and that would be all for his first day. "I almost forgot," said Luther, wiping the sweat from his coal black face. "Make sure you're on the yard no later than seven o'clock tomorrow morning to start your road work."

"I'll be there. Sure enough. Thanks a lot, Mr. Luther."

For six weeks Oliver ran around the yard five mornings a week with the rest of the boxing team. He started out running a mile, the second week two miles, then three, until he could easily run five miles in forty-five minutes. Every afternoon he left his job in the school to go to the gym and work out. The training was agonizing, but he savored every minute of every drill and exercise Luther put him through. He loved, too, the attention and respect he was earning from the other boxers. Every one of them encouraged him and gave him pointers. On the day of his first sparring session, he was feeling ten feet tall when the prisoner he had shown how to do algebra came up to him and said, "You're sparring with my homeboy Disco Bob today. You ever sparred before, white boy?"

"Well, not in the ring."

"Keep your hands up and jab. Don't stand in the middle of the ring and let that niggah tee off on you. You'll be all right."

"Thanks. Thanks a lot, Champ."

Oliver chewed nervously on his mouthpiece while Luther pulled the sixteen-ounce gloves over his hands, tied them and taped the laces. Then Luther adjusted his head gear and tightened the strap under his chin. "You ready, Priddy?" Oliver nodded.

He stepped between the ropes and looked around like a cat in a dog pound. The onlookers were staring at him, pointing and talking under their breath. When he saw the same prisoner who had been following him everywhere he went since he left the Home Block walk through the front door, Oliver's stomach churned and he thought he was going to throw up.

Luther admonished him to keep his hands up and stay loose. "Are you listening, boy?"

Oliver nodded and smiled nervously. Disco Bob stepped into the ring, then leaned back and forth against the ropes to test their slack before he danced around the ring one time. When he stopped at his corner, Champ stood behind him, whispering in his ear.

Moose yelled, "Time!"

The two boxers met in the center of the ring and smacked gloves. Oliver moved to the right, flicking his jab to find his range. Disco Bob moved forward, leaned to the side and shot a quick jab into Oliver's stomach. Oliver countered with two jabs of his own; the first one landed but Bob weaved under the second one. Oliver landed another stiff jab and Disco Bob countered with a solid left-right combination to Oliver's head. He stepped back and adjusted his headgear and as Disco Bob came forward, feigning a jab, bobbing and weaving, Oliver threw a straight right cross that landed on the button of Disco Bob's chin. He followed it up with a left hook to the head that landed and then Bob leaned on Oliver and tied him up. Moose told them to break and Disco Bob nodded to Oliver, acknowledging the power in his punches.

"Time!"

On the way back to his corner Oliver looked outside the ring and stared right into the eyes of Winfield "Fat Daddy" Petaway. "Look at me!" Luther said as Oliver slumped down on the stool. "Are you all right?"

"Hell, yeah, Luther! I feel good."

"Keep your damn hands up and throw more punches. You're waiting on him. You're not a counterpuncher. When you see the motherfucker coming in, set up and get your combinations off before he does."

"Okay. Did you see that, Luther? I got him good twice."

"I saw it. Rinse your mouth out. You tired?"

"Just a little."

"Time!"

As soon as they touched gloves again, Disco Bob threw a right hand that landed with a thump in the middle of Oliver's chest. Oliver blocked the next punch, a left hook to the body, but he wasn't quick enough to block the second hook that landed square on his right temple. Oliver fell back against the rope and covered up in a shell the way he had seen other boxers do a thousand times. Between the stars he saw each time he blinked, he could see the faces of the ringside hecklers who were shouting instructions and throwing punches of their own.

"Knock him out, Bob! Knock that cracker out! I'll take him from there!"

Disco Bob let Oliver off the ropes and the two fighters moved to the center of the ring, circled one another and calculated. Bob did the Ali shuffle and faked like he was going to move in. Oliver went for the fake, lunged and missed wildly with his right. For the rest of the round, Bob danced and jabbed and kept his distance.

In the third and final round Oliver connected with two jackhammer jabs that snapped Disco Bob's head back. Dead tired, he dropped his hands to his side and asked Bob if he was all right. Bob shook his head from side to side, stared wide eyed and moved forward, hitting Oliver with a three punch combination that knocked him senseless. This time when he tried to cover up, Disco Bob applied the pressure, throwing a flurry of precision punches that landed. When it was obvious that Oliver was out on his feet, Moose shouted, "Time!"

Oliver sat on the bench against the wall and stared at the dirty floor as Luther waved smelling salts back and forth under his nose. "You did real good for your first time, Priddy. Lift your head up. You all right? Where are you? What's my name?"

"Come on, Luther. I'm okay." Oliver saw others coming toward him.

"That's a hell of a jab you got," Disco Bob said, tapping Oliver on the shoulder.

"You're gonna be all right, white boy," said another boxer named Shotgun.

"You got a lot of heart, young buck," a welterweight named Sweet Tooth said.

"A lot of motherfuckers didn't think you were going to show up today," said Luther. He draped a towel over Oliver's head. "I'm proud of you, Priddy. Now go get yourself a hot shower."

After Luther walked away, Oliver sat there wondering where the fear had gone. From the instant he had touched gloves with Disco Bob, his fear laid down as though a cage had dropped over it. From there his concentration had been like a seasoned musician playing sixteenth notes at a fast tempo. Intense and effortless. Without thinking about it, he had known what punches to throw and when to throw them. It was a beautiful experience and he was exhilarated. Now he knew what he would tell Early Greer the next time Early asked why he wanted to take up boxing. He would tell him it was the zone, the same zone his brother Skip had once told a sports reporter about when the reporter had asked Skip what he was thinking each time he stepped to the plate and hit the nastiest curve balls for doubles and triples. He would tell Early about it and as sagacious as Early was, he would understand, but he would still frown the way he had weeks ago when Oliver told him he had joined the team. "Well dammit, be careful, Oliver," he had said. "There's a lot of rotten guys over there. Whatever you do, stay out of that shower room. Just don't go in there." He never said why; he didn't have to. Oliver knew.

What he knew was now staring back at him through the ropes on the far side of the ring. Oliver ignored him for now, but kept him in his peripheral vision. He waited until the crowd thinned out before he hooked his long fingers through the handles of his gym bag. Then he slung the bag over his shoulder and headed for the door. He took three steps before he turned sideways and stopped. "You following me, man?" He stared at Fat Daddy with unflinching eyes.

Fat Daddy's smile revealed crooked white teeth. "We going the same way," Fat Daddy said. "I've been meaning to holler at you since we had that little run-in last summer."

Oliver looked up into the clear blue sky and watched a platoon of blackbirds light on the barbed wire over the chapel fence. The afternoon breeze felt cool against his skin as it dried his sweat. He was still feeling exhilarated from his sparring session and the last thing he wanted was a confrontation. "That's over and done with as far as I'm concerned," Oliver said. "So what do you want to talk about?"

"I 'preciate that, letting bygones be bygones. You may not know it, but we have a lot in common, you and me. I'm a lifer too, and I used to box until I tore my shoulder up. I held the welterweight title for two years." His legs were shorter than Oliver's and he had to walk fast to keep up. "I saw something when you were sparring today. Something that could take you a long way in the game."

"Yeah? What'd you see?"

"Heart. You got some heart. Now there's only one question?"

"What's that?"

"Can you take a punch?"

"I took Bob's best shot and didn't go down, so what's that tell you?"

"Bob doesn't hit that hard. You ain't been hit hard yet."

Oliver paused at the front door of the little St. Regis. "I've been hit by guys who could punch a lot harder than Disco Bob and I didn't go down."

"I don't know about that. All I know is I barely hit you last summer and I knocked you on your ass."

"Come on, man. That was a sucker punch. I wasn't expecting you to hit me."

Fat Daddy leaned into Oliver, his hound-dog face twisted with malice as he tugged on two of his corn-rows. "I could have knocked you out, but I gave you a break."

"I doubt that. But what's your point with all this, Fat Daddy?"

"My point is I'm a better trainer than old man Luther. If you join my stable, I'll show you how to take a punch."

"Is that right? Look, man. I don't want any trouble. I'm fine with Luther."

"You think I'm trying to cause you trouble?"

"I don't know, man."

"That's right, you don't. Cause if I was, you wouldn't know it. Trouble's like a sucker punch. You never know when it's coming."

"I'll keep that in mind. Meanwhile, I appreciate your offer, but I'm going to stay with Luther."

"Suit yourself. Just remember what I said, Priddy. It's the punch you don't see coming that spells trouble every time." He winked at Oliver and strolled inside the block.

Oliver was certain he knew the difference between advice and a threat and he was sure Fat Daddy wasn't giving him advice. He walked inside the block and stopped at the sergeant's desk to see if he had mail. While the guard checked, he watched Fat Daddy climb the front stairwell all the way to the fifth tier and when he didn't see him walking down F-tier, he knew the low-life lived somewhere on the riverside.

1979

chapter four

LIFE IMPROVED ENORMOUSLY for Oliver after he began working in the Education Department. Pushing a broom around the halls gave him leave to look through the glass walls of the classrooms and read the chalkboard lecture notes on Shakespearean tragedies, the seventh president's war on nullification, and Freud's Oedipus complex. Oliver was young and handsome and he was friendly, and the professors felt free to tease him when they walked to the water fountain during the ten-minute break they gave the students halfway through their three hour lectures.

"Are you writing down my lecture notes and selling them, young man? They're not free, you know?" said one professor.

"No, sir. I wouldn't do that."

"There'll be a quiz next week," said another. "Any questions?"

"Well, since you asked, that self-fulfilling prophecy can work for you or against you, can't it?"

"Absolutely. As in, if you tell yourself enough times that you're going to be successful, you will be."

"Thank you, sir."

He loved watching the classrooms fill up every morning, afternoon and evening. Each professor brought up to six campus students to every class and they were usually bright, curious girls wearing blue sweaters, yellow blouses, plaid skirts, tight blue jeans and lipstick. Spoiled by his tea and peppermint candy, they talked freely to him about their love lives: Okay, you're a guy so tell me what you think.

He didn't call me for a week so I called him and he wanted to come right over. See? So he does care. Yeah, right. When he got there, I wanted to talk and he wanted to undress me. He practically ripped off my nightgown. You can't blame him for that. You're as beautiful as all outdoors, you know? All he had to do was listen until you made your point, then he could have used his own tongue. Are you seeing anyone else? Not really. He wants to take me home to meet his parents during spring break. I really like him, but spring break? I don't think so. Can't blame you there. You're young. Live and have fun while you can. You want another cup of tea? Want to smoke a joint? Meet me in the Xerox room.

The smell of pine sol, old books and perfume kept Oliver in the building during all of his free time. He painted classrooms, answered telephones and made fresh pots of coffee; he typed memos and put away files and books for the teachers and counselors, and once a week he walked down Turk's Street, crossed Tom's Way and followed the street with no name all the way to the back door of the bake shop where his order was waiting for him. He paid in Kools and returned with sweet nutty rolls, bear claws and donuts. The staff loved him for it. They loved him too, every time he put his mop down to help a student who was preparing for the high school equivalency examination. He knew the rules of grammar and punctuation better than the teachers did, and he was a wiz at math.

At night, alone in his cell, he read books until his eyes crossed and then he laid there thinking about all the new ideas he was gathering. Rather than memorize the meaning of new words, he made a game out of learning them. *Quaint* was the little professor in the green bow-tie, with the flattop haircut and the caterpillar mustache crawling across his upper lip. *Serendipity* was the feeling he got every time one of the campus girls smiled at him early in the morning and said, "There you are!" And *esoteric* was between the lines of the passages he read in a Saul Bellow novel, *Herzog*: "With one long breath, caught and held in his chest, he fought his sadness over his solitary life: '*Don't cry you idiot! Live or die, but don't poison everything.*'" When he read those words it had been as if they were his very own. In his mind's eye he had seen the person speaking and the person spoken to, the watcher and the watched. This moment marked the dawn of his self-awareness and he was excited to tears at the vein of hope that opened up inside him. Now he read like a man in search of a cure for his own terminal illness: stories, novels, biographies, philosophy. He took notes on Emerson, Pascal, James, Husserl, Sartre, and Plato. After he had gone through all the books in Albert's cell, he began finding them in the education building, on window ledges, in storage rooms and cabinets, and on the heaps of garbage. The psychologist he was seeing gave him two self-help books to read and he "got it." He understood that his life script was tragic rather than banal, and he genuinely believed that his life position was, I'm okay, you're okay. When the psychologist suggested that he could improve his conditions by taking up a hobby like drawing or learning to play a musical instrument or enrolling in a college class, it took another year of coaxing from Albert and Early and his boss, Mr. Sommers, before he associated what they were all telling him with the long-term goal he once had.

AFTER FIFTEEN YEARS of teaching behind bars, Professor Stanley Manners told his class of literature students why he continued to volunteer his time to prisoners. He was a free thinker, he said, and he wanted to open rather than close doors. He acknowledged his compassion, but in the same breath he said he was not a bleeding heart liberal. He never got up close and personal into the lives of his students; he merely planted seeds. His goal for the semester was to introduce them to the art of juxtaposing old points of view and new ones, and then determining for themselves which perspective has greater personal value. Professor Stanley Manners had Oliver sitting on the edge of his seat not just because he was blown away by the man's elocution. Oliver was also stunned by the man's physical appearance and one unusual tic he possessed. He was fiftyish, tall and lean, with round shoulders. His gray hair was long and ponytailed and his cheeks were sunken. He had a waxed mustache fanned across his bony face, and chin fuzz. He wore a wrinkled cream linen suit, a pink button-down shirt, and a bottle green bow tie. Cordovan leather wing tips graced his narrow feet, and when he was standing before the chalkboard his left foot never stopped tapping the floor. Rapidly. The tapping seemed as natural to the man as the hand he waved in front of him to emphasize a point. Oliver had enough natural elegance not to stare directly down at the man's foot, but it didn't matter. As he looked intently at the professor's face, he developed a temporary tic of his own. He couldn't stop himself from looking rapidly at the man's foot and then back up at one of his facial features--the chin fuzz, the bright gray eyes, the sunken cheeks, the waxy mustache.

Then he said something that shook Oliver to his core. "The stories we're going to read this semester can touch us as gently as a baby's breath, and, if given the chance, they can encourage us to extend our boundaries and comfort zones, and rattle these bars as fiercely as a caged lion." Oliver was smitten with inspiration.

For the first three weeks of class Oliver listened to his fellow students and learned how the upperclassmen responded to Professor Stanley Manners' questions. He liked the fact that most questions required reflection and elaboration, and some had no right or wrong answers. When the professor asked about the central conflict in D.H. Lawrence's "The Blind Man," Oliver raised his hand for the first time. The professor nodded to him and he rose from his seat but sat right back down after the professor told him he didn't need to stand. "Well, actually," he began. "Isn't there really more than one conflict in this story?"

Professor Manners extended his hands, palms up, his left foot tapping spasmodically. "You tell me."

"Well, actually, yes. You have the conflict of man versus the environment in that Maurice struggles in the world every day with his blindness. Then there's the conflict of man versus self with Maurice's friend Bertie who is very uncomfortable with intimacy."

"Yeah, but *that's* the central conflict," an upperclassman chimed in. "Not the environment conflict. That's a given. There's only one real conflict in this story, Professor Manners, and that's man versus self."

Oliver had no intention of arguing with a third year college student.

The professor pointed at him. "You're Mr. Priddy, right? I take it you disagree with what the gentleman said."

"Actually, sir, I wasn't finished. I don't know if I agree with him or not, but I think there may even be another conflict at work in this story, and that's man versus man. Once Maurice exposes his vulnerabilities to his friend, there's tension between the two of them."

Discussions like this went on for the next twelve weeks and Oliver's confidence soared with each one. He lost his lunch before every exam and bit his nails to the quick after he turned in each paper and while he waited for their return with an A scrawled on top. His final essay called for a lengthy discourse on Kafka's notion that a story serves as "an axe for the frozen sea within us." Not only did he earn a perfect grade on the paper, but the professor said it was so well written that he wanted to publish it in the undergraduate literary journal of which he was in charge on the main campus. Oliver was delighted.

When final grades came out and he saw the A on his official grade form, Oliver said to himself, uh huh, go on, say it! You knew you could do it, didn't you? But around his friends, he downplayed the whole thing. Albert, Penelope, and Early congratulated him until he turned red with embarrassment. His fellow classmates teased him in good taste, and the campus girls said way to go, you scholar.

But what tickled him more than anything was how he was supposed to be doing hard time among hardened cons, and here he had turned his prison into an Ivy League campus. He relished walking down Turk's Street every morning with a bale of books under his arms, flirting with the campus girls who came every day, and staying up until three in the morning, drinking tea and reading Shakespeare, writing in his journal or working on his latest commitment—editing *The Wire*, the lifers' newsletter. Just about everything he needed was right there in the prison and what wasn't came to him once a week, his own college girl Penelope. Tall and busty, with narrow hips, long shapely legs and a well-rounded behind, she had a face that banged drums of envy among the young ladies and awe among the men. Not only was she pleasant to look at, she was bright and witty, too. During their weekly visits, she always brought their conversation around to some political or current topic in the news. Was it right for the United States to do business with the Shah of Iran? Should we give him refuge if he should fall? On both of these questions she answered in the affirmative and proceeded to put forth a sound argument to bolster her position. Oliver was more than impressed by her logic. Her knowledge of major league baseball baffled him, too. She was a Pirates fan, and he was an Orioles fanatic. After she explained to him why and how her team had beaten his twice in the World Series, he quickly changed the subject to the shade of her lipstick. "Is that strawberry?" he artfully asked her. "No. It just tastes that way. See?" she teased, smiling at him three different ways before she gently pressed her lips against his. These moments and other things they shared in common—their Catholic upbringing, broken families, and the universal need to be needed—had metamorphosed their business arrangement into a deep emotional connection. Being with her each week made him feel he still had another part of himself that had not been taken away. He didn't know how long it was going to last and he tried not to think about it. When they were together they made each other feel like they were the only two people in the world. He never asked her if she had someone else out there; he didn't want to know. Her lack of inhibition and unending desire to please was enough for him.

On their first Christmas holiday visit together, she arrived at six o'clock wearing what she knew would arouse him to no end. Her old Catholic school uniform. A white blouse with a little black ribbon tie, a navy blue blazer, plaid pleated skirt, and knee socks and loafers. They stood in the line that led to the back of the room where a Christmas tree display table, covered in a snow white sheet that hung all the way to the floor, awaited couples who wanted their pictures taken and others who wanted ten minutes of privacy. Ten dollars for ten minutes of privacy was what the Jaycees photographer charged. When Oliver and Penelope reached the front of the line other couples hid them from view while they crawled under the table and made clandestine love to the sound of the Lionel train choo-chooing around the Christmas tree overhead.

THREE DAYS BEFORE CHRISTMAS, Freddie the runner brought another visiting pass to his door at nine o'clock in the morning. Oliver thought the word *family* at the bottom of the pass meant his mother June, his brothers, Skip and Huck, and his sister Anna. So he bolted to the visiting room and then pulled up like a buck in headlights when he saw a man who looked vaguely familiar standing there smiling awkwardly at him. With him were two children and a woman who were also staring and smiling as if they all knew something he didn't. And they did.

Surprised you, didn't we? That's what the woman said. As if it were something pleasant. Good to see you, son, the man said. Meet your new family. This is my wife Isabella. This is your brother, Dickie. Dickie's twelve. And this is Lottie. She's thirteen. Fourteen, Dad! I'm fourteen, the nubile girl told him.

Speechless, Oliver shook hands with each of them and did his best to smile. He took a seat beside Ernie Boy the First, whose nervous apprehension showed each time he blinked and forced a smile.

While they took turns describing their hour-long trip from Youngstown to Pittsburgh, Oliver studied Ernie Boy's face until he found the lie he was looking for. It had been sixteen years since this man had skipped town on his family like a fugitive. Oliver was only five years old and Skip was six the day they had stood on the side of 301 Highway waving to their father as he drove away in his new red Ford. See you boys soon. Those had been his last words. Every day for six weeks, Oliver had looked out the front window of their apartment hoping to see Ernie Boy's car pull up into the parking lot. Each time he saw a new red Ford Fairlane coming up the highway, he thought it was his father. Six weeks went by and when his father still hadn't returned, his mother told him to forget about him. "He's gone, Oliver, and he's not coming back. Just forget about him." Every night before they went to bed, he and Skip knelt at the windowsill and watched the tractor-trailers scream through the intersection of 301 Highway and Hawthorne Drive. One night they saw a sixteen-wheeler slice a new red Ford Fairlane in half in the middle of the intersection. The boys put on their sneakers and ran to the scene in their pajamas. Skip stopped at the edge of the highway while Oliver darted around the debris and the men who had come from Mr. Mack's Texaco station to help. He had never seen so much blood. The dead man was lying in front of the car and he was wearing burgundy wingtip shoes. The same kind their father had been wearing when they last saw him. Oliver maneuvered close enough to see that the man's eyes were wide open and were as blue as his father's eyes; his hair was parted on the left side, too, just the way their father parted his, and there was a diamond ring on his left pinkie.

What if it was him? What if God had worked that traffic light to send their father to hell for playing such a bad joke on them? Oliver started to cry. He yelled for Skip. That ain't him, Oliver. But the car's red and he's wearing the same shoes and the diamond ring and... That ain't him, now come on. Oliver wanted to go back and look at the man one more time, but Skip said no. Tears streamed down his face as he watched the ambulance driver pull the white sheet over the man's face. It's him! I know it's him! It is not, Oliver. But this was one time Oliver refused to believe his brother and he was glad his father was gone and he didn't have to wonder about him anymore.

Now he searched the harsh lines on both sides of Ernie Boy's lying mouth—smile lines, but frown lines too and crow's feet at the corner of his lying baby blue eyes. His hair, totally gray, was thick and curly, and he had the great Priddy teeth. He wore a tan suit and a white shirt, with an ice blue tie and high-shine brown Oxfords. Oliver was no more glad to see him than Ernie Boy was to be there. But they talked. They talked and the family went on as if they had just seen Oliver last week and the week before. The kids were beautiful and gracious. Lottie told him at the Coca-Cola machine how she had waited all these years to meet her big brother and how handsome he was. Dickie didn't say much. When it was time for them to leave, they promised to return soon and often.

Oliver went to bed that night using sixteen years of pent up love and anger as the ignition to fire up his memory. Seeing his father had left him feeling nostalgic and longing to see his mother June. Nothing in God's creation could console him the way his mother could.

He was not dreaming nor was he asleep. Rather, he was in that space before sleep comes where thoughts and images were like a random slideshow. Chalk and erasers. Venetian blinds and folded letters. Jealousies and longing. Images heavy enough to entertain but not distinct enough for dreaming. Yet he was hopeful that sleep would bring him a dream, the one that always left him with renewed hope and energy. It always started in the kitchen where his mother June was at her best, cooking and baking and tending to her African violets that thrived on the windowsill over the sink. There was joy and contentment in her lovely face. For as long as he could remember they had played a game, his sweet tooth against her ingenuity. He always won. She hid the chocolate candy, he found and unwrapped the foil. Except that one time when his little arms weren't quite long enough to reach the bottom of the ten-pound cut glass punch bowl. It looked like the biggest snowflake God had ever made when it tumbled off the shelf over the kitchen sink and knocked him off the counter and clear across the linoleum floor. Shocked as any child would be, he sat there in a heap of broken glass and *O. Henry* bars and didn't know whether to laugh or cry. After he felt blood dripping off his forehead, he cried. But there she was. Shocked, too, but she made it all better, and by the time they left the emergency room and she bought him a double scoop of Rocky Road ice cream, she was calm again. He was still seeing stars when she told him to sit in Mr. Winkler's parlor while she disappeared into Mr. Winkler's bedroom to discuss a business matter that had a squeaky rhythm.

It wasn't until years later when he was in the county jail waiting to stand trial for Jimmy Six's murder and Mr. Winkler brought her all the way from Southern Maryland to Pennsylvania to see him that he understood. But it didn't matter. It didn't matter because she was there. With chocolate bars and her beautiful face, she was there. It didn't matter because he and his siblings had never had to eat grits or scrapple for breakfast; there had always been sizzling hot bacon or cured sausages floating beside the sunny side up eggs. Even on Sunday evenings when he and Skip and Anna returned from their weekly visits to their grandfather's farm, after a day of running across acres of honeysuckle and the greenest fields, singing I can't begin to tell you how lonely that song was, even then, she was there. Not June Cleaver in an apron with pearls draped around her neck. But his June, she was there. Hot or cold, in or out, she was there. And he had sooo liked her company, to talk with her, to be around her. Not just because she was his mother, but because she was humorous and witty. They were special to each other. They sang and danced together. She taught him how to jitterbug and when they walked through the side door of the American Legion bar, every man sitting at the bar turned his head to gaze into her big brown eyes. They sat at a corner table with her girlfriends, Mary Jo and Elsie. The women drank Pabst Blue Ribbon; Oliver drank Hire's root beer. And after a dance around the jukebox, Oliver sat on Mary Jo's lap and the first time she pressed his head against her breast, he kept it there for as long as he could because he didn't want the warm feeling that ran through him to end.

When he reached his mid-teens, June and Ernie Boy the Second separated and so did Oliver and his siblings. Anna, who had despised Oliver for as long as he could remember, went to stay with June's sister. Skip, who had always treated Oliver with brotherly affection and relished the role of doing brotherly things, moved to their grandfather's farm and drove a little French car to school. Their younger half-brother, Huck, who was the apple of Oliver's eye, went to live with Ernie Boy the Second and his mother, leaving June and Oliver living in the house. Ernie Boy still had belongings there, but the marriage was over and he only came around occasionally in the middle of the night looking for June. Right around this time Oliver started to do bizarre things to capture June's attention and hold it. On Friday nights instead of taking his girlfriends to the drive-in or to a firehouse dance, he brought them home. One summer evening June came in early and there he was lying on the sofa as naked as the day she had pushed him out of her womb, with a beautiful girl wrapped around him like a vine. June lit an L&M and said who's your friend, Oliver? Oh, this is Marianne, Momma. You're very sexy, Marianne, but not on my good sofa. The kids rose like synchronized swimmers and held hands all the way to Oliver's bedroom. And June saw him. She saw him. And he had never been as proud as he was that night when she saw that he was a man.

That summer, June began an affair of her own with a pint-sized bottle of vodka and Oliver saw less and less of her. She had never been a brood hen and had always enjoyed Oliver and his siblings when the mood struck her. And moods she had. All her life she cried off and on for days at a time and wouldn't talk to Oliver or anyone. But then, just like that, her mood would change and she would feel, once again, natural and easy and playful with him. They talked about piano keys and dance steps, perennials and annuals, cats and stray dogs. They never held grudges, and there was no winning or losing. On Friday and Saturday nights she dolled herself up and in his presence alone she never forgot to ask do I look pretty before she slipped out the door for the evening. There was more than a residue of interest in her big brown eyes as she held her gaze toward him while he told her over and over how beautiful she was.

There wasn't a damn thing he could do that Saturday night when Ernie Boy the Second stumbled into the house at two in the morning and held her hostage in her bedroom. Oliver could hear Ernie Boy punching her and tearing at her gown and when Oliver called out her name from the hall, Ernie Boy dared Oliver to open the door. There wasn't a goddamn thing he could do. After that night though, June got wise and found her way to Oliver's room, knowing perfectly well the bastard wouldn't have the nerve to bother her there. Not in front of her grown son. Oliver, of course, was grateful to tears to protect her. On the morning after the twelfth night he had watched her nightgown fall to the floor, seen the float of her breasts before she crawled into his bed and spooned up beside him, his grandfather called and told Oliver that he was welcome to come and stay for as long as he wanted. June encouraged him to go since they were the only two left in the house and she was often gone for days at a time. Oliver decided to go, but not before he held her like a prom date and promised to stop in every week to see her. He even left some of his belongings there as a reason to return and as a sign to her that his leaving was only temporary. After moving out he spent some part of every night thinking about her living alone in that house. The same house he used to sneak into just before dawn on those nights when he had stayed out all night. He had to admit he liked living in that house when it was just his mother and him. It became his, sort of. A nighttime possession complete with a beautiful mother who let him come and go as he pleased, no questions asked. It was the life. And to think he had traded all that to live on a four hundred acre tobacco plantation just so he could have a little French car of his own.

He had wanted to burn that house to the ground the day he and Skip stopped in after school and found her curled up in a fetal position, rocking back and forth as she stared vacantly at the wall. The boys were terrified. Her jet-black hair, always meticulously coiffed, was hanging in greasy strands. Her eyes were sunken and the skin on her face sagged like dough. At some point she had tried to put on lipstick but had gone wide of the mark. Her face resembled a sad clown. Oliver sat on the side of the bed and held her hand while Skip left the room to call their aunt Harriet, who came right away along with the rescue squad. Oliver and Skip watched helplessly as the attendants loaded her into the ambulance and drove her away to a sanitarium in Baltimore. Ninety-three days later when she returned looking like Maggie in *Cat on a Hot Tin Roof,* Oliver was there to greet her. It was the happiest day of his life.

Pleased once again that he had witnessed her sobriety from the day she came home from that sanitarium all the way up to the day he had broken her antique chair over Ernie Boy the Second's back and fled to Pennsylvania, Oliver finally fell asleep. But he did not have the dream he wanted.

IN THE MORNING he kicked off the rugs he called a quilt and hurled his head in the pillow to keep the sunlight out of his eyes and the man from Youngstown out of his mind. When he finally got out of bed to stare at the icy waters of the Ohio River, the pass-runner showed up at his door.

"Priddy, let me hold the horseshoe you got up your ass," the runner said.

"Freddie, my man. What's up?"

"Here. You got another visitor. That's three this month. What a lucky dude."

Oliver took the pass and saw the word *family* written at the bottom. "I hope that cocksucker's not trying to shock me again."

"Say what?"

"My biological father. He came to see me yesterday for the first time in sixteen years."

"Did you know he was coming?"

"Hell, no! I didn't even know he was alive."

"How'd it go?"

"You don't even want to know." He grabbed his shower kit and towel and opened the cell door.

"Well, just be glad somebody's thinking about you, Priddy. Some of us in here don't have a soul in the world."

"Yeah, you're right, Freddie. Thanks for the pass. I'm going to get a shower. Whoever it is can wait."

By the time he finished showering and left his cell for the visiting room, Oliver had changed his mood twenty times. Should I have it out with him, or let it go? Should I ask the motherfucker why he never called or came around, or let it all be hunky dory? He couldn't decide. When he walked into the visiting room and saw his brother Skip looking out the window his countenance changed again. "Good God, Almighty! If it isn't my brother, Skip!" His voice was full of excitement.

Skip turned around, saw Oliver moving toward him and smiled. "Hey, Oliver."

They shook hands, embraced and patted each other on the back. "How have you been?"

"All right. And you?"

"I'm doing well, Ollie. It's good to see you."

Oliver fingered the sleeve of Skip's leather Washington Redskins jacket, which prompted Skip to say, "I guess you're a Steelers fan now, huh?"

"Are you kidding? I'm not a turncoat." Then, as though he noticed something missing, he asked, "Where's everybody else?"

"Anna couldn't make her mind up and Ernie Boy the Second wouldn't let Huck come 'cause they have a house full of company. And Momma, well, you're not going to believe me when I tell you, Oliver."

"What? Did something happen to her? Is she okay?"

"Couldn't be better. She just got married again."

"To who?"

"A television executive. Real nice guy. You'll like him. He treats her like a queen."

"When did this all happen?"

"Two weeks ago. They're in Stowe, Vermont, right now. They're coming to see you after the holidays."

"Man, she sure is resilient," Oliver said. "Good for her."

Skip smiled at Oliver and said teasingly, "Tell me about this girl-friend of yours."

"How'd you know?"

"Momma. Who else?"

Oliver nodded. "Well, she's real nice," he said. "Her name's Penelope. She goes to Duquesne U. right here in the city. She's one of the smartest girls I've ever met, too. And the prettiest." Oliver tapped his chest bone with pride.

"You always did have the fine ones. You have any plans?"

"For what?"

"I mean, are you two in love?"

"Hell, I'm crazy about her, and I can tell by the way she shows up here every week she thinks a lot of me, too. But we haven't said one word about being in love. I'm a goddamn lifer, Skip. I might never get out of here. She's got her whole life ahead of her. She's not going to stick around forever waiting for me to get out, and I don't want her to." He said it with confidence but he put a period in his voice too. He didn't want his relationship with Penelope discussed and endlessly analyzed, not by his brother or anyone else.

Skip heard the period in his voice but still added, "What about parole?"

"There's no parole for lifers in this state, man. The best I can hope for is a pardon in fifteen years. That's how much time they usually make a lifer do. Did you hear I'm going to college?"

"Yeah, and we're all glad you are."

"I might earn a Ph.D. before it's all over with," Oliver said with enthusiasm.

"That would be some accomplishment, Oliver." They grinned at one another and then Skip asked, "Anyone else been to see you?"

"Yeah, but you'll never guess who," Oliver said, rolling his eyes.

"Give me a hint. One of your old classmates?" Skip asked.

"No." He said it with disappointment. "Happy Ernie." Oliver spit out the word Ernie and his countenance turned sour. "Remember how Momma used to call him that?"

"Our father Ernie?" Skip said in disbelief. "Ernie Boy the First?"

"Yeah. You just missed his ass by a day. He and his *new* family were here yesterday. He wasn't even on my visiting list. The Captain of the Guards let them in because it's the holidays and they came from out of state. Youngstown, Ohio. He's been married for fourteen years. We have a real cute little half-sister named Lottie. She's fourteen. He sure as hell didn't waste any time, did he? And he's got a son named Dickie who's twelve. They're nice kids. His wife's nice too. Isabel, or Isabella."

Skip followed the convoluted flight of a fly overhead. "So, did you give him hell?" Skip smiled faintly.

Oliver laughed. "No. I wanted to show that son of a bitch I had some class, you know? The whole time I just smiled and pretended like he'd been in my life all along. Hell, I could have won an Academy Award the way I smoothed them all right into my morning. I didn't ask him a single question. Not one. I wanted to though. I wanted to say, 'Where the hell'd you disappear to, man? Why didn't you give us a call? Why didn't you stop by?' But no sirree, Skip boy. I had too much class for all that." Oliver was bitter. "And you know what, Skip? He never mentioned a single word about why I was here or what happened in that reform school. Not one word, man."

"I was wondering about that, too."

"About what?"

"You know. What you were doing up here in Pennsylvania in the first place and why you had to rob that store. And we'd all like to know what happened at that training school, why you killed that fellow."

"You didn't hear?"

"Hear what?"

"I broke a chair over that cocksucker Ernie Boy's back."

"I don't get it."

"Aw Christ, Skip. I stopped in to see June one night and his car was in the driveway. This was after she had gotten a restraining order to keep him away. I parked out on the street and looked through the bay window curtains and saw him tying her legs up to the dumbwaiter. When he started tearing her nightgown off, I ran around the back of the house and came in through the basement. You know her favorite antique wicker chair? Well, I tried to knock his head off with it. After he went down, I was afraid he had his gun on him so I hit him a few more times to make sure he didn't get up. Then I untied Momma and I took off. I drove north for two straight hours before I realized I didn't know where the hell I was. I was almost out of gas and I only had a dollar in my pocket. So I pulled into this little country store, walked in the place and told the cashier to give me all her money. Hell, I don't know why I did it, Skip. The whole thing was so surreal, man. Especially when that state trooper pulled me over two miles up the road and told me I was on the wrong side of the Mason-Dixon Line."

"Oliver, that's the craziest thing you've ever done! Did you have a weapon?"

"No. I poked my finger out inside my jacket pocket like I had a gun."

"Okay. So they put you in that reform school, right? And you had, what, nine months to do before you turned eighteen and they had to let you go?"

"Yeah."

"So what happened in that place, Oliver?"

"Look, man. There's no way you could ever understand what it was like in there." Now it was Oliver's turn to stare into the river.

Skip looked at him. "Listen, our grandfather hasn't been right ever since they tried you and put you in here, Oliver. He deserves to know what happened, what made you do what you did. And so do I, and so does everyone else."

"Like who?"

"Your aunts and uncles and cousins. Anna and Huck and Momma. Come on, Oliver."

Again Oliver glanced at his brother, briefly, as though he were a distraction from the major work of looking for an answer. "Remember that big old guard dog in old man Gilbert's junk yard that got loose and went on a killing spree?" Oliver asked.

Skip looked confused. "Okay. Yeah. He killed your collie puppy and two other small dogs in the neighborhood. Go ahead."

"You forget what Ernie Boy the Second did when he came home from work that day?" Oliver pressed his knuckle into the frown between his eyes.

"I remember you were sitting on the back steps holding that dead puppy in your lap and crying up a storm when he pulled into the driveway."

"Yeah, and then the bastard did the one good deed he probably ever did in his life. He went and tracked that dog down and put an end to his viciousness."

Skip scratched his head before he ran his fingers through his hair. "Oliver, I'm sorry. I'm lost."

"Skip, the boy I killed wasn't a boy at all. He was a vicious predator and he made me his prey. He traumatized me something awful."

"I still don't understand why you had to kill him. But listen. We're all sorry you have to be in this place, Oliver. You know you have to pay for what you did, though. The good thing is you'll still be young enough to get on with your life fifteen years from now."

"Let's change the subject," Oliver said. His voice was soft and a little sad.

"Let me ask you one last question. Did you lose your temper?"

Oliver looked at his brother, wishing it had been his temper. Something that easy to explain. But he knew better, and every day since that fatal moment, everywhere he looked—in cell blocks, dining halls, canteen lines, and even his mirror reflection, he saw those dying eyes click shut and while he did not regret the fact that Jimmy Six was dead, he was ashamed for being the perpetrator of the deed.

He continued to look into Skip's eyes when he said, "I didn't mean to, Skip. I mean the killing part. I wanted to kill his viciousness. I didn't mean for him to die, though."

"Wait a minute, Oliver. When you kill something, it stands to reason that it dies."

"Yeah. I went too far." Oliver looked away now and stared out the window into the icy waters of the river. How he yearned at that moment to be sitting in Skip's car and on their way home, or shopping, or to their grandfather's farm—anywhere far away from prison bars and callous men. As hard as he tried to hold back the tears, one rolled down each of his cheeks.

"Come on, Oliver. I'll get us some candy."

Skip bought them each a Reese's Peanut Butter Cup and a cup of coffee and before they walked away from the vending machines, he said, "Can I get you a sandwich, Oliver? Anything you want, name it."

"No, thank you, man. This is fine."

They sat and ate the candy and drank the coffee in silence while they watched a prisoner sitting across from them console the older woman who was wrapped in his arms. After the woman began to cry, Skip dug into his jacket pocket for his keys and curled his fingers around them. "I'm going to be hitting the road soon, Oliver. I'll be back to see you again in the spring and I'll bring Huck with me." He reached into his front pants pocket and pulled out a wad of bills. "I've got some money here for you. Where do I leave it?"

"Give it to the officer at the front desk where you first came in," Oliver said. "He'll give you a receipt. I appreciate it, Skip."

"Well, it's from everybody. So don't just thank me." He got up and buttoned his jacket. They walked to the door and embraced.

Skip stepped back and then reached out and gently touched Oliver's shoulders. "So long for now, Oliver. I'll see you soon."

"Yeah. Listen, Skip. I didn't lose my temper. It wasn't like that, man."

Skip turned around and smiled. "Okay, Oliver. Merry Christmas," he said. He waved his hand and cut around the corner before Oliver could say, "and Happy New Year."

1980

chapter five

DONNIE BLOSSOM WAS STANDING in front of Oliver's cell biting his nails and eyeballing the tier. "Don't be in there all day, Fats," Donnie whined.

Fat Daddy crept into Oliver's cell, closed the door and pulled the curtain across the doorway. "Shut up and keep your eyes open," Fat Daddy said. He looked around the cell and thought the place was cozy right down to the smell. Cinnamon incense and Right Guard. On the clean white wall over the bed were three long words scrawled out in fancy letters: ostentatious, loquacious, salacious. Above the desk was a gallery of family photographs. The Priddy family at Christmas. Mom Priddy, with the Bette Davis eyes and the hourglass figure, had it going on, as did the daughter and three sons. The made-for-television family. Only there was no Ozzie Nelson or Ward Cleaver in the picture. So the boy did need a daddy after all.

A letter on the desk said read me, but Fat Daddy couldn't. The cursive flow was too much for him, so he settled for a peek at the photo inside. The same slim goody who was in one of the pictures above the desk with her arm hooked around Priddy Boy's waist. The come-fuck-me scent of her perfume wafting from the envelope was tantalizing, too. Fat Daddy rubbed his groin and sat on the edge of Oliver's bed. On the pillow was a black marble composition book with the words MY DAILY JOURNAL scrawled in big red letters on the cover. He opened it and easily read the first entry.

I saw the psychiatrist today and the first thing he said to me was I don't give out valium if that's what you have in mind. I told him I was there because my mother asked me to see a shrink. He wanted to know why I caved in "that boy's" skull. First of all, "that boy" was as big as King Kong. Second, my lawyer told me I can't talk about it while my appeals are waiting to be heard. He asked if I was interested in attending weekly sessions with the psychologist. I said my mother thinks I should so I guess I am.

This joint is crawling with booty bandits and they're sizing me up already. I don't want any trouble and I'm doing my best to ignore them, but I sure hope they leave me the hell alone.

This morning when I was returning from the commissary, I found a ten-penny nail in the alley beside the building. Now all I need is some kind of handle to make the perfect ice pick.

Fat Daddy stared at the pages and thought, I'll bet he got fucked. I'll bet King Kong popped his young-ass cherry! He was excited now and flipped to another entry.

After six months, a fractured arm and three ass whippings, I'm finally out of the hole! That lieutenant with the blue eyes came to my cell this morning to let me know they were letting me out 30 days early for good behavior. I thought he was messing with me so I kept right on reading Moby Dick like he wasn't even standing there. But then he said good luck to me and an hour later they were springing my door.

I'm back in the same cell on the little St. Regis. B-49. All my belongings are here except for my two throw rugs. Some thief stole them while I was gone. The first thing I did when I got here this morning was check my stash. My ten-penny nail was still there and I took it everywhere I went today. First, I got a haircut from a barber named Chinaman. Nicknames kill me. The barber wasn't any more Chinese than I am. He was a chubby, high-yellow, hip-talking black dude from North Philly. I liked the scene down there in the barbershop and was glad I had to wait an hour before I got in the chair. I read a couple of magazines and listened to the radio they had tuned to a soul station.

They played Marvin and the O'Jays back to back. And there was that familiar smell of talcum powder and sea breeze and hair after it's been shaved off with electric clippers. It reminded me of Charlie Spalding's barbershop back home.

Tonight I called home. Momma was ecstatic to hear my voice but hounded me because I hadn't called in six months. She knew even before I told her that I had gotten in trouble and couldn't call. I told her this place isn't that bad at all. I didn't tell her I was ready to run a ten-penny nail through the neck of this nasty freak who's been following me around ever since I got here, watching me as if I were his next goddamn meal. The same freak who knocked me down in the yard last summer. Momma's been through enough and I don't want her worrying about me any more than she already is.

Tomorrow I'm going to the gym to join the boxing team and in the evening I'm going to sit out in the yard with my neighbor who I just met, a fellow named Albert DiNapoli. He's a real intelligent guy and he goes to college. He's got more books in his cell than I've ever seen except maybe in a library. I think I'll ask him to let me read a few of them. It's been a long day and I'm tired, so that's all for tonight.

Fat Daddy closed the book and set it back on the pillow. A nasty freak, he thought. I'll show this bitch what a nasty freak is.

What Fat Daddy was planning to do to Oliver other men had done worse to him. The bedroom where his Too Tall Uncle Paul had kept him for two days and nights when he was eleven had smelled worse than nasty. "Cee-lo or straight?" They all said straight at the same time and laughed like a bunch of corner boys over their unanimity. Four corner boys and one Big Momma who went out for fish sandwiches and more Boone's Farm. Too Tall Uncle Paul came in the bedroom first. What you doing, boy? Nuttin'. Come here. Why you crying? I'm thirsty. Drink this. He drank the whole glass of strawberry wine, then Too Tall Uncle Paul said now come a little bit closer. His beard tickled little Winfield's neck. He pulled the child's underpants down and sniffed his hind quarters before he dry-humped him and filled the crack of his ass with warm sticky cream. After Too Tall Uncle Paul walked out, Spook the trash man walked in saying over his shoulder, the next time you stick the dice, niggah! He spooned up beside the child and nuzzled his neck before he dug into his behind. When he pulled out, he said, got to get back to them bones. Kiss me for good luck. Then the nasty niggah slid his tongue inside Winnie's mouth for good luck just as the door flew open. You'd better eat this fast, young'un! Them boys is hungry! Come here to your Aunt Gwendolyn. He devoured the sandwich while she played with him. Lord, child. Yes, indeed. She had him martial and interested when the door flew open again. Where's the food, Big Momma? It's all gone and so are you! Get out! That boy finger fucking you? Get out! Go finger fuck the dice!

Two days later his mother came for him and cursed her former brother-in-law out because the boy smelled so nasty. Stink nasty. They wasn't nice to me, he said. He didn't let his tears or his pain show, but he knew right then at the age of eleven what he wanted to do. He started with a mongrel bitch he found in heat inside an abandoned house at the end of Oxford Street. From there he learned the fine art of becoming as invisible as God hiding behind trees and in them, crouched in the weeds, standing around corners, patrolling school lavatories and public rest rooms. The prey, the predator. He was stalking boys half his size and some twice as big.

"Come on, Fat Daddy! You've been in there long enough." Donnie Blossom's voice startled Fat Daddy. He walked to the door, drew the curtain back and reached through the bars. He squeezed Donnie's buttocks and said, "Shut up, bitch! I'll be out when I'm ready."

Fat Daddy closed the curtain again and took one last look around the room before it occurred to him that he had one more thing to do. He laid on the floor and slid under the bed, moving around until he decided there was plenty of room for what he had in mind. When he got to his feet, he rearranged the marble composition book on the pillow and walked out of the cell.

Early the next morning he got out his trick bag, a baby blue pillowcase, and loaded it with a tube of petroleum jelly, a roll of adhesive tape, a red rayon kimono belt, a yellow cassette boom box, and a homemade shiv. After breakfast he went over the plan with Donnie

Blossom. "When they call work-lines, you follow him to work," Fat Daddy said. "After you see him walk down Turk's Street go to the yard and hang out until he leaves work. Then follow his ass right back to his cell. You got all that?"

"Yeah. I got it."

"You better. Now as soon as he steps in the cell and closes the door, you drop this bolt down through the pin hole. I'll be on him by then."

"Well, what if somebody comes looking for him while—"

"Tell 'em he's using the bathroom. They can't see through the curtain."

"How long are you going to be?"

"As long as it takes to make him mine. Now stop asking me all these dumb ass questions."

Donnie was nervous and his fingernails were bleeding to the quick. "I thought I was yours."

"You are, bitch. I told you. I'm a polygamist."

"You're so bad, Fat Daddy."

"I know it and don't you forget it."

Five minutes later the work-line bell rang. Fat Daddy walked down the back stairwell to B-tier and all the way to the front of the block where he reversed directions. When he reached Oliver's cell he went in and closed the door and pulled the curtain. The cell was much darker than he recalled it being the day before. The lighting was just right. He emptied his rape kit on the bed and went to work. First, he cut a long piece of adhesive tape from the roll and tacked it to the side of Oliver's footlocker for quick access. Then he slid the red cord, pillowcase and yellow boom box under the bed. He stuck the tube of Vaseline down his sock and held on to the knife. Before he slid under the bed, he pulled the curtain open and waited for his eyes to adjust to the light.

Shifting to get comfortable under Oliver's bed, he hit play on his yellow boom box and cued up his favorite Marvin Gaye song. "Stubborn Kind of Fellow." He didn't move for an hour and thirty minutes. When he finally heard the door open, he smiled and grew hard in the groin.

"Fat Daddy! Fat Daddy! Come on out! Come on out!" Donnie Blossom shouted. "He's gone! Meet me upstairs!" Donnie slammed Oliver's door and walked away.

Fat Daddy got to his feet and quickly gathered his tools. He slung the baby blue pillowcase over his shoulder and hurried out of the cell, cursing under his breath all the way to the fifth tier.

Donnie was sitting on Fat Daddy's bed.

"What the hell happened?" Fat Daddy asked. "Where'd that motherfucker go?"

"What happened was he came out of school early and I followed him just like you told me to. When he got to the rotunda he stopped and told this guy he was walking with that he had a visitor. Then he showed his pass to the guard and they let him through the gate."

"Shit! I was ready like Freddie, man!"

"There's always tomorrow, Fat Daddy."

"Yeah, but my dick's hard now," Fat Daddy said. He closed the door and pulled the curtain. "Take off your clothes and get on the bed."

OLIVER WAS ON HIS WAY to the yard to look for Albert. Smoking a joint with Albert would be just the thing he needed. Albert was going home soon and they hadn't spent much time together since Albert had moved to the big St. Regis a couple of months ago because the cells were larger. Oliver had requested to move, too, but his turn hadn't come yet.

It was springtime and the three concession stands were roaring with business. Oliver became excited by the smell of fresh popcorn and fried onions mingling with the fragrance of the hyacinths blooming along the fence line. As he made his way through the throng of prisoners, he stopped to gaze first at Early's flowerbeds that were bursting with color, then at the pigeons pecking at the crumbs of day-old bread Early had spread out for them on the chapel lawn. When he noticed several prisoners heading along Tom's Way for their evening classes, he realized it was a school night for Albert, too, and he was probably halfway down Turk's Street by now on his way to class.

70

Oliver watched the hustlers moving across the yard, announcing their inventories as they went along.

"Laker's jacket! Ten packs! Get your Laker's jacket!"

"I've got new Reeboks with the tag still on them! Size 12! Five packs!"

"Gold Timex! Brand new! Three packs!"

Behind the left field bleachers Melvin was selling hooch by the Tang jar and it was going fast. Those waiting in line knew it was good, too, because the ones who had just copped were coming back for more. "Hey, Priddy. No school tonight, Jim?"

Oliver waved at his co-worker. "Not tonight, Mel."

"You all right? You need anything?"

"I'm good, brother," Oliver said as he passed by.

He found Early and his crew sitting in the bleachers on the first base side of the infield. Oyster, with his headful of snow white hair and the bushy eyebrows that bore down on fatigued lids, and brown eyes that worked their way through a squint, looked down and saw Oliver before the others did. Round-shouldered and soft looking, Oyster was the one who loved to argue, Oliver recalled. Beside him was Peabo, the sensible one, even though he had the face of a man who looked as if he had chosen argument for a career: Battered like a prizefighter, complete with scar tissue over both eyes and leather pockets that sagged under them, he had thick stubby hands and oversized feet. His best feature was a smile that you couldn't help but return. And then there was Bell sitting beside Early. Bell, too, had battle scars. One was a six-inch queue that slanted across his forehead and through his eyebrow and looked like a piece of fishing line. Another was in his aqua-blue eyes that were perpetually sad and distant. Although Oliver had only been around Early's friends a few times, he was left with the impression that Bell was always preoccupied.

As he hopped up on the bleacher and Early saw him, Oliver shouted, "Hey Early! Peabo! Oyster! Mr. Bell!"

Oliver tried to focus on the crisscrossed conversation but he was distracted by a Bobby Womack song playing on a passing radio. Early was reading the paper, and he slapped the pages on his knee when he found the story he was looking for. "You all remember Maurice Wiley, don't you?"

"Yeah," said Peabo. "The guy from Homewood. Killed his wife after he caught her doing the nasty with his dog. What about him?"

"Well, he got off on third degree. They gave him ten to twenty. Looks like I lost that bet. You too, Oyster."

Early peeked over the top of the newspaper at Oyster who was mumbling under his breath. Early grinned and elbowed Oliver in the ribs, then pointed to Oyster. Oliver grinned too.

"You lost too, Oyster," Early said again.

"Like hell. I didn't bet on that man's outcome."

"You sure?"

"I'm damn sure. One thing I'm not is senile. You say he got ten to twenty?"

"That's what the paper says. He got off on account of it being a crime of passion." Before Early could utter another syllable, Bell went off.

"Ever heard the sound of an M-79 rocket launcher! Do I have to draw a picture for you? We are all like lambs in a field, disporting ourselves in the eye of the butcher who chooses one, then another, for his prey."

Oliver kept his nose in the sports section of the newspaper; his concentration countered the uneasiness he felt while Bell was reliving his past.

"Ain't it the truth, Bell?" Peabo said, as insouciant as a wink.

"I'm not saying I shouldn't have come to jail for doing what I did," said Oyster. "That's not what I'm saying. I'm saying a crime of passion's not first degree murder and mine was a crime of passion. Mr. Priddy."

"Oliver."

"Okay. Oliver. How do you define first degree murder?"

"I don't know much about the law," Oliver said, "but I know that first degree murder has to do with premeditation."

"Exactly! And I didn't plan a damn thing! I came home from work and found what I found and then I snapped. It was a crime of passion.

You tell me how that's first degree murder, Mr. Oliver, and I'll never say another word about my case as long as I live:

"I remember it was a Friday 'cause we got paid that morning and the boss sent us home early that afternoon on account of there wasn't any work in the shop. When I got home there was a note taped to the back door from my wife Shirley. See, Shirley wasn't counting on me being home until around 5:30. That's when I usually came in from work. She was planning on stepping out early that night and didn't plan on being home when I got there. 'Oyster,' the note said. 'Your good-for-nothing monkey shit on my sofa for the last time. His brains are in the kitchen sink. You may want to eat them so you can have some of your own. Love, Shirley Bey.' Boy, I swear she was the most sarcastic woman I ever knew.

"Anyway, I opened the back door and stepped into the kitchen and sure enough there was my marmoset, Duke, laying in the sink with the top of his head cut off. His brains were floating in a Tupperware bowl. Shirley's electric carving knife was still plugged in and sitting on the counter. Blood and bones were splattered all over the walls, the cabinets, the ceiling. I had to clear my head so I sat down at the table. I wasn't crying or nothing, I was just shocked out of my mind. It wasn't like losing a dog that was loyal and loving for a lot of years and then up and dies. It wasn't like that at all. I'd won the damn thing in a card game and was looking to get rid of it anyway, only I was counting on turning a profit. So, I was sitting there thinking about what could have made her lose her mind and that's when I heard what sounded like a blues record playing in the back bedroom. I didn't know if it was Shirley or a burglar, so I took out my little .38 and tip-toed down the hall. My bedroom door was ajar when I got there and it only took one look to see it wasn't no burglar or blues record I was hearing. It was Shirley Bey singing and moaning under the high-yellow Blue Sheen Cosmetics lady. I stood there for a minute as frozen as a lawn jockey watching the two of them writhing and moaning all over my king-sized bed. The police said I fired all six rounds; I don't remember firing one. All I remember is standing there blinking and squinting, you know the way you do when you're coming out of a bad dream? Only this wasn't no dream. One of the bullets passed right through Shirley's left eye. That yellow bitch was hit twice, but she lived to tell about it."

Oyster paused and just when Oliver thought he was through he started up again.

"They gave me life. She killed *my* monkey and shared *my* bed with a woman, and they gave me life. Now you tell me, Mr. Oliver Priddy, you tell me that was first degree murder and I'll never say another word about my case."

Oliver didn't know if he could open his mouth without bursting into tears. It was one of the most pitiful stories he had ever heard. "There's no way that was premeditated, Oyster. No way. You must have had one sorry-ass lawyer, that's all I can say."

Oyster didn't answer and this time the silence washed over them like warm rain. Oliver had heard other prisoners' stories before, but this one had to be the sorriest one he had ever heard. As he sat there thinking about Oyster and the way he had told his story, it occurred to him just how theatrical prison life really was. They told stories to one another in order to have something to feel and what they did to others they did in order to make them feel. One day the sun was rising over yellow irises dripping with the blood of someone who needed to know what it felt like to be crossed, and the next day its golden rays were announcing the arrival of some young buck who didn't know which way was up and had to let somebody know it.

Early broke the silence. "Oyster, ain't it your turn to treat?"

"As I recall you just lost a bet," Oyster said. "Besides, I bought all last week. You must be getting senile, Early."

"Okay. Who wants ice cream?"

"Get me a Nutty Buddy," said Oyster.

"I'll have one too," said Peabo. Bell wanted an ice cream sandwich.

"What about you, Oliver?"

"'Preciate it, but I've got to go take care of something. I enjoyed hanging out with you cats. Nothing beats good company."

"You're welcome back any time," said Peabo.

"A friend of Early's is a friend of ours," said Oyster.

Bell waved goodbye. As he walked beside Early down the third base line, Oliver listened to the crickets chirping in the ivy that crawled over the walls of the Home Block and the pastoral sound reminded him of spring evenings long ago on his grandfather's farm. He recalled the game he and his brother Skip had made out of seeing who could silence the last cricket in the patch of ivy that grew along the main pasture's fence line. The boys' methods couldn't have been more different. Oliver would run along a path that was parallel to the fence while clapping his hands and shouting, "Shut it up! Shut it up!" Skip's tactic had been to step inside the pasture and run beside the fence while sharply rapping a tobacco stick against the wooden fence posts. How Oliver missed those days now.

He looked over his shoulder as the pitcher released the ball and was braced to protect Early and himself from any foul balls coming their way. A tall, stocky prisoner in a green cap pushed Early in an effort to get past him and Oliver grabbed his arm. "Hey, what's the big hurry?" Oliver asked.

"Get the fuck off my arm," the prisoner snapped, moving on through the crowd.

Oliver left Early standing in the ice cream line and headed for the auditorium. He stood inside the doorway and checked his watch. It was almost time. Through the glass in the door he watched the door to the little St. Regis and at eight o'clock sharp Fat Daddy came strutting down the ramp dressed in his apple green hospital uniform and shiny brogans, just as he had for the last three nights Oliver had been watching him. When he passed by the auditorium doors, Oliver followed him from a distance. Prisoners were returning from the evening medication line and Tom's Way was crowded with Thorazine shufflers and other drug-induced prisoners walking in Oliver's direction. At the intersection of Turk's Street and Tom's Way he stopped and watched Fat Daddy cross Main Street and head up the hospital driveway. When he saw Fat Daddy enter the lobby, Oliver fell in with the crowd that was moving back toward the cellblocks.

Inside the little St. Regis, he took the front stairwell all the way to the fifth tier and started down E-tier, walking slowly and reading each name tag as he went along. When he reached the divide, he stopped and draped his arms over the railing to watch a speedboat racing down the river. Behind him, two prisoners were emptying their trash into fifty-five gallon barrels; another was washing clothes in the deep sink. There was only one other prisoner on the tier at the far end, but there were several men moving up and down the four stairwells at the divide, so he waited. After a while he realized no one was paying any attention to him and headed down the back half of the tier.

He only had four cells to go when he noticed that the prisoner who was hanging out on the tier was now watching him curiously. Oliver read him fast. He was dressed in tight white shorts and a tank top and he had shoulder length hair that looked as if it had just been brushed a thousand times. His eyebrows were plucked and shaped in a high arch, his legs were tan and hairless. Except for the protruding knot in his throat, he could have passed for a girl. His cell door was open and Oliver read his name on the door card. *Blossom, Donald*, E-63.

"Hello," Donnie Blossom said, leaning against the black iron railing with his slender arms spread out.

Oliver nodded as he passed by.

At the next cell Oliver found what he was looking for. *Petaway, Winfield*, E-64. He turned the corner and hurried down the back steps all the way to the flats. An excellent arrival and escape route, he thought. And right there was the shower room. He could go right in, strip down, wash the blood off his body and out of his clothes, wipe his prints off the nail and drop it down the drain. He would chuck the wooden handle in one of the trash barrels at the divide. He returned to his cell and started to put on his water stinger for a cup of coffee but stopped short and squeezed his balls with his right hand in anticipation of the relief he would feel once he annihilated Fat Daddy. When Early had first told him about Fat Daddy's success rate in turning out white boys, Oliver had taken little heed to the warning. After all he had dealt with this kind of threat before and he was confident his reputation would work to his advantage now. It wasn't until his new neighbor told him he'd seen a "skinny yellow coon" coming out of his cell two mornings in a row last week that fear had run through him like an Indy car race. He knew then that only a preemptive strike would quell his fear.

Excited and restless now, he walked out on the tier and watched more speedboats go by while he tried to imagine how it would feel when the ten-penny nail entered the side of Fat Daddy's neck for the first time. The second time. He pictured the purple-red blood gushing out of the holes and wondered if the nail punctures would distort Fat Daddy's voice when he called out for help or to say you white motherfucker. His imagination was suddenly interrupted by the flip-flop of sandals on the stone floor down on the flats. He looked down and saw Donnie Blossom walking at a fast pace to the front of the cellblock. Oliver leaned over the railing and watched as Donnie pulled up at the end of the phone line and folded his arms. Oliver quickly closed his cell door and hustled to the back of the tier and up the three flights of stairs. He eased around the corner of E-tier, pulled open Fat Daddy's door and stepped into his cell.

The first thing he noticed was the squadron of model airplanes hanging from the ceiling by various lengths of thread. Each one was beautifully painted with a decal tag affixed above it that identified the kind of plane it was. A B-17, a P-51 Mustang, an F-86 Sabre, an F-4 Phantom II. The only one Oliver recognized was the F-4 Phantom II that had been so superior against the Soviet Mig-17s in the Vietnam War. There were stars and a half moon covered in glitter hanging strategically between and around the planes. The overall look was aesthetically pleasing. A freak with a seventh grade hobby, Oliver thought.

He took a good look around the room and stopped when he saw the iron bed frame standing from floor to ceiling in the front corner of the cell. The frame was covered with a navy blue mover's quilt and made a perfect privacy panel. And a perfect place to hide behind. Oliver turned his body sideways and eased between the wall and the frame. He pictured the point of attack, the angle of the blows. He was excited.

He opened Fat Daddy's cell door and stepped out on the tier.

"Hey, what are you doing?" Donnie Blossom asked. He was standing there with his lips apart, eyebrows arched, one hand on his hip.

"I was looking for a friend's cell," Oliver said, "I think I'm on the wrong tier."

"You're the same guy who passed by here fifteen minutes ago." Donnie didn't say it accusingly. "I remember your face. And those green eyes."

"Sorry, man. I got the wrong cell. Do you live here?"

"I live next door. It's okay. Everybody makes mistakes. You didn't take anything, did you? Maybe I should frisk you." Donnie smiled salaciously when he said maybe I should frisk you.

"No, I didn't take anything. I wouldn't steal from another convict."

"Okay, then. No harm done."

Oliver slid his hands into his front pockets and walked away. "No harm done," he repeated. "See you around."

"I hope so."

Oliver descended the back stairs two at a time. When he got to his cell he let out a heavy sigh of relief. He had started smoking a couple of months after quitting the boxing team to go to school full time and now he reached for the Camel package. He stretched out on the bed letting his long fingers rub his shirt pocket where his lighter should be. Everything's cool, he thought, before he lit up. He closed his eyes and threw his arm over his face to keep the light coming through the bars from overexposing his thoughts. In the darkness he could see a rain of ten-penny nails coming down faster than hail pellets had when he had tried to catch them in his hands as a boy. Ten-penny nails that would puncture holes in everything he had going for him. His runway model, the job he loved so much, his friends and all his books and new ideas were about to go south.

chapter six

AT EIGHT O'CLOCK in the morning, the setup committee for Prisoner Appreciation Day was putting up a canopy over the outdoor grills, and Little Freddie the sound man was wiring the outdoor stage for the live bands that would play all day: Paul Savoy's Motown Memories; Faruq Wideman's jazz quartet, Mellow Mood; and Al Byna's classic rock band, Red Licorice. In two hours the yard would be transformed into one big festival complete with hidden wine stands, reefer parties and an array of scheduled activities: sack and bicycle races, softball throwing and pass, punt and kick contests, handball and chess tournaments, and a game of softball played on the backs of ten rented donkeys.

Prisoner Appreciation Day was the one day of the year when the three prisoner organizations were able to give something back to the men who had supported them throughout the year by paying dues and patronizing their concession stands. The first round of hamburgers and hot dogs, sodas and popcorn, and ice cream sandwiches was on the house. Seconds would cost.

It was also, unofficially, the one day of the year for a truce between all rival parties. For the five years Prisoner Appreciation Day had been taking place, not a single fight or dispute had been settled on this day. The beauty of it all was that even with five hundred men in the yard at one o'clock in the afternoon, not a single guard would be in the mix. Why would they be? What would they accomplish? Two with shotguns kept watch on the catwalk outside the number one and two gun towers, and who knew how many pairs of eyes were watching through binoculars from the top floor of the administration building? It didn't matter anyway, for the administration believed in the old cliché, let sleeping dogs lie.

The scene outdoors was picture-perfect for a prison picnic: a cool breeze, sunny blue skies, birds singing in the hundred year old oak tree, on the barbed wire and in the rooftop gutters. The sidewalks were still wet from Early's garden hose and plastic garbage cans were being set out along the fence line and wall of the big St. Regis.

Inside the two cellblocks, some prisoners were still sleeping while others were just waking up and heating water for their morning coffee, or on their way to the shower or curled up in their beds watching cartoons. The guards patrolling the tiers stayed on the move for the entire hundred yards down the tier, around the back and up the other side. They didn't stop when they smelled overripe fruit, hashish or reefer, or when their peripheral vision picked up six in a cell or a curtain blocking the entire view. The guards believed in a variation of another cliché: hear no evil, see no evil.

When Oliver returned from his morning shower he was setting his Brute shower kit on the shelf when he heard sudden footsteps behind him. In the time it took him to shift his feet he felt the palm of a hand slam against the side of his face and then his world went black. The culprit rammed Oliver's head into the brick wall a second time and watched him crumble to the floor. Then he closed the door and pulled the curtain, grabbed Oliver's legs and slid his body to the middle of the floor. Oliver was bleeding from his nose and a gash over his left eye. Fat Daddy stood over him smiling while he touched himself. "Got you now, you white bitch!" he said softly.

Slowly, Oliver began to move. As he pressed the palms of his hands against the floor, Fat Daddy stepped on his neck and held him down while he dug in his back pocket for the red cord. After tying Oliver's hands behind his back, he grabbed a handful of Oliver's hair and yanked his head back. "You yell or try to fight this and I'll put you to sleep, you hear?"

Fat Daddy knelt between Oliver's legs, lifted Oliver's bathrobe over his back, and then reached for the tube of Vaseline in his sock. He was unscrewing the cap when the steam whistle over the boiler house suddenly blasted one long shrill note, paused and blasted again and again.

"Come on, Fat Daddy! The guards are at the front of the tier! Hurry!" Donnie Blossom yanked open Oliver's door. "Come on, Fats! You didn't hurt him, did you? Oh God!"

"What the fuck's going down?" Fat Daddy asked, his face flush with anger.

"Come on! They're telling everyone to lock up! Something happened! I don't know! Is he okay?"

"Why the fuck do you care? Get your ass out of here!" Fat Daddy kicked Oliver's footlocker and looked down at him. "I'll be a motherfucker!"

"Come on, Fat Daddy!"

Fat Daddy started to untie Oliver's hands, but changed his mind. He stared down at Oliver's bare buttocks one last time before he said, "You're mine, Priddy! I'll be back!" Then he hurried out of the cell, carefully closing the door behind him.

Oliver lay there trying to distinguish left from right. Stars flashed in his head and random words surfaced. *Help! Momma! Get up!* The left side of his head throbbed and pulsated; he could hear a high-speed train and the wail of a whistle. *Oh, shit!* He rapidly blinked his eyes and the more he did, the more the stars faded. He tried to move his arms but they were fused together behind his back. He moved his hands, wiggled his fingers and turned on his side. Something familiar brushed up against his fingers. *Soft strings. Shoelaces.* He touched his sneakers and heard shouts and an awful banging, then the loud rick-racking of a train hightailing it down the track. He managed to sit up, his back pressed against the cold steel of the bed frame. It was making sense now. He traced his memory. In the shower. Singing. Up the steps, down the tier, into his cell and *wham!* He vomited into his lap—two waffles and Rice Krispies. *Get up, get up!*

He moved his wrists back and forth but there was no give. He heard voices drawing near, shouts, more banging. "This is an emergency lockdown! Everyone take it in immediately!" The banging he heard was the long iron lever at the end of the tier the guards pulled to secure the cell doors. The guard was striking the bar against the wall, that much he knew.

It took several tries before he was able to stand. He backed up to the sink and felt for the razor blade he kept on the ledge. With his thumb and index finger, he picked it up and slowly touched the blade close to his wrist. Feeling the restraint, he pressed the blade into it and sawed away. Halfway through he nicked his thumb. His fingertips were wet with blood now, and he lost his grip on the blade. Frustrated, he balled up his fists and with a violent jerk he forced one fist down and the other one up at the same time. No sooner was he free then he heard the guard's boots thumping down the tier. He turned his back to the door and when the guard stopped in front of his cell, Oliver was sure he was going to be told to turn his light on, but the guard said nothing. Oliver stood there until he heard the guard's footsteps fade away down the tier and then he went to the mirror.

The gash over his eye wasn't deep, but the blood was still oozing from the wound. He filled the sink with cold water and stuck his face in it, shaking his head from side to side to loosen up the blood that had dried in his nose. When the water turned pink, he emptied out the sink and repeated the process.

He looked at himself in the mirror again. His eye was swollen but no more than it would have been on his worst day of sparring. The side of his head was swollen, too, and he could still hear a train running through it. He had a splitting headache and wanted to lie down and go to sleep, but he didn't. He had read somewhere that it could be dangerous to fall asleep after suffering a head wound. He was sure he had a concussion.

After a moment he sat on the toilet and noticed that his feet were wet. When he looked down and saw the puddle of urine in the middle of the floor, he put his head in his hands, leaned forward and began to cry. Not for Oliver the Victim, but for Oliver the Optimist, the Oliver who had thought he could put off for tomorrow what he should have done weeks ago. He had thought through the details like a battlefield strategist, first exchanging the ten-penny nail for a ten inch lead pipe, then practicing the force of the blows on a balled-up mattress so he wouldn't kill the nasty freak, but merely maim him so he'd drool spit and slur his words for years to come. The one important thing he had failed to do was mark the calendar and the time of his attack. He had been having too much fun studying and going to college and flirting with girls to carry out a preemptive strike. As he wiped his tears in the crook of his arm and consoled himself at the same time, he was firm in his resolve not to play the waiting game a second longer than it took for the doors to open again.

After washing his feet and cleaning the floor, he got dressed and listened to the conversations around him. Someone up the tier was relaying information down the tier. Police boats had been spotted near the banks of the river in front of the administration building. A coroner's van had just pulled up in the visitor's parking lot. "Somebody drowned!" a man up the tier shouted.

But there had to be more to it than that. Someone drowning in the Ohio River had nothing to do with the orderly running of the prison. Swimmers had drowned right in front of the prison before and they'd never locked down the joint.

Five minutes later the sergeant's husky voice boomed over the PA system and the prisoners thought they had the answer. "Count time! Count time! This is an emergency count! Stand by your door! Lights on!"

Maybe someone had escaped and couldn't swim. It had happened before and they'd locked down the prison just like they did this morning. More chatter along the grapevine confirmed that they had found a body. The body bag was coming up over the riverbank just now. Oliver looked out the window and could see two speedboats from the McKee's Rocks side of the river heading straight toward the prison. As they came closer they veered off toward the administration building.

Even though they had all been gypped out of a free picnic, the prisoners were excited over the events that were unfolding. The media had come to Riverview. Channel Two news trucks were in the parking lot, along with real cops and the county coroner.

"Holy fuck! This is serious, y'all! They just found another body! They're bringing it up the bank right now!" Some fool yelled they were probably just filming an episode of "Hill Street Blues," and that was what the commotion was all about. Someone else discredited the fool when he yelled back, "'Hill Street Blues' ain't filmed in Pittsburgh, dumb ass!"

"Oh yeah? Well, this episode is! And who you calling dumb ass?"

"You, dumb ass!"

It went on like that all morning until the reporter Cindy Burns of KDKA news brought them the truth on the twelve o'clock news. "Two bodies were found floating near the banks of the Ohio River this morning in front of Riverview Penitentiary on the North Side of the city. An unidentified white female believed to be in her late twenties, and a black male in his early thirties were discovered a little after nine by passing boaters. Both victims were fully clothed. Police have identified the male victim, but are not releasing his name at this time. We'll have more details on this story tonight at six."

After hearing the story the prisoners' emotions were jolted from excitation over the speculation that one or two of their own had almost gotten away to sheer indifference over learning that the victims were probably just some white trash hooker and a trick, and then to blatant anger over their day having been ruined for no good cause. The mood in the cellblock reminded Oliver of being in the dining hall on evenings when liver was the main entrée—in a fume. It stayed that way for several hours.

To take his mind off his own anger Oliver wrote two letters. One to his mother June telling her he might be losing his phone privileges and not to worry if he didn't call for a while; he was fine, just a blunder in judgment. He would let her know when it was okay for her and Skip to visit. Then he wrote a letter to Albert and told him the whole story about Fat Daddy and what he had to do to settle the matter once and for all. When the doors opened again he would give Early the letter to deliver to Albert before he climbed the back stairwell to the fifth tier and split Fat Daddy's head open to the bone.

Others around him spent the day turning the wheel on the rumor mill. The dead woman was the superintendent's daughter. The black man was a former con named Bub Dukes. But it would take one ignorant prisoner to believe that story, for Bub Dukes was a notorious dope addict who had been out on parole long enough to have a heroin habit so vicious he couldn't get a hard-on if he'd wanted to. No, it wasn't that. It was simply two lovers who had been walking along the bank and fallen into the river. Maybe one fell and the other drowned in the rescue. And then there was the one about a white woman who was kidnapped and raped by a black man, and somehow they had both ended up drowning. With all their clothes on!

Before the six o'clock evening news came on, every gambler in the cellblock had put down a bet on the lead story. By the time Ed Burns told it all, the five hundred men in the little St. Regis were rattling their cages and laughing hysterically. The dead woman had been identified as thirty-two year old Melinda Cain, third wife of forty-five year old cult leader and polygamist Virgil Cain, a prisoner at Riverview. Virgil Cain was serving fifteen to thirty years for having sex with underage girls. The black male, thirty-one year old Caesar Holmes from Lock Haven, Pennsylvania, was a professional welder by trade. He had apparently been hired by the Cain wives to help break Virgil Cain out of prison. The medical examiner said the two had been dead for up to three days.

From there the story took on the details of a Hollywood blockbuster. There was a labyrinth of tunnels under the prison, the newscaster reported, and one of the tunnels led to the banks of the river. The opening was closed off with a two-inch thick steel grate that had been welded and padlocked shut for a hundred years. Apparently, the victims had climbed down the bank and entered the niche that led to the tunnel grate after the tide had gone out sometime late Wednesday night. Found ten feet from the sealed grate was a set of portable welding tanks, complete with a cutting torch tip. According to Port Authority investigators, the two victims were trapped and drowned when the high tide came in suddenly sometime around twelve thirty a.m. on Thursday.

A spokesman for the prison said that Virgil Cain had been moved to another prison upstate and that Riverview would remain locked down until investigators could determine how and where Virgil Cain had planned on entering the tunnels inside the prison.

The hype was enough to hold everyone's attention for the next two days. Virgil Cain was both hated and revered by his peers. Hated for being a low-life pedophile who, for reasons that baffled everyone, had been allowed to bounce his thirteen-year old stepdaughters on his lap during weekly visits; and revered for having whatever it was he had that made women worship him. This polygamist had a word game that Billy Graham would envy, or else he had a very long tongue.

But the novelty wore off with the passing of each meal—a bag lunch consisting of a bologna and cheese sandwich, an orange and a half-pint of milk. By Monday evening those who didn't have food in their cells that they purchased from the commissary were feeling the hunger pains and letting the guards know it. "Take it easy, men," the sergeant told them when he was making his rounds. Chewing a wad of tobacco, he stood in front of Oliver's cell and spit a stream of the liquid shit over the tier and down the side of the wall. "You'll all be out in the morning."

Two hours later the same sergeant placed the prisoners' mail on the bars of their doors. Oliver received two letters. A message from his mother June telling him they would be up to see him soon, and a notice from the communications office informing him that he would be moving to the big St. Regis, cell L-14, when the institution resumed normal movement in the morning.

Oliver sighed long and deep, grappled with his obstinacy, then smiled as wide as a farmer who had prayed for rain and been rewarded with a downpour. Before he changed his mind and Winfield Petaway's fate, he quickly packed everything he owned into his footlocker, thinking with absolute certainty that the big St. Regis was far enough away from the vilest thing he knew.

AFTER LUNCH the next day, Champ the boxer was standing in front of his cell on M tier when Oliver showed up to see him. "Come on in, Priddy." Champ stepped into his cell, sat down and started rearranging piles of folded laundry. He was dressed for his morning roadwork. Purple sweatpants, two dingy gray sweatshirts, and black brogans. Champ stared at Oliver's swollen eye and grinned. "I thought you quit boxing a long time ago."

"I did," Oliver said, eyeing the six grapefruits on Champ's desk.

"Looks like you just had a sparring session with someone."

Oliver had momentarily forgotten about the mouse under his left eye and the fresh scab over it. "Just a little misunderstanding, that's all."

"Everything all right?"

"It is now."

"That's good. I want to ask you a serious question, Priddy. You feel safe in this joint?"

Before Oliver could answer, someone tapped him on the shoulder and said, "Are you coming or going? Let me get by, please."

Oliver stepped out of the way to let the prisoner enter Champ's cell. He was carrying a jug of steaming hot coffee wrapped in a yellow dishtowel. He wore blood-red Japanese slippers with gold thread and a white terry cloth bathrobe. His long black hair hung loose halfway down his back and over his shoulders, black curtains billowed around a strikingly feminine face. He had black almond-shaped eyes, flawless skin and thick lips, a delicate frame, but his hands were strong and marked by work.

"This is my boy, Little," Champ said. "Little, this is Oliver."

"How's it going?" said Oliver.

"Nice to meet you," the boy said. "Excuse me again."

After he was gone Champ said, "You want some coffee?"

"No thanks." Oliver stood at the threshold of the cell eyeing the posters on Champ's wall. Mohammad Ali, Dr. J, and the Honorable Elijah Mohammad. He looked around the room and two things impressed him: the racks of clothes hanging from several hooks on the walls—sweat suits, silk robes, jeans, shirts, jackets, and sweaters; and two waist-high stacks of books inside the door. The room had a strange smell to it, though. Oliver wasn't sure, but he thought it was a combination of dried sweat and cocoa butter.

"Well, do you, Priddy?"

"What?"

"Feel safe in here."

"Anybody would be a fool to feel safe in a penitentiary, Champ. I watch my back everywhere I go, but I'm not afraid. Just smart. I'll tell you one thing, though."

"What?"

"I feel a lot better now that I'm over here in the big St. Regis."

"Why's that?"

"Well, let's just say I was real close to fucking a dude up over there and now I don't have to."

"Lemme guess. Was it a niggah named Fat Daddy?"

"Yeah. That's the dude."

Champ smiled and dropped a pile of clothes into a cardboard box. "How do you think I knew that?"

"I don't know, man."

"Cuz I know everything that goes on in this joint. You think you're safer over here?"

"All I know is I'm glad to be away from that guy. He was stalking me everywhere I went. I didn't have any peace of mind except when I was at work or locked in my cell at night. It was nerve racking."

"Well, this is why I wanted to talk to you, Priddy. See this block's no different, man. There's guys over here tougher and crazier than Fat Daddy and they're everywhere. In the stairwells, the showers, around every corner, ducking behind the trash cans. All they're looking to do is pounce on something young, white and fresh. No disrespect intended, but you're a good looking dude, Priddy, and you're gonna have trouble over here too."

"Yeah, but there's something those guys don't know about me, Champ. I had to kill a guy already for that shit, and I'll do it again it if I have to." Suddenly, Oliver was feeling queasy, his adrenalin was pumping fast and the butterflies were fluttering in his stomach. He was relieved when he heard the work-line bell ring. "I've got to be getting to work now, Champ."

"Hold up, Jack. You still got ten minutes. I called you up here to ask you a question. How'd you like to be my partner?"

Oliver couldn't hide his disappointment or his fear. His jaw dropped and his eyes were wide. A red scald rose up his neck and into his cheeks. "What kind of question is that, Champ? I thought you and I were cool, man. I ain't no punk."

Champ grinned and shook his head. "Calm down, Priddy. We cool. I like you. You're all right for a white guy. Look. You get visits, right?"

"Yeah, every week."

"All right. Get your girl to start bringing you reefer. You smoke?"

"Yeah."

"Okay. Keep a little for yourself each time and give me the rest. Let's say a couple ounces a month. I'll sell enough to pay your girl back for the stuff and keep the rest for myself. We can be business partners. You won't ever have to worry about another niggah in this joint even looking funny at you."

Oliver sighed slowly, relieved to learn that Champ wasn't interested in trying to demoralize him. He knew what his answer would be. He admired Champ and enjoyed hanging out with his squad in the Young Guns Boxing Gym. They had never ridiculed or teased him after he quit the team to go to school and when he came in to work out on the heavy bag and jump rope once or twice a week, they welcomed him with open arms, treating him like a brother. Big Jake. Brother Melvin. Disco Bob. Blue Light. Cheese. Soul Train. And Champ. These North Philly boys, notorious not just for their gang-warring prowess, superior boxing skills and unflinching courage, also had a gift for talking jive and ribbing one another. Oliver loved hearing them play the dozens. He felt a real kinship when he was around these fellows. There was no reason why he couldn't help Champ make a few dollars for himself while at the same time gain the one thing in the world he needed to prosper. Albert was going home in a few months and he had already arranged for Oliver to continue receiving packages once he got home. Oliver's part of the deal would be a cinch.

"Yeah. We can do that, Champ. But what happens if my girl leaves me? What do we do then?"

"As slick as you are, I know you'll find another chick sooner or later."

"Okay. It's a deal," Oliver said.

"Wait. There's one more thing, Priddy. I've come a long way in math and I appreciate all the help you've been giving me up in that school. I'm going to try one more time to pass that GED exam but if I fail it again, you're going to have to find a way to take the math test for me the next time. I've got to get my diploma, man. That's all there is to it."

"You'll pass it, Champ."

"Yeah, but if I don't, you've got to find a way to take the exam into the bathroom or somewhere and complete it for me."

"Okay. If it comes down to that, I will."

"Solid. So it's a deal?"

"Yeah."

"All right. Let's shake on it."

AFTER MAKING HIS quid pro quo deal, Oliver immediately stopped reading and sleeping with one eye peeled to the door. No longer did he squeeze his anus tighter than a vise or walk around checking over his shoulder every time he turned a corner. Now he threw himself into his studies. Now he could concentrate with the precision of a microscope. During his childhood it had been easy for him to become enthusiastic about a new hobby or adventure only to grow bored and lose interest when the novelty wore off. Baseball cards had lost their importance the minute the bubble gum lost its flavor. Winning every cat's eye and steely in the circle wasn't as much fun as giving the whole sack of marbles away in the end. Bringing home pockets full of Mary Janes from Woolworth's was a strong second to the excitement he experienced when he had first shoplifted them. But that didn't happen when it came to pursuing his education. His hunger for knowledge was relentless.

Every night after the dead bolt dropped on his door, he withdrew like a hermit crab into his inner world. For the next four years he studied subjects ranging from religions of the world to personality disorders, multicultural poetry, criminal justice, calculus, satire, public speaking and many others. Though he was more interested in literature and philosophy than he was in mathematics and history, he still earned straight As in calculus and the history of Western civilization. So in awe of the academic world and so concerned about his status within that world was he that he was compelled to master every subject he took up. His greatest passion of all was literature, though, for it was through the vicarious experience of reading that he had come to recognize a truth and internalize it. *The Count of Monte Cristo* may have been a condemned man, but hope still ran through his prison. If the protagonist in *The Red Badge of Courage* was a coward, Oliver wanted to be one too. After reading the novels of a Russian writer named Dostoyevsky, he found a book of letters the author had written while he had been in a Siberian prison. One particular letter Dostoyevsky sent to his brother gave Oliver permanent assurance that it didn't matter whether he was in prison or out in society because, as Dostoevsky had so eloquently put it, "... life is life everywhere. Life is in ourselves, not in the world that surrounds us." Oliver read these words and the epiphany moved him to tears.

Discovering life inside himself eventually led Oliver to grapple with his Catholic upbringing and reject original sin as the source of his suffering. It was original ignorance, he believed, that was the root of all suffering. He rejected, too, the father, son and holy ghost, and the rest of the supernatural kingdom. Pascal's wager was fascinating, but it went against the grain of his own thinking. If we live our lives as believers and find in the end that there is no God, we have lost nothing, Pascal proposed. But if we live as non-believers and find ourselves face to face with a supernatural God at the end, then our proverbial goose is cooked for all of eternity. *Cela vous fera croire et vous abetira.* ("This will make you believe and you will be stupefied.") Oliver disagreed that there was nothing to lose by believing blindly, for to do so, as the Church demanded, was to stop searching for the truth.

With every book he opened he found a reason to turn the page. When he studied Greek mythology, Mnemosyne, the goddess of memory, became his heroine and led him to other books where he learned advanced mnemonic tricks for remembering formulas, dates and important names and geographic regions. In philosophy, Husserl's idea of intentionality became his grail: "If our 'gaze' toward a thought or idea is a stone thrown toward its object, then meaning depends on how hard we throw the stone." Eureka!

During these years his increasing sense of inner freedom led him to write in his journal about the aesthetic side of his daily life:

October 9, 1982. Today while I was sitting in the bleachers reading Emerson's "Self Reliance," I saw a blind man standing near the wall. He was a gaunt and gristly looking man with blotches of pink and brown skin covering his face and hands. For a while I watched him standing there tapping his red-stick-of-a-cane to the rhythm of the blue handball the prisoners were hitting against the wall. What disease, I wondered, had caused his black skin to turn pink like that and his hair to fall out in patches, leaving the bald spots a hue of sickly pinkish-brown? I thought to myself this man would curse God's ass up one side and down the other if he knew how horrible and pathetic he looked. Dostoyevsky said that denial of self-expression is death to the soul, so when I came in from the yard this evening I wrote this poem about discovering a blind man among us:

STUDY OF A BLIND PRISONER
The Blind Man who stands
near the cracked asylum wall
and tap tap taps his red
stick-of-a-cane is as lonely
and lame as the old guard
who stands above the wall,
chained, hour after hour,
to his gray and gloomy gun tower.

It was a little over a year later when the blind prisoner tapped his way up the steps of the education building and into the classroom where Oliver was explaining the Pythagorean theorem to a group of GED students:

February 21, 1984. Today I finally met the blind prisoner face to face. His name is Milo and he's from right here on the North Side of the city. He came up to the school this morning to inquire about a system of learning mathematics by finger counting. I asked if he knew how to read Braille and if he had enough books to read. He hesitated for a few seconds and then he said, "I have a disease in my nervous system that causes my fingertips to be numb, so I can't feel the Braille." I can't even begin to describe how sorry I felt for him when he told me this. Wasn't it bad enough that the man was blind? Did he have to suffer even more? I told him I would ask my boss if there was anything he could do to help him with his needs. He seemed like an easygoing fellow. After we got to talking, I found out he's an avid jazz fan. I told him I'd look for him on the yard over the weekend so we could talk more and listen to some of his jazz tapes on that giant boom box he lugs around.

After that day Milo turned Oliver on to the Jazz Crusaders and Oliver gave Milo his Jackie Wilson's Greatest Hits tape to listen to. One day Oliver's boss, Mr. Lionel Sommers, brought a woman from the Pennsylvania Society for the Blind to meet and teach Milo how to calculate math on his fingers. A week later the woman brought him stories and magazines on audio tapes and Milo thanked her over and over. Then he thanked Mr. Sommers who later thanked Oliver. "You're a real asset to this school, Oliver," his boss told him one morning as the sun glinted through the half-open Venetian blinds. "You've become a fine teacher, too, and I think it's time you had your own classroom. Why don't you move into the learning skills center? You can set the room up for your high school classes and you can clean out that storage closet in the back of the room and use it for an office. How's that sound?"

"Man, you don't know how much I appreciate that, Mr. Sommers," Oliver exclaimed.

"Well, you've earned it, Oliver, and let me tell you something else. A professor named Dr. B.J. Dallet is coming to our graduation this spring. She's a good friend of mine. I've told her all about your academic achievements and the great progress you've made getting through to some of our most difficult GED students. She's interested in talking with you about attending graduate school. Now if you can get admitted into her program and earn your Master's, I think you'll be in an excellent position to go home one day. I'm not going to be working in this godforsaken prison forever. A few more years and I'm out of here. You should be finished earning your graduate degree by then. As long as I'm not working for the DOC, I can attend your pardons hearing and speak on your behalf if you'd like me to."

Oliver was dumbfounded. "Are you serious? I'd be grateful as hell, Mr. Sommers. That's how Garfield Gilly got out. A retired police commissioner from his home town vouched for him. I can't wait to tell my family."

"Just make sure you keep doing the right thing. Don't let me down."

"I won't. Thanks, Mr. Sommers." Oliver took Mr. Sommers' hand and shook it jubilantly. "Hey, before I go, there's a rumor going around that we're getting a new warden. Any truth to it?"

"It's true. He's a troubleshooter from central office. The deputy warden told us at yesterday's staff meeting that a lot of changes are coming down the pike and they're sending this guy down here to initiate them."

"Changes? Like what?"

"For one thing, and you didn't hear this from me, Oliver, they're talking about putting two men in a cell to help relieve the overcrowding."

"Two men living in one of these little ass cages? They're out of their minds. These men aren't going to go for that, Mr. Sommers."

"What do you think they'll do?"

"I don't know."

Mr. Sommers shook his head in frustration. "In your opinion, Oliver, is Champ Burnett capable of keeping the lifers under control?"

"Not all of them, he's not. He might be the most respected guy in this prison, but that doesn't mean everyone will listen to him. He wouldn't expect them to either. Not about something like this."

"At some point, they're probably going to be calling Champ in to see if he'll help them keep the guys calm when these new changes start taking place."

"You mean there's more? What else are they talking about?"

"Well, they're going to restrict varsity sports teams from traveling every week, and they're talking about doing away with the Christian family masses and cutting back on the number of hours you men get for your organizations' annual picnics. There's some other things too, but they're not finalized yet."

"Like what, Mr. Sommers?"

"The DOC is asking the legislators for money to build three new prisons. With this new governor backing them, they'll no doubt get it too, I'm afraid. It's really a shame. They've slashed my educational budget to hell."

As Oliver twisted his face in disgust, thunder shook the roof and was followed by the first spatters of rain. The raindrops sounded hard, like someone flinging handfuls of pebbles into a washtub. Prison could seem like a boring place, about as dangerous as a maternity ward when everything was going well. The days and weeks and months could pass without cause for alarm, and then something like a memo could appear announcing the slightest change and someone would go down with the speed of a kamikaze pilot. The slightest change and someone reminded everyone else just how dangerous prison really was.

But what worried Oliver more than the threat of these new changes was how they appeared to be in sync with the new wave of politicians who were getting elected all over the state by running on a campaign that promised to get tough on crime and criminals. Every night on the six o'clock news these politicians were resounding the same theme: "It's time to lock 'em up and throw away the key."

WHEN IGNATIUS MELROSE WHITE showed up in the winter of 1983 with a briefcase full of new policies, the lifers' newsletter box swelled with complaints about the man and the changes he was putting down. Formerly the warden at White Hill Penitentiary, Ignatius Melrose White was now the new "Superintendent" at Riverview. The title "warden" had outlived its purpose and a new euphemism was now in place. The new warden's stationery read, simply, Superintendent I.M. White. That was the first change.

Second was the initiation of a noon count. For a hundred years the prisoners had been counted at six in the morning, four in the afternoon, and nine at night. In his first month, I.M. White added a noon count to the other three and the prisoners were infuriated. Another hour locked in their cells each day was another hour of punishment. Another hour of recreation lost. The prisoners filed their complaints to I.M. White and later to his bosses in central office. This noon count, argued the lifers' president, was nothing but a way to keep them locked down an hour or two more each day. I.M. White responded by telling Champ that times were changing and the men were going to have to get used to the changes.

The third change was an attempt to begin a mandatory standing count. The memo said that any prisoner who wasn't standing by his door when the guard came around for each count would be issued a disciplinary misconduct. The guards had never complained before if a man was sitting on his bed or lying on the floor during a count as long as he could be seen. Why make him stand now? But the prisoners didn't go for this mandatory standing count, and the guards never pressed the issue.

After that came a notice that the varsity sports teams would no longer be traveling weekly to compete with other prisons. Due to budget cuts and security concerns, the softball, basketball, track and field and boxing teams would only travel three times a year.

But the change that most infuriated everyone was having to stand in the rain, snow and bitter cold just to receive clean linen. At six-thirty in the morning every Wednesday, prisoners who wanted to exchange their sheets and towels for clean ones would have to walk down Turk's

Street and stand in line outside the clothing exchange room until they made it to the door. When Champ asked I.M. White what was wrong with having the linen delivered to their cells the way it had always been done, the new Superintendent told him the new procedure was more efficient for the laundry workers. "Maybe so, but you're pissing off the whole population," Champ said.

I.M. White didn't feel the threat. "Well, they'll just have to get used to it, Mr. Burnett. And, by the way, I hope you're training hard for your upcoming fight. I'm betting on you to win."

"So am I," Champ said, walking away and spitting on the ground when he was six feet up the sidewalk from the most arrogant black man he'd ever met.

Every one of these changes led to a mound of angry submissions to *The Wire* and while Oliver had been careful not to publish a single one, when the prisoner whose sobriquet was the "Greek" died in the license plate factory, he included a story about the tragedy on the front page of the March '84 issue. The author of the story had started out paying tribute to his friend but ended up lambasting the Department of Corrections. No one but the DOC was responsible for the three-inch thick bolt that came loose from a high-speed machine and burrowed through the Greek's forehead and into the back of his brain. The friend urged every reader who knew the Greek to write a letter to his family and encourage them to demand an investigation into the unsafe conditions inside the plant. He ended his tribute with a promise to write to the people at OSHA and demand an inspection of the prison industries plant. It was this last pledge that had Oliver sitting in the hot seat in the deputy superintendent's office.

"You lied to me, Priddy. Why'd you lie to me?"

Oliver was clueless. "Lied about what, Deputy Maroney?"

"When you started this newsletter project four years ago, you told me you wouldn't piss me off. You remember telling me that? You said, 'This newsletter will feature informative and entertaining news.' That's what you said, Priddy." The deputy held a copy of the newsletter in his hand. "This article on Jerry Coustopoulos's death is anything but informative and entertaining! It's downright offensive and inflammatory!"

"It was supposed to be a tribute to the Greek, sir. I guess I didn't read it close enough before it was typed up. It won't happen again."

Perpetually stooped and with the grace of a wading stork, Deputy Maroney shook his crooked finger in the air. "It won't happen again, Priddy, and here's why! From now on, I'm going to review the contents of every newsletter before it's distributed. I want a final draft of every issue on my desk by the third Friday of each month. Is that clear?"

"Yes, sir."

"Are you sure?"

"Absolutely, sir."

"Good. That's all. And Priddy?"

"Sir?"

"Keep up the good work."

"Yes, sir. Thank you."

A week later, two Black Panthers in a former life stood up at the lifers' monthly meeting and demanded to know why their articles on I.M. White and his new policies had been left out of the last two issues of *The Wire*. Brother Key-su swung his dreadlocks over his shoulders and said it was time they fired the editor and hired someone with a little backbone. The newsletter was too soft and too pro-administration. Oliver got up and said, "Anyone who wants my job can have it! But let me just tell you a couple of things first. I got my ass chewed out last month for printing that story on the Greek. Does anybody really think they're going to let us print stories that criticize them and get everyone hyped up? I'll gladly step aside if somebody thinks they can do a better job."

Champ, who was knocked-down tired from going seven rounds in the gym that afternoon, recalled the information Oliver's boss had shared with him and he, in turn, had shared with Champ. Oliver's loyalty had given Champ time to think and surreptitiously plan a strategy for confronting the issues the prisoners were facing with this new administration. "Ain't nobody replacing nobody," said Champ. "I have the same concerns you two Brothers have about all the shit that's going down. We got to talk about it, but we got to find another way of doing it than through that newsletter. Key-su, how about you and the other Brother seeing me right after this meeting? All right. That's the end of that. Mr. Secretary, what's the next item of business?"

1984

chapter seven

THE APRIL, 1984, ISSUE of *The Wire* paid homage to the one hundred and forty-two graduates who were scheduled to march down the aisle of the auditorium the first Saturday evening in June, in that grand old tradition known as graduation:

"SPRING GRADUATION COMING TO RIVERVIEW"
by Oliver Priddy

Next month the auditorium at Riverview will transform itself into hallowed grounds for one evening. One hundred and forty-two graduates will march down the aisles to the tune of "Pomp and Circumstance" and be awarded their just deserts for years of hard work and dedication. Forty-nine will receive high school diplomas while their homeroom teacher, Ms. Rhoda Cherry, will receive a year's supply of aspirin to treat the chronic headaches these brothers gave her. This year's class valedictorian is Junior Thompson, who scored a whopping 257 on his exams. Junior, you're the man! Junior will be starting classes this fall in the University program. We wish him continued success!

Another distinguished member of our GED graduates is also our state heavyweight boxing champion and president of the lifers' association, Brother Theodore "Champ" Burnett. For six long years, Champ kept his tenacity to learn as sharp as he keeps his punches. In addition to receiving his well-earned diploma, Champ will be honored with "Student of the Year" accolades. Congratulations, Champ!

Twelve proud barbers will march down the aisle with undoubtedly the best shaped heads in the building. How many of us guinea pigs paid the price for these brothers' success! How many high fades went too high before Chinaman finally got it right? And who among us isn't familiar with his favorite line: "Aw, Brother, don't worry about it. It'll grow back"? You all deserve a shout out. (Run those Kools in!)

The vocational school classes will send fifty-six graduates down the aisle this year: seven welders, eleven plumbers, fifteen auto mechanics, and twenty-three electronics technicians. The most noteworthy member of this entire group is Erie Sticks, who singlehandedly blew up more television sets and radios while trying to repair them than all the students combined in the history of the electronics class (and this statistic came directly from his instructor!). I know you all remember Sticks's patented line: 'The diodes must be bad!' Okay, Sticks! You've got your props now, baby!

Last to march across the stage will be the twenty-five new members of the University of Pittsburgh's alumni association. Thirteen men will receive Bachelor of Science degrees, and twelve, their Bachelor of Arts degrees. The valedictorian of this distinguished class is Gordon Welch, who is graduating with a 3.91 grade point average. A sincere and hearty congratulations to you, Brother Gordon! This year's keynote speaker will be Dr. B.J. Dallet, from the University of Pittsburgh's School of Education.

Expected to be in attendance are Superintendent I.M. White, Deputy Maroney, the entire academic and vocational staff, including tutors and janitors, various counselors and clergy and a sea of University faculty members. Each graduate will be permitted to have two visitors in attendance.

On behalf of the three prisoner organizations, *The Wire* extends a warm and sincere congratulations to all of the 1984 graduates. And to you graduates who are going home soon, as the one and only Mr. Ray Charles would say, "Don't you come back no more, no more, no more, no more. Hit the road, Jack!"

ON THAT DAY IN JUNE, in typical June weather, warm and bright, they swung open the auditorium doors, put away the dominoes and card tables, and poured boiling water on the gray cement floor. Scrubbed. Rinsed. Waxed. Folding chairs were brought out for the occasion. Fifteen rows of fifteen chairs on each side of the aisle. Color-coordinated pansies, impatiens, and petunias lay in long wooden boxes, painted in the University's colors, blue and yellow. Early placed the boxes across the front of the stage and then dressed the front and sides of the podium with fresh clematis vines. When he was finished, he arranged three dome-shaped birdcages made of papier-mâché and pipe cleaners between the flower boxes. Perched on a swing inside each cage was a perfectly sculpted bright blue songbird. What was possible to say about that was already in print on a banner being raised over the stage, a quote from the poet Maya Angelou: "I Know Why the Caged Bird Sings."

Early's helpers brought in more flowers arranged in large plastic pots covered in blue and yellow foil. Early arranged two pots on each window sill and one on each side of the five double doors.

As James Brown's song, "I Don't Want Nobody To Give Me Nothing/Open Up The Door And I'll Get It Myself," piped through the sound system, the workers danced up and down the aisles while they transformed the building from a finger-popping, dice-rolling, card-playing recreation gallery for thieves and murderers to a hall worthy of receiving two hundred and fifty distinguished guests and a hundred and forty-two convict graduates singing "Ain't No Stopping Us Now" as they marched across the stage to receive their diplomas.

Oliver stood outside the auditorium in Stick-Up Alley helping Mr. Ocheltree, the academic counselor, line up the graduates for the final walk-through. Whereas the morning air had been cool and sharp, by mid-afternoon the edge had worn off the sun and the day was blue and gold and exciting. As the graduates' names were called in the order they would march into the building, Oliver handed each one a slip of paper with a number written on it. "Don't lose that paper, gentlemen!" Mr. Ocheltree said. "You'll need it tonight in order to line up properly."

Oliver noted the irony of standing in Stick-Up Alley with some of the same prisoners who had contributed to its name. Situated between the auditorium and the commissary building, Stick-Up Alley was the home of more strong-arm robberies than anywhere else in the prison. Today it was part of hallowed ground; on Monday morning it would return to being a danger zone for new arrivals coming from the canteen for the first time with bags full of groceries and cigarettes. Those with their mind on court dates and home would be candidates for a strong-arm robbery. Oliver recalled the first time he had walked out of the canteen building and down this alley with two grocery bags in the crook of one arm, a ten-penny nail held tightly in his free hand and a deadly glare in his eyes. He had certainly come a long way since then, he thought, as he smelled the hibiscus riding on the breeze through the open side-door of the auditorium. Though he was mindful that the environment he thought of as a college campus was still a hundred year old prison filled with dangerous men, it was a distinction without a difference, for beauty, harmony, color and fragrance were all around him.

And magic too, he hoped. Tonight, he would have the keynote speaker, Dr. B.J. Dallet, all to himself after the ceremony. A month ago she had sent him a handwritten note on cream-colored stationery offering him the chance of a lifetime:

Dear Mr. Priddy,

It is difficult enough under normal circumstances to earn a C.S. Award; you have done it under the most trying conditions. Congratulations!

Mr. Sommers has shared with me your interest in our School of Education's Master's program. I look forward to meeting and talking with you about this at next month's graduation.

Best wishes,

B.J. Dallet

If you were a prisoner who had just received a note on cream-colored stationery offering hope and upward mobility—well, then you taped it to the wall, telephoned all the people you loved and planned to make the impression of a lifetime. It was the most hope-filled day of his prison life the day Professor B.J. Dallet recognized his scholarship on a cream-colored note with a light fragrance. More than anything in the world, he needed this *rara avis*, as rare as tamarind rinds on a prison yard, for only two prisoners before him had ever attended graduate school, and that was because, one, most were as indigent as the homeless and, two, the discerning eye of graduate school professors didn't usually extend beyond the main campus. Though Senator Claiborne Pell's grant did not cover tuition fees for graduate school, with his Chancellor's Scholarship and his mother June's resources he had the financial part in tow. What he needed now was a humanitarian in need of a protégé and by the end of the night he hoped to have her.

He had learned from his grandfather, Ernest Priddy, Sr., how to shake hands with just the right firmness and how to stand as straight as a plumb line. His grandfather had taught him many things. Work, save and study hard. Say grace and be it. Don't chomp into your food or the reputation of your friends. Laugh at the things that are funny and those meant to be. Look the devil in the eyes, and others, too.

He had another gift he didn't inherit from his grandfather. The charm of a lady's man. Six three and lean, with wide shoulders and thick brown hair perpetually in his face, a quick, contagious smile, and large green eyes, he was what women called a beauty. Tonight he would wear his new light blue button down dress shirt, tan slacks, and Weejun penny loafers, and hope that in his finely pressed collegiate clothes she would see not a murderer-man or a prisoner-therefore-con-man, but a where-did-he-go-wrong, man, and all-he-needs-is-a-chance, man.

HE HEARD HER high heels clicking across the tiles in the main corridor, heard her say, "Yes, this is my first time here." He didn't turn around to look. He pulled the next cap and gown off the rack and shouted over the crisscross of conversations going on around him. "107…108!"

"Yo, Butch. I never thought I'd see the day you'd be wearing a gown."

"Hey. Watch it, fella."

"Come here, homeboy. You look like a real scholar. Your momma's going to be proud of you tonight."

"Yeah, yours too."

"Fix your hat, Leroy."

"It's not a hat, it's a cap."

"Whatever you call it, you can't wear it cocked all to the side like that."

"Who says?"

"I say!" Ms. Rhoda Cherry shouted. "Now straighten that cap out! You're not going to be a jitterbug tonight, young man. That's the way. Thank you."

Oliver handed out the last cap and gown and turned around, adjusting his eyes to the crowd. He looked over the prisoners and saw bits of Professor B.J. Dallet. Wide, watching eyes. Her smile. The other prisoners were checking her out, too. Mr. Sommers waved his hand. "Can you come here for a second, Oliver?"

He took a deep breath, smiling nervously, then walked across the room. As he approached her, he thought she was the tallest woman he had ever seen. Not quite his height in black pumps and high heels. She wore a royal blue suit with gold buttons. Her straight blond hair was pulled back and held together with a black ribbon. She had aqua blue eyes that were wise and familiar. She looked the way he imagined she would. Haute couture. Like one of June's girlfriends. A woman's woman, a man's woman.

"Oliver, this is Dr. B.J. Dallet. B.J., this is our scholar, Oliver Priddy."

"It's a pleasure to meet you, Oliver," she said, extending her hand and a firm grip. Her smile was full and confident.

"Likewise, Dr. Dallet," said Oliver.

"Mr. Sommers has told me a lot about you," she said.

"All good, I hope."

"Yes, it was."

"Oliver, make sure you get with Dr. Dallet right after the ceremony. We're going to head over to the auditorium now," Mr. Sommers said.

"I will. I'll be waiting for you when you come off the stage, Dr. Dallet."

Dr. Dallet said, "I'll be looking for you, Oliver."

Twilight distilled blue into purple and reduced purple to crimson by the time all the proud and giddy graduates were lined up in Stick-Up

Alley. Oliver stood at the end of the procession humming a song his brother Skip had hipped him to in high school. An R&B version of "Some Enchanted Evening," in four-part harmony. He hummed the tune in his head until he heard the swell of "Pomp and Circumstance" echoing through the alley. Then the procession started moving forward. Oliver walked behind the last graduate in line and when he entered the auditorium he closed the double doors behind him. The room was a sea of teary-eyed mothers. A grandfather leaning on a cane. A nun smiling solemnly. Siblings. Wives. Professors. Clergy. The top brass of the administration. They were all there. Oliver stood in the back row with his fellow school workers. Father Kelly Reese said a prayer and then everyone sat in unison.

Mr. Sommers' opening remarks chimed with paternal salutations. When he introduced Junior Thompson, Mr. Sommers embraced Junior before taking a seat behind the podium.

Junior, tall, dark and sharp-looking, paused and stared at his mother and sister who were sitting in the middle of the audience. First, he thanked his teacher, Ms. Rhoda Cherry, for her patience and endurance and for believing in him. Then he told a love story about a mother and older sister who had toiled all their lives to keep their family together and fed through the worst of times. Homeless twice, they had found shelter in the back of a car one night, and an abandoned building the next. Subsidy housing had worked until the building's structure was found to be on the verge of collapse, and he and his mother, grandmother and three siblings were homeless once again. This time his older sister Jackie quit school—she was in the eleventh grade—to take a full time job in a supermarket. Her selfless act had not only led to keeping the family together and in a decent home, but had enabled their mother to quit one of her three jobs. As tears flowed among the mothers in the audience, he went on about how his father had come and gone over the years like a midnight burglar. How he had rocked in their mother's cradle and left with the rent money so many times the children thought he was the landlord. He paused again and looked across the audience. His mother Val and sister Jackie were here tonight, he said, and he wanted to thank them for loving and encouraging him every day of his life. He thanked them and they wept openly, as did his teacher, Rhoda Cherry, and every other woman in the building.

A standing ovation for Junior.

Rhoda Cherry, toothpick thin and as cute as a mannequin, stood at the podium, drying her eyes and smiling. When she was finally composed, she thanked Junior for thanking her and said it was now her pleasure to introduce a man who had come to Riverview several years ago fresh off the streets of Philadelphia with all the potential in the world to succeed at whatever he set his mind to. And succeed he had. Eight years ago he had captured the Tri-State amateur heavy-weight boxing title and still held it. At the same time, he had been the most tenacious student in her classroom, never giving up after failing the high school equivalency examination by only a couple of points each of the four years he had taken the test before he passed it. She was moved to tears again as she called Theodore "Champ" Burnett, Student of the Year, to the podium.

Champ shook Rhoda Cherry's hand until she frowned and said, "You better show me some love." Then she all but disappeared when Champ wrapped his arms around her. The sight of a prisoner embrac-ing a female staff member was enough to make Superintendent I.M. White pull on his necktie and fidget in his seat.

"That woman there," Champ said, turning and pointing to the still tearful Rhoda Cherry, "is a real saint, another Mother Teresa. She puts up with more of our crap than anyone I know. I want to thank you, Ms. Rhoda, for taking me back in your room after all those times you threw me out for not doing my homework. I also want to thank my tutor, Oliver Priddy, for spending all those hours up in the school showing me how to break down algebraic equations. If it wasn't for that man, I would never have gotten a grip on learning algebra. Thanks, Priddy. You're one hell of a tutor, Jack." Champ pointed to the back of the auditorium.

Oliver nodded. Why did he have to mention me? he thought. Oliver had deliberately held back taking his last college course so he wouldn't have to walk down the aisle this night and draw attention to himself. It wasn't that he didn't want to be acknowledged by his family and peers and professors for all his accomplishments and scholarship. He did, and they had, at every milestone along the way. What he didn't want was to be recognized publicly by Champ or anyone else for the same reason he didn't want to be up on that stage and called the next prison scholar to be heading for a master's program. He didn't want the story getting out before he could get in and finish it. It would only take one uninformed citizen to complain that his tax dollars were being used to finance a murderer's graduate school tuition and then for some politician to pick up on the story and stump with it. Better to not be seen or heard from until it was all over. Oliver was a little embarrassed as several members of the audience looked over their shoulders and smiled at him. A little embarrassed, but proud nonetheless.

"I also want to thank the school administration for giving me this award," Champ went on. "I never thought in a million years I'd be student of the year. Thank you very much."

The graduates whistled and cheered while the rest of the people clapped for Champ as he returned to his seat.

Now it was the keynote speaker's turn. When Mr. Sommers introduced Dr. B.J. Dallet, she approached the podium as if she owned the real estate underneath her feet. Oliver's heart pounded as he watched her look across the audience, smile radiantly, and wait. He tried to guess her age. Thirty-five? Forty? Whatever it was, she was exquisite. Her blue eyes were still intoxicating from thirty yards away.

When she began, she looked directly at the graduates as if they were the only people in the room. "Good evening, graduates. Hopefully, each of you has a favorite writer whose words and ideas have affected you in some significant way. One writer whose writings have always moved me is that lovely sage, Maya Angelou. The words on the banner above and behind me are, as I am sure you are aware, her words. Tonight, as we celebrate each of your successes, I think it would be appropriate to take a few minutes of your time to talk a little about *why* the caged bird sings.

"Simply put, the caged bird sings because it *can*. It sings because without a song there is no inspiration. Without a song there is no hope.

By a song, I do not mean one on the radio or the eight track. Though surely those songs are important, too. The kind of song I am referring to is the one in your heart. The song of your daily lives. Like the song on the radio, the song in your heart has a beat and a rhythm, too. The rhythm can beat fast or slow, smooth or rough, hard or soft, loud or quiet. And just like the song on the radio, there is a tone and a mood to the songs of our daily lives. Dark or bright, happy or sad, cowardly or courageous, forgiving or resentful. We all write our own songs. You write yours and I write mine.

"Let the lyrics of your song represent your goals and dreams. Let the lyrics of your song define how you treat others and yourself. And let those lyrics be a testimony of change for the better. If you write your lyrics well, they will comfort you when life gives you the trombone blues and life surely will, for the blues is an integral part of life. When the blues plays, it tests the quality and arrangement of our own individual songs, it reveals our characters.

"Never stop writing new verses to your songs, people. And never stop revising the old ones, for that is what life is truly about. Arranging and rearranging so that, in the end, our song, our contribution, is the best it can be. Make your song one of hope and inspiration and endurance, for you alone have the freedom to do that. It is your choice and no one can take that away from you. No judge, no jailer, no prison walls.

"I want to leave you tonight with these words from one of my favorite songs on the radio: Keep your heads to the sky. Never stop believing in yourselves, for each of you is a mighty, mighty person. Each of you can be all you dream of being. Thank you and congratulations!"

At that very moment every prisoner in the building rose from his seat; the cheers and clapping went on for five minutes, and Dr. B.J. Dallet was a star among thieves. Oliver was mesmerized by her maternal aura and her elocution, and couldn't wait to stand beside her.

After the last diploma was handed out and the closing remarks were made, the prisoners pushed and pulled one another to be the first to shake Dr. B.J. Dallet's hand and thank her for coming. Oliver waited patiently. Kept his composure and waited. The more the line thinned out, the closer he got to her and the more his heart raced. As the prisoner in front of him shook her hand and walked away, Victor Lejeune, a fellow tutor, stepped in front of him. "I'm waiting to talk with her, Victor," Oliver said.

"So am I. You're after me."

"I've been standing here—"

"Excuse me, Dr. Dallet. My name's Victor LeJeune. That was a great speech."

"Why, thank you." Dr. Dallet smiled warmly.

"I was wondering if you can help me. I'm trying to get some information on a graduate program."

Oliver smiled and held his countenance in check. He moved a little closer to Dr. B.J. Dallet, but not so close as to be rude or intrusive.

"In what department?"

"Criminal justice."

"I'm sorry but criminal justice is not my area. I'm in the School of Education. The best I can do is try to pick up a brochure from our criminal justice department and bring it over here the next time I come. I can leave it with the principal, Mr. Sommers. I'm sure he can get it to you. Your name again?"

"Victor LeJeune. And I work for the principal. I'm his head tutor. I'd really appreciate it if you could do that for me. Do you know when you'll be coming back?"

"I have to come over on Monday for orientation, but I may not have the information for you by then. We'll see."

"Well, I'll be looking for you. It was nice meeting you."

"Nice meeting you, too, Victor." She smiled genuinely and then turned to Oliver. "Mr. Priddy, is there a quieter place where we can talk?"

"Yes, ma'am, but first, would you like something to drink, something to eat?"

"How about coffee? A little cream, no sugar."

They got in line and one graduate's mother told her how stunning she looked in the Yves St. Laurent suit she was wearing. Dr. Dallet smiled and thanked her.

The refreshment line was long and moving slowly. While she stood in front of him receiving wonderful comments about her speech, Oliver leaned over her shoulder and told her he would be right back. Then he walked to the front of the line and behind the serving tables.

"Priddy, grab me a couple packs of those napkins from the box under the table," said Big Jake.

Oliver got on his knees and dug into the box. "Here. Need anything else?"

"No. How 'bout you?"

"Yeah. Fix me two coffees with just a little cream, would you? And put three or four of those ladyfingers on a plate for me."

"Got you."

"'Preciate that."

Dr. Dallet was watching as he made his way toward her juggling a plate of pastries and two styrofoam cups of coffee and weaving gracefully through the crowd. He motioned for her to follow him, but no sooner did she step out of line than Victor LeJeune appeared again.

"Just one more thing, Doc."

"Yes?"

"What if I decide to apply for my Master's in the School of Education? Would you be willing to be my advisor?"

"We can talk about that sometime," she said. "I'm not really sure at this point the extent to which I'm going to be involved in the program here. I do know I'm scheduled to teach an introductory linguistics course over the summer."

"Linguistics? Isn't that about where language originated and all that?" Victor asked.

"Well, yes, but there's more to linguistics than the history of language."

Victor LeJeune ignored Oliver's glare. It was every man for himself and Victor was armed. Not with a shiv or a lead pipe or a shard of glass, but armed just the same. He was armed with a superiority complex. But Oliver wasn't threatened, he was irritated. He knew Victor didn't have a chance. His posture was wrong. His tongue slithered and his lusterless black eyes were uninviting.

"Victor, you're going to have to excuse us," Oliver said, finally. "There's not a lot of time left before Dr. Dallet has to leave and we've got things we need to discuss."

"Yeah. One more thing, Doc. All the fellows think you're wonderful and beautiful and classy and we all hope to see you around here on a regular basis. Thanks for coming!"

Victor extended his hand and pumped hers several times before letting it go.

Dr. Dallet followed Oliver to the front left corner of the room and sat down. She sipped her coffee and said, "You handled that so well, Oliver. Is he always that persistent?"

"Yes ma'am, he is."

"Oh, please don't call me *ma'am*, Oliver," she said, with a light chuckle. "I'm too young for that. Call me B.J."

The lilt of her laughter pleased him and instantly reminded him of his mother June.

"Before we get started," she said, "I want you to know my schedule is clear this coming Monday afternoon. I have to come over for orientation in the morning, and then I'm having lunch with Mr. Sommers. I can come back in the afternoon and meet with you and have you fill out some forms and applications. Will you be free then?"

When she said the word "free" they both laughed. There was no uneasiness between them, the kind that often accompanies first meetings. She smiled like a friend.

"Sorry, Oliver. Poor choice of words."

"Actually, free is a great word. And, yes, I'll be free on Monday afternoon."

"Good. Now why don't you tell me a little about yourself? I know you're a lifer. I've seen your academic transcripts and I've read the brilliant essay you wrote for the C.S. Award you earned. So I already know you're a scholar. Tell me some other things you'd like me to know about you."

"Where would you like me to start, Doctor?"

"Wherever you'd like."

He set his cup down and licked the sugar from his fingertips. She was waiting and studying his eyes while he swallowed the last of the ladyfinger. He wondered if she noticed his left pupil was slightly larger than the right one, and if she thought that flaw was remarkable. He wasn't sure where to begin. Being too easy on himself would be just as embarrassing as being too hard, so he thought he would balance the good with the bad. He was from the state of Maryland, he began. He had three siblings and a father he didn't know until a few years ago. His mother June was a horticulturist and a recovering alcoholic. Bicycles, marbles and spin-the-bottle had all been staples of his youth. His first love was a gaggle of Sisters of the Immaculate Heart of Mary, followed by his mother's girlfriends. Juke boxes, Nehi sodas, and pool halls had been his haunts after school; the movie theater on Friday nights; dance halls and drive-ins after he reached puberty. He had been incorrigible from day one and enjoyed just about every minute of it. His favorite movie was "Cool Hand Luke," his favorite president, LBJ, and his favorite poet, Langston Hughes. What he despised the most in life were bigots and a stepfather named Ernie Boy the Second. He would save that story for another time, he said, as well as the one about how he wound up in Pennsylvania. He ended by telling her that discovering higher learning had saved him from wolves and himself and he was hoping she would help him continue his quest for higher learning and another college degree.

He paused and looked at his watch. "It's getting close to that time," he said.

"Oh, my. How much time do we have?"

"A few minutes."

Her face was animated even when she frowned. "I'm so glad I got to meet you tonight, Oliver. I feel honored that you shared a part of your life with me. Now let me share with you that one of my reasons for accepting the invitation to come over to this prison and help you with your graduate studies is that one of my own two sons could have very well been your next door neighbor a few years back." She leaned into him and lowered her voice. "He had a serious drug problem. Cocaine," she whispered. "I'll tell you more about it some other time.

114

I just want you to know before we have to leave that I'll do anything I can to help you further your education. I understand you only need one last course to finish your bachelor's degree."

"And I'm taking it now, Dr. Dallet."

"Good. We'll get you started in my program this summer." She smiled at him with unwavering assurance and then looked away to observe a half dozen guards moving through the entrance doors. After the guards had taken up positions along the back wall, the captain of the guards announced that all guests were to begin making their way to the back exit.

Dr. B.J. Dallet stood and extended her hand. Oliver took it in both of his, thanked her for coming and told her he was looking forward to seeing her on Monday. When he released her hand he hoped the gesture was a little more personal than a formal handshake.

"Thank you," he said.

"You're quite welcome, Oliver. And thank you. I'll see you on Monday afternoon."

While he watched her go he smiled to himself, suddenly realizing that he had forgotten what a woman looked like moving in a crowd.

1985

chapter eight

TRULY DISCONTENTED PROFESSIONALS know they are. Know when the money and the years invested in their careers have ceased to bring fulfillment or happiness. Seldom dreaming of change, they often resign themselves to believing, as dream-bitten people do, that a gold watch and the final exit are the only destinations left to them. Lucky are the ones who find an epiphany whispering that they themselves are responsible for their own well-being. When this happens, change is often seen as a definite possibility. It might be an appetite for a makeover, a hobby or some weekend adventure. Or it may be as simple as an urge to do something benevolent.

As a young girl, B.J. Dallet had been driven by the completion of tasks, one after another in a variety of fields: academics, arts, music, sports. No sooner did she finish creating a collage out of the *Saturday Evening Post* covers than she went to her mother's piano and practiced one Broadway musical arrangement after another until she could play each fluently. If working out with the high school track team so she could be the best seventh grade high jumper in the state was overdoing it, her parents couldn't tell. Home by six, she ate dinner, completed her homework and still had time to read a good book before going to bed. She was a prolific reader all her life and having received a fine education, she learned, among other things, the true meaning of the word "philosopher." Knowing that this label provided her with both drive and courage, she believed that to conceive of a possibility was to begin it.

During her formal years of training to become a doctor of philosophy in education, she unfolded a great paradox of learning: Students are imaginative but lack experience; pedants are full of knowledge but have feeble imaginations. Rote learning had its purpose, but active interest was the key to engaging a student's imagination. Just as she knew that staring too long at the sun would make a person go blind, she knew there could be no mental development without interest. Interest was the sine qua non for attention and apprehension. Whether one endeavored to excite interest by means of birch rods, or coaxing it by the incitement of pleasurable activity, without interest there was no imagination, no progress.

Her career was quite successful. Early on she achieved a lifetime of tenure by writing illuminating philosophical treaties on the organization of thought and the foundations of childhood education. Her most celebrated work, a tome on the role of classics in education, was translated into seven languages and won her international recognition. She loved her career and her life. Together she and her husband Stanley raised two wonderful sons, Malcolm and Cab. Both boys grew up to have successful careers and families of their own. Malcolm, now thirty-three, was a cabinetmaker; Cab, thirty, was a watercolorist. After twenty-two years of university life, she was still teaching her two graduate courses every semester, supervising young teachers in the local school districts, and advising a half-dozen graduate students each year. Her income was large, but she had no taste for luxury outside of fine clothes. Having never lost her drive to stay fit and look attractive, she worked out three days a week at the same health club she had belonged to for the past twenty years.

Her life was an arabesque of harmony, complexity, and balanced proportion, except for one thing. The careful construction lacked physical love. She had no preference for celibacy but had succumbed to it after her second child was born. That was when her husband Stanley, world renowned for his wood sculptures, began devoting all of his waking hours to his art and career as a professor of fine arts at a competing university. Their marriage gradually dissolved into one of convenience. Even if they had not been Catholics and had believed in divorce, they would have stayed together for the sake of the boys and their own careers. As it turned out, separate bedrooms and separate social lives gave him the freedom he needed to be happy. She adapted and they eventually developed a unique friendship, one in which they talked and listened to each other, and went out for dinner together once or twice a year.

After moving out of the master bedroom, Stanley had crawled back into the marriage bed at least once a month during the first year. As time went on he came less frequently until he didn't come at all. She had always enjoyed making love to him but the last half dozen times they did it she noticed he could not experience sustained erections and she began to wonder if she was the problem or maybe he had become a homosexual. In any case she was relieved when he stopped coming, for she had begun to abhor his flesh on hers. The sight of crust in the corner of his eyes, his earwax, his moles and blackheads, repelled her. Her attention therefore gradually settled on raising her sons, advancing her career and occasionally having a go at self-manipulation.

She could not remember when her season of discontent began. Because she had not attended a conference or published a paper in years, some of her colleagues were whispering burnout. Others were saying her imagination had withered, and still others that she was resting on her laurels. Her closest friends, Alice Proctor and Shirley Knot, told her she simply needed a change of scenery. She still enjoyed teaching and she loved her students, but she longed for something more. Being highly acquainted with existential philosophy, she felt that finding the right cause would cure her of her ills. So when she heard about a bright and promising young prison scholar who was in need of an academic mentor, her interest was piqued. She thought it might be just the thing she needed to shake off her mid-life doldrums. She had watched *The Birdman of Alcatraz* more times than she could remember and had always been fascinated by the convict Robert Stroud. She had been more than a little curious about prison life. Over the years whenever she drove past the towering walls of Riverview Penitentiary on her way to one of the city schools where she supervised new teachers, she had felt the same chill and reverence she felt whenever she passed a church or cathedral. Her adrenaline rushed through her fine veins each time she fantasized about going inside. On her initial visit to the prison she was in awe of what she had found there: civility, respect, gratitude. And to witness such depth of commitment to post-secondary education inside a prison had far exceeded her expectations. Moreover, she was excited about the time she had spent getting acquainted with the handsome scholar.

The second time she signed him up to be her protégé and then lectured him on etymology, semantics and rules of transformational grammar. After two hours she stopped and told him that a broad knowledge of the fine arts was also essential to a well-rounded education. They would therefore reserve the final hour of each class to discuss anything from current events to books, art, their personal lives and prison life, which she said she was very interested in learning about, that is, if he didn't mind sharing that part of his life with her. No, he didn't mind at all. She wanted to know how dangerous prison life really was and asked him not to spare a single detail. He didn't. He told her about the homicides and suicides, gang rapes and love affairs, and all about the underworld. In the middle of his story about an orderly named Handsome Johnny, they were interrupted by the same prisoner who had interrupted them the first time she visited. "Hello, Dr. Dallet. That's a beautiful blouse you're wearing." Victor LeJeune stared at her long curvaceous legs.

She recognized his ruddy face with the off kilter nose, but she couldn't remember his name quickly enough. "Thank you," she said, smiling tentatively.

"The boss just gave me the brochure you brought for me. Thanks. I have a couple of questions. I was wondering—"

"Hey, you ever heard of knocking, Victor? We're having a meeting here," Oliver said.

Victor LeJeune's coils of curly black hair flew from his temples and his hostile black eyes remained focused on Dr. B.J. Dallet. He ignored Oliver completely and she could see from the change in his countenance that Oliver was angry. Victor stood directly in front of her and when she looked down at his shoes and glanced upwards, she saw a bulge in his groin and felt a strange fear, and another response that wasn't fear. Something more like repulsion. Because the front of his pants were stained in some areas and wet in others. And he stank. Really stank. Ripe. God, what a nasty smell! And he was practically right up in her face. He stood there with his hands in his front pockets fondling himself and staring at her like an animal. That was what repelled her.

"I was wondering if you could give me about fifteen minutes of your time to explain some things to me," he said.

She shifted her body in the chair and pulled on the pink collar of her blouse. She tried to sound regretful when she answered. "I'm in the middle of working with Mr. Priddy, right now."

"It won't take long. Priddy, would you excuse us for a few minutes?" Victor started to sit down.

Oliver got up suddenly and bolted toward the door. "Come here, man. Let me talk to you out in the hall. Right now!"

Through the crack in the door she heard Oliver say, "Do you want all your teeth in your head? This ain't your gig, man! Now get the fuck out of here!"

When he returned to the room his voice was soft, breathy and refined again. "I apologize if what just happened shocked you. He was way out of line barging in here like that."

"You didn't shock me, Oliver, but he is one strange character. Did you see the stains on his clothes? And the way he smelled, my God, I almost gagged."

"Personal hygiene is not a priority with guys like him."

"What is it with him anyway? I saw the way he jumped in front of you that night at graduation. Does he have a feud with you, or is he just naturally rude?"

"To be honest, Doc, the guy has no manners."

"If you think he's going to cause problems, I can say something to Mr. Sommers if you'd like?"

"Please don't. I can handle it."

"I know you can. I just don't want to see you get into any trouble," she said, surprised at the steadiness of her voice and even more surprised with what she said.

"You have to understand something, Doc. This isn't a college campus. This is a penitentiary. This is where the term con artist comes from. He's a prime example of one. Every time a pretty woman shows up, he comes around looking for a way in the door. But you don't have to worry. As long as you come here, I've got your back."

"I believe you wholeheartedly, Oliver. One of the first things Mr. Sommers told me was I can trust you and I do. I feel completely safe with you. I just don't want to see you do anything that might jeopardize your studies."

"I won't. I can assure you of that."

In her bed that night she tried to reconcile his outstanding refinement with the physical threat he had made to Victor LeJeune. Hadn't he just explained to her all about prison codes and turfs? Wasn't he just protecting his own interests and her at the same time? After all, she was his guest. She was surprised at herself. She seldom judged people. Victor LeJeune had violated one code or another, she was sure, and Oliver had merely put him in check. Strangely, she was both pleased and startled to know that what was so unique and green-eyed handsome was also volcanic.

THE THIRD TIME she came he sat at the table across from her and tried to focus on the complex theories of psycholinguistics she was explaining with such intensity he couldn't help but be spellbound. When he wasn't gazing into irises so blue he thought they were heaven, he was watching the thirty-five ways she could smile. How was he supposed to think about morphemes and phonemes when her very presence was a study? It would take some getting used to. Thank God for the textbooks he could read later.

True to her word, every week she lectured for the first two hours and then they spent the third hour rounding out his education and getting to know each other better. She brought him large picture books containing the works of Cezanne, Monet, van Gogh, Hopper, and her two favorite American painters, Wyeth and Bartolozzi. She taught him how to distinguish romanticism and realism, impressionism from postimpressionism. He was instantly affected by the intense moods of despair in van Gogh's self-portraits, so she used van Gogh's works to teach him about light, atmosphere, color, form and mood.

In these sessions they talked about war and politics and he tried hard to impress her with his knowledge of past presidents, the civil rights movement and the two party system. She showed him the folly of seeing things in black and white. She was a Republican, so he was shocked to learn she supported Head Start and other entitlement programs. He thought only Democrats approved of entitlements. She was also against the death penalty and that, too, surprised him, for he believed that all Republicans were proponents of the death penalty. She had an abundance of patience with him and constantly challenged him to postpone arriving at conclusions until he had all the facts.

A staunch ambassador of multicultural experiences, she often brought along her Chinese, African and Middle Eastern graduate students and he was always mindful of making a fine impression.

Among other things, what he loved about the time they spent together was the way she blended art and books and theories right into conversations about their personal lives. One minute they were discussing the Bay of Pigs incident, and the next she was telling him about her husband Stanley. She wanted to know about Oliver's friendships, so he told her about Early and Champ the boxer and Albert DiNapoli who had remained a close and loyal friend even after being home for two years. He showed her pictures of his girlfriend Penelope who had recently moved out to California to attend graduate school at UCLA. Just as he was about to start bragging about his mother June he changed his mind and said, "Enough about me, what about you?" The contentment he drew from watching her reaction made him smile.

"Well, I've been teaching at the University for the past twenty-plus years now, and I've been married for the past thirty-three years. My husband Stanley is a professor of fine arts at Carnegie Mellon. He's also quite a successful wood sculptor. I believe I already told you we have two sons, Malcolm, who's thirty-two, and Cab who's thirty. Malcolm is a highly successful cabinetmaker; Cab is a watercolorist. They're both great boys. I think you and Cab would get along well. As I mentioned to you before, he had an addiction to cocaine a couple of years ago and he almost lost everything. My husband and I found out about it on the opening night of one of his watercolor exhibitions when he showed up bug-eyed and talking a mile a minute. To make a long story short, his father took him aside and told him to wise up, and he eventually did but not before he overdosed twice, depleted all his savings and stole money out of my purse. But that's another story."

"We have time. Why don't you tell me about it," Oliver suggested.

"We do? Well, that's a relief. To begin with, he was still living at home at the time. I had been curious and concerned for a long time, as his mother, you know?" She lowered her voice as she remembered, and then continued. "I wanted to find out what was so alluring about this cocaine stuff. Of course, I had never taken anything stronger than an aspirin in my entire life. Now, I'd been to several parties back in the seventies where other artist friends of Stan's and professors I knew were snorting, is that the right word? Anyway, snorting cocaine right out in the open. But I didn't once entertain the notion of trying it myself. Not until I entered Cab's bedroom one morning and found his stash. The first thing I felt was shock. And then, strangely enough, I was excited and nervous at the same time. There I was squatting in his closet and staring into a sandwich baggie half-filled with white powder and thinking, I need to find out what this is all about. And I did. I took the bag downstairs and snorted a little pinch and then a bigger pinch and I kept right on going in a complete state of rapture. Later that day Cab went ballistic when he woke up and discovered his cocaine was missing. He came running downstairs and there I was cleaning the house from top to bottom in a complete frenzy. We argued for a while and he was so irate I thought he was going to hit me, but he didn't. Instead, he ran back upstairs and a few minutes later he ran back down again and stormed out the front door. Later, I discovered he had taken nine hundred dollars from my purse."

"That's a heck of a story. So did you find out what the hype was all about?" Oliver asked.

"Oh God, Oliver. It was sheer nirvana. The most blissful experience I've ever had. Not to mention the fact that I've had chronic back pain for years, and that cocaine obliterated any hint of pain for two days. But I'll tell you the God's honest truth, Oliver. It scared the heebie-jeebies out of me."

"It did? Why?"

"Because every time I took some I wanted to do a little more. And I did, that is, until it was all gone. The euphoria was … well, have you ever tried it?"

"Can't say that I have."

"Well, it's like this, Oliver. Once you start, you don't want to stop, you know? It was better than sex."

Oliver's jaw dropped to his chest. "Nothing in this world's better than sex." He smiled and stared into her baby blues. She blushed and grinned. He could have watched her all day.

"Okay. Maybe I'm exaggerating. It's just that it's been so long."

"What has?"

"Well, that's another story, too."

1986

chapter nine

THE AIR WAS SO CHARGED with astonishment the blackbirds came to see. At one o'clock in the afternoon a platoon of blackbirds circled the hospital sun deck three times before disappearing over the wall. The nurses and orderlies came out to look, too, but didn't stay. Handsome Johnny sat in his wheelchair but never looked up. Fat Daddy stared at him, oblivious to everything except the summer of 1978 when they took Handsome Johnny away. And though he could never mistake that face for another's, Fat Daddy asked, "That you, Handsome Johnny?"

Johnny's face was slow to form a smile and when he spoke his tongue was thick and heavy. "Whooo…you…think?" Though Handsome Johnny's words came out heavy and slow, Fat Daddy thought he recognized the sarcasm and was glad.

"How you been, Johnny?"

Handsome Johnny rolled his head in figure eights and said, "Goood…Fa-Fat…Da-a-ddy." He stood slowly, shuffled over to the rail and looked down into the flower beds. In his eight years as a hospital janitor, Fat Daddy had been around enough mental patients to recognize the Thorazine shuffle." They got you on that zombie juice, Johnny? They got you on that shit, man?" Fat Daddy walked over and stood beside his old friend and business partner.

Johnny's lower lip slid to one side and slowly over his upper lip. He looked at Fat Daddy with limp, pitiful eyes, looked away and back again.

Fat Daddy looked back at him, slowly. The last good memory he had of Handsome Johnny was when he'd shown up at Fat Daddy's favorite crime scene seven years ago with the prettiest nineteen-year old white boy Fat Daddy had ever seen. Posing as a hospital pass runner for the tenth time, Handsome Johnny had escorted the blue-eyed boy across the hospital lobby to the abandoned basement where Fat Daddy, dressed in a dirty white doctor's smock, complete with a broken stethoscope draped around his neck, waited to play doctor. "You Mr. Blossom?" he had asked the boy.

"Yes, I am, Doctor," Donnie Blossom said.

"You got to have a physical. Go behind that screen and get undressed, then sit up on this table."

Donnie Blossom had followed Fat Daddy's instructions to a tee. When he came from behind the screen, he was shivering and his milk-white skin was covered with goose bumps. He sat on the table, hiding his privates with his hands. Fat Daddy took the broken stethoscope and pretended to listen to his breathing while Handsome Johnny guarded the door. After a minute or so, Fat Daddy said, "Now stand up and bend over. I got to check your anal cavity."

No sooner did Donnie stretch his arms out in front of him and bend over the table than Handsome Johnny appeared in front of him and threw an extension cord tied into a noose around Donnie's wrists. After securing the cord to a brace under the table, Handsome Johnny said, "Now pay me, Fats, so I can go get mines."

Fat Daddy was so tricked up over what Handsome Johnny had brought him that he told Johnny to take five instead of two packs of Kools out of his gym bag that was sitting on the countertop. Handsome Johnny stuffed the cigarettes into his pockets, then be-bopped out of the room just as Fat Daddy pulled Donnie's ass cheeks apart and told him to buck back.

Later that day, a faulty elevator brake ended Handsome Johnny's career as well as his own love life. Whereas Fat Daddy could mop and shine floors like nobody else, Handsome Johnny had been a highly skilled orderly with certification to prove it. He could feed a needle into a collapsed vein quicker than any nurse and his fists were more adroit than any defibrillator. A fine black nurse named Veronica had depended on Johnny for everything: coffee, gossip, hot sandwiches, the daily newspaper, clean bedpans, Kools, monitoring her patients, good conversation and a heads-up whenever her supervisor was on the prowl. He had asked for only one thing in return: to be the only Handsome Johnny to ride in her elevator. And he was. For four years, twice a week at about the same time (seven-thirty pm), the hospital elevator shook and trembled to a stop between the first and second floors long enough for them to beat out a rhythm on all fours or standing up against the back wall. Rumors and gossip abounded. "He got it made, don't he?" "She carrying his baby?" "Takin' a big chance, ain't she?" Rumors and gossip, that's all it was until that evening when the elevator brake slipped and that steamy hot box descended all the way to the first floor lobby. Veronica heard the ring-a-ling of the elevator door as it slid open, and then she looked right up into the eyes of Captain Ned Twyman who was staring at her pretty black buttocks.

"Help me, sir! Help me!" Veronica unlocked herself from Handsome Johnny, got to her feet and threw her arms around the captain's waist. "He forced me down there, sir!" She cried like a little girl.

Captain Ned Twyman consoled her.

Handsome Johnny cried too. Then he laughed. But the laughter was serious. Astonished, he got to his feet, pulled his pants up and sighed before his laughter broke out again. He had to lean against the elevator door to keep the laughter from pulling him down to the floor.

"Look how he bruised my breast," Veronica cried. She showed Captain Ned Twyman the martialed nipple of her left breast.

Handsome Johnny should have hated the woman, rose to his feet and hated her, but what he felt was just as relevant. Guilty and beaten.

And he was. The guards came and hauled him off to the redbrick Home Block. When they were finished beating him late into the night, there was nothing left unbruised or unbroken. They broke and scattered him into pieces and hurled him back together in a meaty ball of pain. His mind was gone, too, shattered into a thousand halls, each with its own echo.

The next morning the prison ambulance carried Handsome Johnny away, and that evening his name appeared on the most-dangerous-patients ledger at the hospital for the criminally insane.

Now the doctors had declared Johnny harmless and returned him to the same prison hospital where he had once been the best orderly they ever had. Fat Daddy wanted to see how far his friend was gone so he said, "You want to know what happened to her, Johnny? Want me to tell you what happened to Veronica?" Handsome Johnny frowned before his eyes got wide and he turned and stared at Fat Daddy, who took it as a gesture of sanity. "A bullet from a drive-by shooting sliced her jugular vein in half while she was standing on the corner of Hamilton and Homewood Avenue. Happened about a year after you was gone, man. It was in the paper. I cut the story out. I'll bring it to you if you want. Oh, here, look. There's somebody I want you to say hello to. Come here, Donnie. You remember this boy, don't you, Johnny?"

Handsome Johnny swiveled his head in the direction of the roof-top door. "I-I-I…re-memm-berrr…yeah, I dooo." Handsome Johnny's smile was twisted.

"Hello, Mr. Johnny. Nice to see you."

"Yeahhh." Handsome Johnny maintained his twisted smile while he looked up in the sky.

"I've got to get you right, Johnny boy," Fat Daddy said. "We got to get you off that shit, man. You going to let me help you, Brother?"

This time Handsome Johnny laughed like a house on fire. "Yeahhh, yeahhh, yeahhh! Help meeee!"

WHEN HE STARTED receiving three sticks of reefer every morning in exchange for his daily dose of Thorazine, Johnny's mind was grateful but his body was confused. The joints in his knees locked up and his tongue shot out of the side of his mouth uncontrollably. Fat Daddy stayed with him day and night for an entire year, altering his treatment as he saw fit. He fed him valium and Percodan he purchased on the black market and increased the reefer from three sticks a day to five. After a year, Johnny started picking up his feet again instead of shuffling them and his sentences contained both a subject and verb.

Handsome Johnny was grateful for having been saved. Except occasionally. Occasionally, when he smelled perfume in the hallways or heard the pulleys turning on the nurse's elevator, or when he watched Fat Daddy bartering for rouge, lipstick and bobby pins—he wondered if it would have been just as well to have died in a psychotropic stupor than to feel so much loneliness.

He had a solid year of school in Rhoda Cherry's special needs class, a bed in the big St. Regis, and a job as a groundskeeper before he got the courage to whistle again, and when he did, it all came back to him. Once again he started shining his shoes and polishing his nails with clear coat floor wax. He went to the barbershop and told Chinaman to give him the works—shampoo, shave and a high fade. Now he was ready. Now when the secretary with the bright colored skirts swished by him in the mornings as he squatted to pull weeds from the cracks in the sidewalks, he stopped and squeezed his groin.

With his groove back, Handsome Johnny started a friendly garden rivalry with Early. The front and side yards of the hospital grounds, for which Johnny was the official keeper, were given over completely to growing flowers. Irises, poppies, daffodils and peonies took up his time.

Though he wouldn't take credit for the buckwheat and clover patches that had been flourishing there for years, he laid claim to them just the same. Early gave him tips on mulching and showed him where to find soil so rich it made Early's biennial foxgloves grow six feet high. Early even brought Johnny jewel flowers and nasturtiums from his own garden and showed Johnny how to replant them.

Handsome Johnny was completely content with his multicolored poppies and peonies until the morning he visited Early's flower beds that surrounded the prison chapel. He was amazed at the sight of the orange wing butterflies etched with black lace hovering in Early's pansies and violets. And why, he wondered, why didn't those blues and viceroys flutter and feed in his own buckwheat and clover patches? He was determined to import those giant butterflies and hummingbirds from Early's garden to his own, and he thought he knew just how to do it. Using his connections, Handsome Johnny ordered up an array of exotic plants.

But the plan was a disaster from the start. Ignorant of certain horticulturally important specifications such as light and temperature, Handsome Johnny failed to cultivate a single new plant. He under watered the tropical slippers and over watered the begonias. When the panda ginger, string-of-hearts, and Jack-in-the-pulpit were almost parallel to the ground, Fat Daddy helped him haul in wheelbarrow loads of the rich, black soil Early swore by. In the end, though, only the peonies, pansies, poppies and two rows of pink and lavender irises survived. Fat Daddy told Johnny that the clay and rocks in the soil weren't his fault and that the plants still standing and prospering were proof of Johnny's green thumbs. Fat Daddy drew the line when Johnny asked him to help him replace the dead verbena with radishes and peppers. Fat Daddy had something else to do and told Johnny to let it go.

FAT DADDY WAS TOO BUSY doubling his dedication to being deviant. Every morning when the doors opened, he and Donnie Blossom found a new place to link themselves together. Standing in the one-man shower stall they moved to the frenzy of a brown-tail moth beating its wings against a 60-watt light bulb. The flickering light arched Fat Daddy's back; the water warmed Donnie's tongue.

There was no way to mistake them if you knew where they were. In the outdoor toilet stall Donnie rode up and down on Fat Daddy's lap like he was riding a carousel. They did it easy and sometimes rough. And they never stopped. Not for droves of shit-dropping pigeons or heat hovering at 102 degrees. If you happened to spot them curled up in the ivy during one of those intermittent summer showers, you could see their bodies changing hues. And they kept right on doing it in the pure summer rain.

Nothing could stop them. The born-agains wanted to. Over and over Tommy Lovechild told Deacon Bob how they looked and where to find them. They could have been, should have been, a sideshow, a tourist attraction, he said, except they were an embarrassment to decent Christians. A posse of born-agains plotted to lay hands on them and pray in tongues. They started to do it, but the movement died before they could go on their first stakeout. The born-agains said their objections were not aimed at sex at all, but at perversion. These two were as bad as Sodom.

Swanee said, "It's not like they're doing it on the forty-yard line or on top of home plate. You have to go out of your way to find them."

The born-agains wanted to get rid of these homosexual deviants, but they wanted them to be there too. Even a bunch of repressed pedophiles, too scared to have wet dreams of their own, knew they needed these two. Even if they never went near them, they needed to know they were out there.

The one brave soul who did approach them challenged Fat Daddy to give up his debauchery right in the middle of the act. When he should have been attending a Wednesday night prayer meeting, Barney Lee Russell III was pulling open Fat Daddy's cell door and shouting, "Heal, in the name of Jesus!" Jolted and buck naked, Fat Daddy rolled off Donny Blossom's back and ran into so much resistance that he had to kill. Those who were there said Barney Lee Russell III held his own until his body succumbed to twenty-seven puncture wounds made by a finely honed welding rod.

The other born-agains were standing on the corner of the street with no name and Tom's Way when the gurney carrying their brethren's body rolled by. Night school had just let out and the students and their professors were being held up on the other side of the intersection. "Everybody step back!" shouted Tommy George, the schoolhouse guard.

Dr. B.J. Dallet dropped her books and gasped at the sight of blood dripping from the gurney as it passed by. Twenty feet behind the trail of blood, two guards had Fat Daddy handcuffed and jacked up between them. Every few feet his bare feet touched the blacktop long enough for the guards to jack him back up while he pedaled his skinny ashen legs faster and faster.

Passing by the professors and students, Fat Daddy turned his head in their direction and twisted his face into a monstrous grin. Everyone on the corner could hear Dr. B.J. Dallet exclaim, "What in the world happened? And why does that man look so evil?" Oliver's green eyes glinted with disgust. "Because he is," he said. "As evil as they come."

AT ABOUT THE SAME TIME the coroner's van showed up the next morning for Barney Russell's dead body, every booty bandit in the little St. Regis appeared at Donnie Blossom's door to lay claim to him. Donnie looked repeatedly at the players and then told them he already had a new home. One squeezed Donnie's ass as he went by. Another didn't believe him and said he'd be back for him later that night. Donnie walked out of the little St. Regis and through the doors of the big St. Regis. The empty cell on Champ's right was clean and ready for him when he arrived.

Three weeks later, he was shelling pistachios and popping them into his mouth when the Home Block janitor appeared at his door with a written message from Fat Daddy. The message read, "I'll see you in five years and nine months. You better stay true."

Donnie belched, softly, purringly, amusingly.

1987

chapter ten

WAYNE ST. PIERRE TURNED the keys to the front gate of Riverview Penitentiary as if he owned the locks. A third generation turnkey, he loved his job and took great pride in seeing to it that no visitor, official or otherwise, got inside the front door of the prison after two o'clock in the afternoon, Monday through Friday, without his scrutiny.

There were certain things about his job that irked Wayne St. Pierre more than others, like when black men showed up at his gate to visit other black men. In some form or fashion he was sure a conspiracy was in play. A drug transaction, a robbery or burglary plot, or just more conversation about how the white man ain't right, never was and never will be. For these visitors he gave extra scrutiny, turning up the sensitivity scale on the metal detector, double-checking identification cards.

Black women—mothers, wives, sisters, daughters—stood a better chance of obtaining a morsel of humanity from Wayne St. Pierre, but that was only because he was a natural born skirt-chaser and didn't discriminate when it came to the color of the skin. He had been staring into the eyes of female visitors for so long that he could spot the broken ones without a second look. The desperation came off them like a morning fog, a desperation you could almost touch. And he often did. They didn't have to turn their heads to know his eyes were searching for cleavage or that his fingers were drumming the scars on the hundred-year old oak counter, all the while anticipating the opening of buttons, clasps and zippers. His aftershave told it all. And to those he thought were desperate enough, he would whisper, "Nice tits," "Sweet ass," "Fine girl," "What do you say?" More understanding than a regular John. He got his sex from the crying ones. Who needed a white man wearing a correctional uniform with a black tie pointing down to something that couldn't please a house cat, but for his few dollars.

Working six to two overtime one overcast Saturday in June, he honed in on a high-yellow woman in her thirties as she sat in the waiting room holding her three-year-old son and dabbing her sleeve at the tears rolling down her cheeks. She was slender, with prominent cheekbones, and she was put together. She had a bad bruise, as deep as a burgundy wine stain, on her left cheek. The bruise excited Wayne St. Pierre.

"Excuse me, ma'am. Are you all right?"

The child slid off her lap and Wayne St. Pierre's eyes followed the woman's smooth yellow thighs all the way up to the hem of her short black skirt. "Is there something I can help you with?" he asked her, offering a paper towel.

"Thank you," she said. "I'll be all right." She said it with confidence, but then she lowered her head and cried some more.

Wayne St. Pierre said, "That's a terrible bruise, ma'am. It looks fresh."

She nodded and looked at her son. "Ray-Ray hit Mommy with a belt buckle, didn't he?" She glanced at Wayne St. Pierre, held back her tears. "He... He slapped Johnny Boy's son here with a belt buckle, too. Look." She snatched her son between her legs and yanked his shirt up. The welts were fresh on his back.

"Ah, jeez," said Wayne St. Pierre.

"We're going to show your daddy as soon as we get inside what that no-good Ray-Ray did to you, aren't we, Ty?" The boy shrugged his shoulders.

"I'm sorry, ma'am. Ray-Ray's the man you live with?"

She nodded and then said, "Not anymore. I'm leaving him. He took my money. I ... I got but two dollars to buy Johnny Boy a soda and a bag of potato chips, and a bus pass to get across town with. That bad ass Ray-Ray took my money."

Wayne St. Pierre looked down at the sign-in sheet, then up at the clock, then at her. "Jasmine? Jasmine Teal? That's a pretty name." He lowered his voice. "My name's Wayne, Jasmine, and this shift I'm working ends in an hour and a half. If you're out front on the Ohio River Boulevard when I'm leaving work, I'll be more than happy to drive you across town and buy you some groceries."

Jasmine Teal dabbed away at her tears.

The child watched him as he looked around the room and then took out his wallet and removed a bill.

"Here's five dollars. Get you and your Johnny Boy and son here a sandwich when you get inside. Now mind you, I could lose my job for helping you so it's best you don't tell anyone."

She took the five dollar bill and looked him up and down. He was a tall, heavily built man in his forties, with thinning gray hair and a tanned face scored with lines. He would be considered attractive even with the wrinkles and extra pounds. "Thank you, sir," she said. "That's very kind of you." She smiled. Her teeth were white and straight.

"Call me Wayne," he said. "We know each other now."

The top button of her blouse had come undone and she leaned forward, crossing her legs slowly.

Later that afternoon, while the child soared higher and higher in a park swing, Wayne St. Pierre locked Jasmine Teal's leg around his waist, leaned her against a great white oak tree and entered her. When he was finished, he let go of her breasts at the same time the child let go of the swing and shouted, "Whee! I'm flying!" The boy smacked into the tree twenty feet above the ground and dropped like a duck riddled with buckshot.

Jasmine Teal dropped her leg to the ground, sighed and walked around the tree where her child lay unconscious and bleeding profusely from his nose and ears. There was a six-inch gash across his forehead. Wayne St. Pierre came to look, too, and frowned when Jasmine fainted in his arms. He threw her over his shoulder and carried her to the bed of his navy blue Chevy pickup. Then he retrieved the child and laid him at her side.

By the time the truck screeched to a halt in front of the emergency room of the Allegheny General Hospital, Jasmine Teal had revived herself and was cradling her child in her blood soaked arms. She handed the boy to Wayne St. Pierre and jumped over the tailgate. He handed the child back to her. "I'll be waiting for you."

He waited impatiently in the cab of his truck and when mother and child didn't return after two hours, he hauled the bag of groceries through the emergency room door and inquired about them. A tired looking nurse directed him to the elevator, fourth floor, room two twenty-two.

Jasmine Teal was sitting beside the bed with her eyes closed, her small hands folded in prayer. The room was cold and the low light made it difficult for Wayne St. Pierre to see. After he blinked and squinted several times, he peered through the transparent walls of the oxygen tent and gasped at what he saw. The child's head, wrapped in a mile of gauze, was the size of a basketball. He looked away and cleared his throat. He shifted the load in his arms and the crinkling of the paper bag startled her. When she looked up, he said, "I brought your groceries. I can't stay. I have to go. I'm really sorry. I have to go now."

She stared at him through a curtain of tears.

"I'd really like to see you again," he said.

With red-eyed rage, the woman screamed, "Get out! Get out, you!"

He walked out of the room. A nurse entered the elevator ahead of him. Her countenance was soft and sympathetic, his was shock. When the door closed he looked up at the ceiling, then at the nurse. "She could have thanked me for the groceries," he said.

B.J. DALLET HAD BEEN AROUND enough snakes in her life to know what kind Wayne St. Pierre was. She knew because every time he had made a pass at her, he gave himself away. His rattlers were anything but subtle.

"Haven't I seen you on campus before?" he asked her the second month she entered his gate. "I could swear I've seen you on Fifth Avenue."

"It's possible," she answered. "But my office is on Forbes."

"Maybe that's where I saw you."

"Do you attend the university?" she asked.

"No. Not me. I go over there once in a while just to walk around and take in the scenery. I've been all through the Cathedral of Learning. That's some building."

"Isn't the architecture breathtaking? I often teach my classes in the Early American room."

"Maybe we'll run into each other over there one day," he said.

"Maybe," she answered. "You never know."

Several months later he was checking her tote bag one evening when he brought up the subject of her car. "I sure do like that sweet little Mazda you drive. I'm thinking about getting one myself. I imagine it gets good mileage."

"Oh yes," she said, steadying her eyes on his, smiling genuinely. "Much better than that gas guzzler my husband drives. An Imperial."

She saw him staring at the finger where her wedding band should have been.

"I didn't know you were married."

"Well, sometimes I have to remind myself of that very fact. I've been married for thirty years." She laughed. He laughed harder. She slid her hip to the side as she reached for her bags. Waving the fingers of her left hand at him, she said, "I take off my rings at night when I bathe. If I don't they slide off my fingers. Plumbers are expensive, you know?"

"Your husband's a lucky man," Wayne St. Pierre said. "You're a very attractive lady."

"Why thank you." She hooked her tote bag over her shoulder. "You have a nice evening, Officer St. Pierre."

"Call me Wayne."

"Okay, Wayne. Call me B.J."

The next time she came he said, "How are you this evening, B.J.? Nice dress."

She was wearing a burgundy dress with a two-inch wide patent leather belt that accentuated her shapely hips and flat stomach. She wore black high heels.

"Thank you, Wayne."

He looked at her left hand, now a ritual. No rings. "You look stunning in it, woman. But you'd look that way if you were dressed in a burlap sack."

She laughed.

"You ever been boating, B.J.?"

"Years ago. My brother Mickey had a speedboat he kept docked at a North Side pier right up the street from here. Back in the early seventies. Why do you ask?"

"Well, I just bought a new boat myself. I'd love to take you out for a ride sometime."

She looked at him regretfully. "That's sweet, Wayne, but I really can't."

He leaned into her. "Let me tell you a secret. I'm married too." He cocked an eyebrow at her and grinned.

"Oh." She acted surprised. "It's nice of you to offer, but I can't. I really can't. I'm old-fashioned, Wayne. But I'm flattered, I really am."

"Well, you can't blame a man for trying." He smiled lightly at her.

For two years she placated his ego with her friendly gestures and innocent flirtations. Her singular goal had been to instill within him the notion that things might have been different between them if it weren't for the fact that she was happily married. And she thought he believed her. She had bought him issues of *Boating Illustrated* and homemade jars of honey she purchased for him in the Amish country. She had single-handedly milked the venom right out of this rattlesnake.

Or so she thought.

Six months into her third year she stood at the counter waiting for him to check her bags. She looked as glamorous as ever, but there was no greeting, not even the slightest eye contact.

"Here to tutor that lifer again?" he said, removing the contents from her bag. Books. Tablets. Pens.

She didn't know what to say. A moment of silence and he added, "I don't know why you professors waste your time. Those lifers are never getting out, you know? This new governor is putting a stop to that."

She was shocked. "Well, Wayne. His mind can certainly be free. And he is making a genuine contribution to society. He's writing a book, too, you know?"

He moved his finger like a windshield wiper. "You're not allowed to take anything that belongs to him out of this institution. That's against policy. No legal documents, no letters, no manuscripts."

"I understand. But I *am* allowed to take his class assignments with me. I have since I started. How else can I evaluate his work?"

"They need to be inspected each time."

"I'm confused, Wayne. What's going on?"

He looked at her for the first time that evening. "Well, Dr. Dallet, you may not know this, but those lifers are dangerous criminals. We know their angles."

AND SHE KNEW HIS. No way was a disgruntled prurient going to distract her from savoring the whipped cream that had been missing from her bowl-of-cherries life for so long. Now that she had someone who was, all in one, a protégé, friend, confidante, playmate and simply there, she gloated to her boon companions, Shirley and Alice, who had been hearing about Oliver's intellectual prowess for two years now. They had been more than impressed. Now, when she told them about the love affair they were having and that he was twenty-five years her junior, their mouths dropped open so wide you could have fit a peach inside.

Shirley, who was a plump fifty and having an affair of her own with a younger man, said, "My God, he's practically a baby."

"He's no baby, honey!" B.J. said. "He's a stud."

Alice added, "Just think, B.J., all these years you've been sweating in the spa to keep your tummy flat and your muscles toned and now look at you! You're beaming like a school girl. Can you keep up with him?"

"Hardly, girlfriend. I have love bites in places you wouldn't imagine."

Alice and Shirley wanted to know every detail of the first time they had made love.

"Let me be clear. He didn't make the first move until long after we had acquired a great mutual admiration for one another," she said. "And long after he had finished his courses I was responsible for teaching him."

"Uh huh."

"Oh, do tell."

"Well, one evening while we were sitting together in his office having a discussion about what I don't recall, I felt his calf rested against mine. I didn't think anything of it except that it felt familiar, you know? As warm as toast. Anyway, I was sure he was testing the waters when he moved his leg away and then pressed it even closer back against mine. I didn't move a muscle. I went right on talking. Then he did the sweetest thing. He slid a note in front of me that said, 'I'm dying for you to hold me in your arms.'"

"No, he didn't! What a risk taker," Shirley said.

"He has his own office?" Alice asked. "What kind of prison is that?"

"Yes, he did. And Alice, you wouldn't believe the place. On the outside it's a fortress. On the inside it looks just like any other education department, nothing but classrooms and offices. And wait until you hear this. There's only one guard in the entire education building and he stays downstairs manning the door. Oliver has his own classroom and his own office because he's a gifted teacher and worker."

"One guard? You're kidding!" said Alice. "Okay! Go on!"

"So he slid this note in front of me, and I scribbled 'go for it!' on the bottom and slid it back to him. That's how it all started."

"What happened after you held him, hon?" asked Shirley. "Did you rock him to sleep?"

"You did hold him, didn't you?" asked Alice.

"We held each other. And then we squeezed each other a little tighter until I could feel his prick throbbing against my thigh. He had his long arms wrapped around my waist and without saying a word we looked into each other's eyes and he kissed me. He kissed me like I've never been kissed before. It was so gentle and so passionate. Then he stopped and I was terrified."

"Well, don't stop there, girlfriend! What did he do that terrified you?"

"He picked me up and sat me on the edge of his desk. Oh, God, the intensity in those green eyes of his, coupled with that strange environment and my lack of experience, you know, frightened the living hell out of me. Then he told me to lie across the desk and when I did, he went under my skirt and slid my hose and panties off my waist. Well, I almost wet myself. I don't have to tell either of you how long it had been since I'd had a man between my legs. My whole body turned to jelly. I couldn't have stopped him if I'd wanted to. And then, when he got on his knees and became my very own Valentino, I wasn't afraid anymore."

"I guess you weren't, honey. That's the most romantic thing I have ever heard," said Shirley. "You are one lucky lady. My lover hasn't discovered what his knees are for yet."

"That man-child of hers is the one who's lucky!" said Alice.

Of course they wanted to know all there was to know so she told them more. How every Saturday morning since their affair began she had gone on shopping sprees for new lingerie. She now owned silk panties and garters in just about every color under the rainbow. Dozens of pairs of thigh-high stockings, lace bras that opened in the front and teddies she couldn't wear anymore because he had destroyed the hooks trying to open them. She told them how nefariously thrilling it felt to walk through the front gate of a maximum security prison every week dressed in Victoria's Secret and black velvet high heels, only to be waved through by a guard who had befriended her the first time she came; how her anus puckered up every time she strolled across the courtyard filled with muscle bound men and into the private office of her handsome young murderer, all the while thinking that the volume of her heart was up way too loud.

There were plenty of things she didn't tell them, too. Like how delicious and exciting it was to make love in a dark room right next to a window where even on the darkest nights she could lean her head back and see, just fifty feet away, the armed guard pacing inside his red gun tower. And how being with him once, sometimes twice, a week now just wasn't enough. She was touching herself every time she found a private moment. In the ladies' room. At the water fountain. Sitting at her desk. She was fifty-five doing a thirty year old man who had been incarcerated since he was a boy. That was enough to make any woman twitch and look out the window every morning. He had awakened cravings in her that were equal to his own and his were endless. Not only did she want him; she needed him.

And the beauty of it all was that he was easy to love. She lined up his professors, he impressed them with his hard work. She lived for the hours she could be with him each week, he made it all worthwhile when she got there. And on only two occasions did she ever have to reprimand him. Once when he was feasting on her nipples, he looked up and whispered, "Does that feel good, Mommy?" She didn't interrupt their lovemaking, but later told him she wasn't his mother and please don't call her that again. He was hypersensitive to begin with and his feelings were naturally hurt. He knew what she was thinking, he said, but he didn't mean anything like that. She assured him everything was okay. The second time was when he had tried to penetrate her anus. Like trying to push a flashlight through a keyhole. It was just too painful.

But it wasn't just the way he had brought to life nerve endings she didn't know she had that compelled her to love him. The pure youthful innocence he exuded was both genuine and contagious. He was full of love and mischief when he laughed and teased her and that too filled her with happiness. Every time she thought of him her heart pounded like a drum. He made her feel seventeen again.

"You truly are the luckiest girl in the world, B.J., honey!" Shirley said.

"I suppose she is," said Alice. "But what about him? He would be twiddling his thumbs if it weren't for her. He has it all. He has his cake, and he's eating it too."

1988

chapter eleven

OLIVER KNEW THE DAY was going to be prosperous when the one person he loved more than anyone in the world showed up to see him before the visiting room guard had gotten comfortable in his seat. June Priddy got to him before he could hand his pass to the guard and turn around. "There you are!" she said, spreading her arms. He entered them for a long, swaying hug. When he let go, he handed his pass to the guard and turned to gaze at his mother. "Look at you!" June said. "You get more handsome by the day. Oliver, this is my husband Joe, Joe Michael."

"Hello, Oliver. It's nice to finally meet you," the man said. "I'm sorry we haven't made it up to see you sooner."

"That's okay. How're you doing, Joe?" Oliver smiled at the handsome man, thinking that he looked more like a professional golfer than a television producer. His golden hair and deep tan reminded Oliver of Jack Nicholas.

Oliver hugged his sister Anna and then said, "Come here, kid!" He bear hugged his younger brother Huck and when he let go, he tousled Huck's neatly combed hair. Huck wrestled to remove Oliver's hand and smiled impishly. "Ollie, you want anything?" Huck asked before they sat down. "A soda? Something to eat?" Oliver said no.

"First things first," June said. "We can't stay long. Joe goes back to work tomorrow. We've been traveling through New England for two straight weeks. Skip couldn't come this time. He had to work." She paused and smiled uncomfortably before she went on. "Now, Oliver,

I hate to put you through this." Her glance swept across her two boys and Anna.

"Oh, Momma. I'll tell him. Oliver, we talked to your lawyer," said Anna. "The news isn't good. He said the timing couldn't be worse. Apparently, you haven't served enough time yet and on top of that, he said the new governor doesn't believe in parole for lifers. You may have to wait up to eight more years to apply for your pardon." Anna moved to the edge of her chair and cleaned her fingernails of Fritos dust. Oliver put his arm around his mother's shoulder.

"This is just terrible," June said. She leaned forward and swung her foot.

"Not really, Momma," Oliver said, trying to reassure her. "It's not like I don't have a million things to do. I've got a lot of responsibilities in this place. My boss, a bunch of college professors and all kinds of students depend on me for one reason or another."

"Oh, we know. When your Dr. Dallet came to dinner she couldn't stop talking about you. You're going to be a college professor some-day. We're so proud of you, Oliver. She asked me a thousand questions about your childhood. Is she a psychiatrist?"

"No, ma'am, but I hope you made a good impression on her anyway."

"Of course we did. I even invited her to come back the next day. She couldn't though. She was giving some kind of speech at the conference she was in town for. But she did call me that next night and we talked for over an hour." June widened her eyes. "That woman thinks very highly of you, Oliver."

"How's your girlfriend, Ollie? I got the pictures you sent."

"She's fine, I guess, Huck. She just moved to California to attend graduate school."

June held her forehead in the palm of her hand, then looked up. "Does that mean you're all alone, son?"

"Not me, Momma. I have a new girlfriend."

June smiled and smoothed Oliver's collar down.

"Oliver, there's one other thing," said Anna. "That lawyer can't represent you without knowing why you did what you did."

Oliver looked perturbed. "He said that?"

"Yes. He said the pardons board is going to want to know your side of the story."

"All right, Anna. So what's your point?"

"Why don't you explain to us what happened? We're your family, for God's sake. Don't you think you owe us an explanation?"

"There's nothing to explain, Anna. My life was threatened, and I had to put an end to the threat. I had to defend myself. That's what happened. Now you tell that lawyer if he wants more details than that, he can ask me himself."

They didn't speak for a while but later, when Oliver followed his brother to the candy machine, Huck said, "Anna keeps telling everyone your temper got the best of you and that's why you're here."

Oliver said matter-of-factly, "She doesn't know what she's talking about, kiddo."

Huck gave Oliver a worried glance. Not nervous, just worried. "What's it like in here, Oliver? Momma said it's like you're away at college."

"She did?" Oliver asked, affectionately patting his younger brother's shoulder. "Well, I think that's a good way to look at it, Huck. One thing's for sure. I'm making the best of it. You can count on that."

When they returned to their seats, June and Joe were having a friendly conversation and Oliver took note of how happy his mother looked before her countenance turned serious again when he sat down beside her. She smoothed out an imaginary wrinkle on the front of her chartreuse chiffon blouse. "We'll have to be leaving soon, Oliver. It's a long drive home. Do you need anything? Clothes? A new radio? How's your television working?"

"Fine. I don't need anything." Oliver smiled confidently.

"Well, I'll leave you some money in case you do. We'll be back to see you again real soon, son."

Oliver shook Joe Michael's hand and thanked him for visiting. He hugged his siblings and then held his mother in his arms. When he let go, she held on tightly for a moment longer before she released him and backed away, her eyes locked on his. "I'm going to get you out of here, Oliver, if it's the last thing I do," she promised, before she turned away and walked quickly toward the exit door.

EVEN IF HIS FUTURE was uncertain, the present was where Oliver wanted to be anyway. At seven thirty that night, he dismissed his high school math students and ten minutes later he was in the arms of his superfine woman whose fifty-something face looked two decades younger. In the privacy of his office he kissed her and ran his hands up and down over her curves. She traced the angles of his strong jaw, lingering on the corners of his mouth. Then she ran her fingers through his long brown hair and kissed his neck tenderly. She stood back to look at him and asked, "Can you keep a secret?"

"Can I! Like nobody you ever knew," he said.

"Good. I've been craving for you since I left here last Tuesday." She loved to tease him.

"Well, you must have some appetite. Come here."

"Wait, there's something else. I made some changes to my schedule. I can come in on Thursday nights, too, for the rest of the summer."

"That'll put me in heaven two nights a week instead of one," Oliver said. "I'm not going to know how to act."

"I brought you a gift," she said. "It's in the bottom of my tote bag."

"Oh, yeah? Let me see the top of your thighs first. Pull your skirt up real slow. Take your time. I like it better when you go slow."

"Like this?" Slowly she started raising her skirt, carefully, as though to drive him wild.

"Higher," he urged her. "Come on."

Quickly then, she revealed the milky skin above her thigh hose. "Look at that," Oliver whispered. "Lemme touch you."

"Later. Let me show you what I brought you first."

She lowered her skirt and walked out of his office and into the classroom. They sat down and as she fumbled through her tote bag, Victor LeJeune walked into the room and sat down at the table across from them.

"Excuse me, Doctor. There's something I need to discuss with you and Mr. Priddy here," Victor said. "Something real urgent."

"We're right in the middle of a lesson," she said. "Can you come back at eight thirty?"

Victor leaned forward, jowls, dewlaps, heavy shoulders slumped. His bloodshot eyes were bulging, the bags under them large enough to make a pair of leather pockets. His lips were chapped, his breath sour. "No, I can't come back at eight thirty, Doc, and here's why." He reached inside his jacket and pulled out a small cassette player. He plugged it in the wall socket behind him, then leaned back in the chair.

Oliver bolted out of his seat. "What the hell do you think you're doing, Victor? Get out of here, man!"

"Sit down, Priddy. This is business."

Victor pressed the play button on the cassette player, and turned up the volume.

"… take off your panties, B.J. …"

"… I'm not wearing any, Oliver, honey … See? …"

"…What a pretty ass … Sit on the edge of the table and lie back …"

"… Oh, Oliver …Oh my God! I want you!...I want you now!"

Victor shut the machine off and snatched the plug from the wall. "In case you want to know, the tape's fifteen minutes and forty-two seconds long," he announced casually.

Before Oliver or B.J. could compose themselves enough to speak, Victor rose from his chair, removed the tape from the machine and stashed it down the front of his pants, then calmly walked out of the room.

Oliver kept his rage to himself. In that moment he could have killed Victor LeJeune. What would she think of him if he beat the man senseless? Did she even know what violence was up close? No, she didn't. There was a better way to deal with this, Oliver was certain of that. He looked down at the floor, incredulous, shocked. The nerve of that motherfucker! He glimpsed a shaft of light coming through the removable baseboard in the corner of the room where they had made love, and he knew instantly how Victor had done it. He had removed the baseboard in the adjacent classroom and slid the tape recorder's microphone through the hole. Now he looked at her and she was on the verge of tears.

"This is my worst nightmare," B.J. said. "What do we do now, Oliver?"

Oliver was about to tell her when Victor walked back into the room and leaned against the wall. Oliver glared at him. "Before this gets ugly, Victor, you'd better—"

"Shut up and listen, Priddy." His stony black eyes turned to B.J. Dallet. "If you want this tape, Dr. Dallet, it's going to cost you a thousand dollars in cash and I want it by next week. That's all there is to it. It's as simple as that." Victor's face was creased with a smirk as he walked back out of the room.

Oliver moved quickly into his office. She followed him, crying, terrified. A rash had broken out on her neck and arms.

"B.J., you've got to get a grip! What if George, the guard, walks in and sees you like this, baby?" Oliver picked up the phone and dialed 3-6-2. "Moose? I need to talk to Champ. Is he there?"

"Hold on. Who is this?"

"Priddy." Oliver pulled her close to him and held her until he heard Champ's voice.

"What's up?"

"Theodore, this is Oliver. I got a problem, man. I need your help. Meet me outside the school in two minutes." Oliver hung up the phone and grabbed B.J.'s arms. "Listen, B.J., I'm going to let the guard know I'll be right back. Don't open the door for anyone except the guard if he happens to come back."

"There's not going to be any violence, is there, Oliver? I cannot be a part of any violence."

Oliver grimaced. "You once told me you trusted me, didn't you? Well, now's the time to show it. You've got to trust me." He put his arms around her waist and held her and he was almost unable to let go. She was perspiring profusely and he was attracted to the scent of her sweat. "I'll be right back."

The streetlights cast Champ's long shadow across Turk's Street and Oliver moved quickly toward it.

What's going on, white boy?" Champ said, shifting a toothpick from one side of his mouth to the other.

"That no good cocksucker Victor LeJeune recorded Dr. Dallet and me in a private moment. Now he's trying to blackmail her. He just came in the room and played part of the tape to us. Then he demanded a thousand dollars from her."

"Oliver, how the fuck did you let him record you two?"

"I'll tell you about that later. Right now I need you to go up there and get that tape from him, man. He slid it down the front of his pants before he left the room."

"Where's he at now?"

"He was sitting in Rhoda Cherry's classroom listening to music with one of his boys when I just walked by."

"All right. Where you gonna be?"

"Back in my classroom waiting for you."

Champ checked his watch and looked back up the street. "I'll be behind you by a minute or two. Who's on the door? George?"

Oliver nodded and looked up at the sky. It was brilliant with stars that dwarfed the crescent moon, high over Turk's Street. "I owe you, Champ," Oliver said. "Thanks, man." Oliver took off in a trot.

B.J. Dallet was standing inside the door of his classroom as Oliver hurried across the main corridor. She unlocked the door for him and he took a seat at the table in the front of the room. "You said you had a gift for me?" he asked, perfectly serious.

"Oliver, this isn't the time," she admonished. "I've never been so afraid in my life. Tell me what's going on, please." She was about to cry again. "Maybe we should just go to Mr. Sommers and tell him everything. We can trust him. I know we can. We're very close. He thinks highly of you, Oliver. He'll know what to do."

Oliver saw Champ stalking across the corridor. The collar on his black jacket was turned up and the sleeves were pulled up over his forearms. His face was stoic. He was now wearing his wrinkled brown prison cap, the beak positioned slightly off-center the way the North Philly men wore them.

"Oliver, talk to me."

"Listen, B.J. I respect Mr. Sommers a lot, but he can't ever know one goddamn thing about this. It would mean the end of everything. Nothing bad's going to happen. This is all going to be taken care of. You have to trust me."

They sat in silence for a long while. She took out a pair of aviator-style sunglasses and put them on. He was about to reassure her when Champ knocked on the door and walked in. "How you doin', ma'am?" His smile was reassuring.

Her hello was a whisper. She looked at Oliver when Champ turned to him.

"Here. Get rid of this thing." Champ handed Oliver the tape.

"Champ, this is Dr. Dallet, the lady who spoke at your graduation."

"I know that, dummy. Nice to see you again, ma'am." Champ smiled at her.

"Nice to see you too," she said smiling back meekly. She was starting to regain her composure now.

"I've got to go," Champ said. "I'll holler at you later, Priddy."

When Champ left the room, Oliver walked back into his office and inserted the tape in his own machine to make sure Victor hadn't pulled a switch. When they had listened to it long enough B.J. told him to turn it off. She felt deeply violated, she said. And what if he had made a copy of the tape? What then? It wasn't possible, he told her. There were no duplicating machines around. What if he'd had it smuggled out of the prison to make a copy? No way. He didn't have those kind of connections.

"Oliver, do you know what this means?" she whispered, closing his office door.

"What?"

"It's over. I could never make love to you again as long as he's around. I just couldn't."

"Why? We got the tape back. There's no harm done."

"Are you serious, Oliver? Who's to say he won't run his mouth to his friends? And now this Champ fellow knows about us. How do you know he won't try something?"

Oliver walked to the window, his back to her. His mind raced, tripped and raced again. "You don't trust me, do you?"

"You think I would have given myself to you the way I have if I didn't trust you? Yes, I trust you, but you don't have control over what happens next, Oliver."

"Well, I trust Champ with my life. He's a thug but he's an honorable thug. He put the fear of God in Victor LeJeune, I know he did. Victor isn't going to open his mouth to anyone about this. I can promise you that."

"How can you be so sure? You can't! And I can't chance losing my career either. Oliver, I love you and I won't stop coming over, but—"

"This was my fault."

"How was it your fault?"

"Come here, let me show you something." She followed him back into the classroom and up to the front corner of the room where they had made love. "You see that hole in the baseboard? I know that's how he did it. He was in the room next door. If we had stayed back in my office this would never have happened."

"It's not your fault." She walked in front of him and he watched her go, instantly aroused at the sight of the sensual tension of her back legs and buttocks as she walked into his office. He could see both their reflections in the window. She never took her eyes off him and he doubted if she was all that interested at the moment in how her backside and long legs looked in the black knee-length skirt and matching stockings she was wearing.

"What if I told you we could get rid of him?"

She stood there with her hands folded across her stomach. They exchanged glances, her eyes begging for restraint, his promising none. "Oh, come on. How could you possibly do that? Or do I want to know?"

He sat at the edge of his desk in front of and a little to the right of her and looked at her steadily. He went on. Went on trying to make an impression. "One of Champ's people is a clerk in the major's office. He's made transfers happen before. The guy wouldn't even know who he's doing it for."

"I don't know, Oliver. I'm all nerves right now. I don't know what to think." She looked at him, trying to figure out if he was the man who understood theories of multiple intelligences or the one who worked his way through one catastrophe after another. Or both.

"There's only one catch." Oliver said.

"And what's that?"

"It would cost money to have it done."

"Everything costs money. How much?"

"I don't know. I would have to talk to Champ." He dropped the cassette on the floor and brought his heel down on it with force. The case cracked and scattered across the floor. He gathered up the spool of tape and tore it to shreds.

"Here, give me that." She opened the top two buttons of her blouse. He watched her left breast rise as she stuffed the ball of mangled tape inside her bra. "Tell me more about this Champ person."

"What do you want to know? You want to know about the stories I've heard or about the things I've read about in old newspaper clippings?"

"Both."

"Well, they say when he was thirteen he cut a boy's face from his earlobe to the corner of his mouth just for being in the wrong neighborhood. And when he was fourteen he took a screwdriver and made three evenly spaced holes in the chest of a rival gang member. Now what I read about him is even worse. He came to prison for hanging a storeowner in the back of his store. Then while he was in prison waiting to go to trial, he killed an informer inside the prison. He hanged that guy, too, from what the papers said, and then he buried a ten-inch knife in the guy's rectum. He's the most feared man in this prison. He's also the most well-liked. He and his crew have their hands in everything that goes on around here. Victor LeJeune's not in his league, B.J., believe me."

She combed her hair with her fingers while looking at him. "So what's the catch, Oliver? He's looking out for you, why? Because you tutored him in math?"

"That's one reason. Remember the guy we saw two years ago being escorted across the walkway in handcuffs?" She nodded yes. "His name is Fat Daddy Petaway and he's a notorious sexual predator. Okay. Remember the guy on the gurney who was bleeding like a stuck pig? Well, Fat Daddy stabbed him like twenty-seven times. The guy on that stretcher could have been me, B.J. Fat Daddy had been stalking me since the first day I got here. To make a long story short, a few years ago I found out he had been in my cell two or three times looking around when I was at work. The minute I found out, I decided to get him before he got me. I was less than twenty four hours away from bashing his head in when they moved me off the block."

"My God, I had no idea you'd been through this sort of thing. But how does Champ fit in?"

"It's a long story. He came at me with a deal that I couldn't turn down. He knew Penelope was visiting me every week so he offered to make me a member of his crew in exchange for a couple of ounces of weed every month and some math lessons. I took the deal and it was the best thing I ever did for myself. Champ made it so I didn't have to carry an ice pick around everywhere I went and sleep with one eye open all the time. Penelope got the weed from my friend Albert. Champ paid the wholesale price of the weed and it didn't cost me a dime."

"Maybe not, but he was using you just the same. Now I know how you've survived this place all these years. You've been through so much, my God." She pushed the door closed with the point of her high heel and moved to him slowly, her hand reaching out for his. She pressed herself against him and brought his hand to her lips. After several seconds, he replaced his hand with his own lips and kissed her gently. When he moved his hand up between her legs she said, "We can't, Oliver. Not as long as he's around."

chapter twelve

THOUGH IT HAD BEEN a moneymaking enterprise since its in-
ception in 1972, the Pennsylvania Lifers Association was never a
very productive organization until around 1980. That was the year
the membership acquired a large enough constituency of Philadelphia
voters to oust the old president, sixty-four-year-old Homer Dunn, and
install Champ Burnett as their new one. Champ's first order of business was to change the organization's constitution so that its main
mission statement no longer read, "merely to encourage members to
become model prisoners." Its new mission became "to change the
public's perception of convicted murderers." Champ embarked on this
formidable task by setting up generous annual donations to several
local charities—a North Side homeless shelter, an after-school community center, a nursing home for retired veterans, and the Ohio River
Boulevard Volunteer Fire Department. His next step was to increase
the organization's productivity by making its members more productive. To that end, he created a new legal committee, a public relations
committee, a newsletter committee, an entertainment committee and
a welcoming committee that showed up at each new lifer's cell door
with greetings and a goodwill bag stuffed with toiletries and other
daily necessities. When Champ had difficulty finding willing volun-
teers to fulfill these committees, he resorted to the one asset that had
never failed him—his guile. When asked to head the legal committee
because he had the best legal mind in the state, Omar Ali had flat-out
declined until Champ told him that all the legal books he wanted, plus

a brand new Olivetti electric typewriter, came with the job. And when Oliver was recommended to head the newsletter committee, he said he needed time to think about it. Champ gave him ten seconds, glared at him and said, "Time's up, Priddy. Here's the file. Now get the show on the road."

Many thought Champ's first real challenge would come after he fired the five concession stand workers from Pittsburgh, who had been on the job for as long as the organization had been in existence and skimming graft for just as long. Complaints among these men flared like snake cowls: Whatever happened to respect? We've been here a lot longer than those Philly guys. Who in the hell do they think they are, anyway? This is some geographical bullshit! But when it came time to hand over the keys and records they were as cordial as church ushers.

Six months after Champ installed his own people to run the year-round soda and popcorn concession stands the organization began churning out record profits, and morale among its members actively engaged in making a contribution to one committee or another was at an all-time high. Champ's ingenuity had brought a measure of pride and stature to the organization that had never before existed. The Pennsylvania Lifers Association was functioning like a big city Chamber of Commerce.

For the next nine years, while the organization and its members thrived, life in the free world experienced an explosion of violence and crime in every major city across America. As the usual swarm of talking heads sounded off about the best way to handle the problem, op-ed editors found themselves in a buyer's market. While one side of the page demanded more prisons, longer sentences and harder time, the other side pointed out the obvious root causes to the problem: poverty; truancy; media violence; poor nutrition; the erosion of family values; godlessness; the absence of moral training in schools; insufficient funding for social programs; and the unrelenting infestation of drugs in the inner cities. By 1989, a steady rise in Riverview's population, along with the accompanying daily violence, underlined the growing discontent within the penitentiary walls. A reduction in food portions and other amenities added to this undercurrent of tension, which only reinforced and heightened the rumors that the worst was yet to come. Consequently, every anarchist, misanthrope and conscientious objector among Riverview's four hundred and three lifers were urging their peers to store up knives, razor blades, matches, rope and jars of paint thinner. Champ, a natural leader, urged the membership to come up with a nonviolent plan of action. "Aw, no!" shouted a former Black Panther at one of their monthly meetings. "That shit didn't work for Martin Luther King! How you think it's going to play out hear? By the way, I thought you had a reputation to keep."

Champ pursed his lips and let his tongue stroke a gold inlay before he replied, "Don't let your mouth overload your ass, Jack."

STAMPED OUT INTO THIS WORLD under the name Theodore Elijah Burnett, Champ was raised on a street in Philadelphia called Oxford. Early on he learned that a brick was as good for keeping other boys in line as it was for building a house. His father Jerome had managed to keep Theodore close to the front stoop of their Oxford Street row house and out of any real trouble until he died of a heart attack when Theodore was thirteen years old. After that, Champ's mother and older sister Shirley gave up trying, though not for lack of love. It was a matter of practicality. Who could expect a thirteen-year-old boy with ants in his pants to sit on his front stoop all summer when ten other boys were instigating him to "come on"? So he took to the streets with the other boys from Oxford Street, and together they refined their skills in a sport called gang war. After gang-warring with the boys from the Valley, the Zulu Nation up on Diamond Street, and the 16th and Norris Street gang, Theodore and his Oxford Street pals played a one-round elimination of fisticuffs to determine their leader. Theodore was the last boy standing.

Though he wasn't the biggest or strongest member of the Oxford Street gang by any means, what he lacked in those areas he more than made up for in his viciousness. One or two blows with a length of pipe was never enough. He loved to hear the crunching and splintering of bones. One slice with a knife led to two—and another and another. He wouldn't stop the assault until his mind registered the urgency in his fellow gang members' voices when they shouted that the sirens were getting close and it was high time to beat feet.

Theodore's troubles with the law began in the spring of his fourteenth year, when he and three other gang members went to see a Temptations concert at the Uptown Theatre one blisteringly hot Saturday afternoon. Waiting in line right behind him was a pretty red-boned girl from Norris Street, who was eyeing and vibing with Theodore when her older brother told him to find somewhere else to stand. Theodore smiled at the older boy and told him he didn't want any trouble. But the boy wouldn't just leave it at that. He profiled on Theodore, stuck out his chest and sneered, "I know motherfuckin' well you don't, chump!"

After the show Oxford Street followed Norris Street down Broad Street and into an alley that was supposed to be a shortcut home but ended up being the scene of a homicide. On the day of Theodore's preliminary hearing the prosecutor sighed and told the judge there were no witnesses and no evidence other than the three evenly spaced holes in the dead boy's chest. Theodore and his homeboys were free to go.

A week later Theodore's mother placed him on a Greyhound bus, destination Orangeburg, South Carolina, to spend the summer with his Aunt Beulah and cousins Joanne and Leon. They were waiting for him when the bus pulled into the small college town, and though he had only met his aunt once when he was five years old, he recognized her immediately for she resembled his mother right down to her marcelled silver-gray hair. She embraced Theodore tenderly and then introduced him to her beautiful eighteen-year-old daughter Joanne, and son Leon, who was Theodore's age. A chubby boy, Leon wore a mini-Afro, baggy bib overalls and peach fuzz on his chin.

Aunt Beulah and her family lived in a two-story yellow clapboard house on the edge of a farm two miles outside of town. When they got out of the car, Theodore could smell the simmering aroma of food before he saw the steam rising from the pots of potatoes and collard greens on the stove, and the sizzling country ham and two hot fruit pies waiting on the counter.

For the two months he was there, Theodore enjoyed the food the most and his cousin Joanne's complacency the least. She was a student at South Carolina State University in Orangeburg, and on Friday evenings her college friends came to the house to eat pizza and talk. One evening while they were discussing a tragedy that had occurred on campus a few months back, Theodore and Leon were sitting at the kitchen table eating blueberry pie and drinking ice-cold milk chasers while they listened. Apparently, there had been some kind of demonstration on campus and the police arrived to try and break it up. When the demonstrators refused to leave, the police opened fire on them killing three students. With a mouthful of blueberries and a scowl across his face, Theodore told Leon he wanted to know the whole story. Leon informed him that Joanne had been on campus the night of the incident and she could relate all the details.

And she did the next morning at breakfast. For three nights in February, she said, students had been peacefully protesting the failure of the town's only bowling alley to racially integrate. On the fourth night the students had lit a bonfire to stay warm, then the police came and extinguished it. Her friends started another one, and when the officers attempted to put out this second fire, some of the students threw rocks and bottles at them. What followed was a barrage of gunfire with students running in every direction. In the end three young black men were dead and twenty-seven other students lay wounded.

"Most of them had been shot in the back," she said.

Theodore was enraged. "Why didn't the brothers have guns?"

Joanne shook her head calmly. "We don't believe in violence, Cousin Theodore. At least the majority of us don't."

"Violence! You got to protect yourself, don't you? You can't let those honkies get away with that kind of stuff!"

"Cousin Theodore, that's exactly the kind of thinking some of those young men over on campus have right now, and it's only going to lead to more violence."

"As Christians, Theodore, we don't believe in violence," said Aunt Beulah.

"What about an eye for an eye? Isn't that what the Bible says?" Theodore couldn't believe what he was hearing.

"It does, son, but we are dignified people and must abide by the law."

"I'm leaving now, Momma," said Joanna. "We're having a meeting with the Dean of Students this afternoon."

Aunt Beulah hugged her Bible and trembled. "Child, don't you be on that campus past dark. You make sure you're back in this house. I'm not fooling now."

"I'll be home, Momma. I promise."

The day was so hot that the cotton planters had come out of the fields early to find shade. The boys tried to beat the heat off with the breeze they caught while riding their bicycles as fast as they could down the back roads. When they met up with two of Leon's friends, one of them said the best place to be on such a hot ass day was in a swimming hole. "How bout old man Tucker's pond?" said Leon.

"Too many of them water moccasins," said one of the boys. "Let's go to the creek."

Theodore, who was deathly afraid of snakes, watched the boys ride off without looking back. When they were out of sight, he pedaled back to Aunt Beulah's house, propped Joanne's bike beside a shed and then did the strangest thing. He bolted as fast as he could through a cotton field without a clue into which direction he was running. When he got to the end of the first field, he ran straight into the next. At the end of this second field, he encountered a patch of woods and ran right through it. He tried to stay close to the road that led into Orangeburg, but he wasn't sure. With each twig his Pro Keds trampled and snapped, he ran a little faster.

When he finally came out of the woods, he saw a garage up ahead on the edge of town. A black boy about Theodore's age was changing a tire on a rusted out pickup truck. The boy was barefoot and wore grease-stained overalls. The sweat on his ebony skin glistened in the sunlight. Theodore asked him where the University was located.

"Straight down yondah on Main Street, pass them there traffic lights. All them buildings is the University, heah?" The boy looked at

Theodore curiously. There was no mistaking him for a local boy, for most of them wore their hair thick and nappy, and Theodore's haircut was close to the scalp, in a high fade. That, and his jeans were pressed, tighter fitting, and double cuffed.

"Good looking out, my brother," said Theodore, and then he pressed on as if he was on his way to fight a rival gang.

Beyond the traffic light he saw a large sign on the corner—Campus of South Carolina State University. Beyond the sign lay a maze of sidewalks and buildings. Young black men and women were walking in every direction. Theodore crossed the street and walked down the sidewalk until he reached the heavy shade of a magnolia tree. He could smell lemons and charred wood in the breeze and he could hear a conga drum faintly beating a steady rhythm. He looked around and saw groups of students sprawled out under the shade of the tree, some reading, some eating sandwiches, others napping and listening to music. There wasn't a white person among them and he was flabbergasted. For a while he stood there under the heavy branch of the magnolia tree where the air was cool and sweet. Fifty yards in front of him he noticed several students with books and backpacks leaving the main walkway and disappearing behind the administration building. Curious, he headed in that direction.

When he turned the corner of the building a large group of students was gathered in a semicircle listening to one of their own who was shouting into a megaphone. The brother wore a blue and orange dashiki and a matching Yoruba hat.

"...are African Americans citizens with rights just like anybody else, brothers and sisters! We are not animals to be slaughtered! Those racist pigs murdered three of our innocent young brothers only a few hundred feet from where we now stand! Right over that hill!" The speaker pointed in a northwesterly direction. "Henry Smith! Murdered! Samuel Hammond! Murdered! Delano Middleton! Murdered! And twenty-seven others were shot in the back! Why? I'll tell you why! Because they were exercising their right to gather in a peaceful manner! Because they were protesting the illegal segregation of a local bowling alley! They weren't carrying guns! Or knives! Or pipes! They were carrying schoolbooks! They weren't bothering any-body! It's time now! It's time to wake up, brothers and sisters! We've been sleeping for four hundred years! The white man will continue to annihilate our people until we wake up and take matters into our own hands! I say!... I say to hell with the president of this University. I say we demonstrate tonight! Now what do you say?"

"Power to the people!"

"Black power!"

"We want justice!"

"We want it now!"

Theodore joined in the shouting. "We want justice now!" He punched his fist into the air. Someone had placed a stack of books on the grass and he picked one up, waving it above his head. "We want justice!" He weaved through the crowd until he approached the front. That's when he saw his cousin Joanne shaking her head in frustration. As she turned in his direction, she saw him and shouted his name. "Theodore! How did you get here?"

"I ran," he said. "All the way."

"Let's go! You can't be here. And where did you get *Invisible Man* from?"

"What?"

"That book. Ralph Ellison's *Invisible Man*. Where did it come from, Theodore?"

"I found it in the grass."

"You can't just take it. That book belongs to one of these students. You have to put it back."

She followed him through the crowd to the place where he had been standing when he picked up the book. He tossed it on the ground. "Why can't we stay?" he asked.

"We just can't."

"Why not? These are my people too."

That was true, she told him on the way home. But the campus was no place for a fourteen year old boy who didn't know the first thing about white people from the South, even if he did know how to take care of himself, she added for his benefit. He asked her if she was

166

going to attend the demonstration that night. She told him that holding another protest against the orders of the University president was just asking for more trouble and, no, she wasn't going to attend.

"I wish I could go. That brother was right, you know. We have to start fighting back."

WITNESSING THE WRATH of those who had experienced the Orangeburg massacre lit a revolutionary flame in Theodore's heart and made him hate the white man even more than he already did. Three years after he returned from his trip to the South, he traded in his birth name for one that better suited his anger. Theodore Elijah Burnett became Brother Aziz X. Mohammed when he joined the Nation of Islam's Masjid Number Twelve located at Park and Susquehanna. It was the black pride and militant aspect of the organization more than the religious doctrine that appealed to him.

At home his sister Shirley was first amused by her brother's new-found commitment to pressing his own clothes, polishing his shoes, and laying out his bow ties neatly on top of his scarred dresser. But when she gradually noticed the once-playful side of his personality was nowhere to be found, she began to take him more seriously. For hours at a time he practiced standing at attention in the middle of the living room, frozen like a statue, unblinking, a piece of handsome granite. Once a cockroach crawled all the way up his body and across his face and he never flinched. After that, Shirley gave him plenty of room whenever she passed his way. His mother, a devout Christian, was disappointed in his new religion, but pleased with his newly acquired discipline.

Brother Aziz X. Mohammed was not just another new convert at the Masjid Number Twelve either. He was also the newest and young-est member of a squad that meted out discipline to the brothers who didn't have enough of it. It was a position at which he excelled and took more seriously than anything he had ever done. On his nineteenth birthday, he walked through the front gate of the Philadelphia House of Corrections, a full-fledged lieutenant in the Nation, and his fellow Muslims in tow addressed him as Brother Minister. Once again he was charged with murder, but this time it was no gang war murder. This time he was accused of killing a corner storeowner, motive unknown. The cause of death—strangulation. The dead man was found fully disemboweled, hanging from a rope tied to the ceiling in the back room of his store.

Inside the House of Corrections, Theodore's problems were compounded when he received word from the streets that there was a rat inside among the rank and file. One morning, the rat was spotted entering the security office after having just told his brothers he was on his way to the visiting room. Two days later the rat was found hanging in his cell with his guts dangling out in front of him and a finely honed shiv buried in his rectum. The story in the *Philadelphia Inquirer* revealed that the rat had been an FBI informant waiting to testify against a group of Muslims from Masjid Number Twelve, who had allegedly driven a van to the Nation's Capital and massacred a room full of people. Brother Minister Aziz X. Mohammed and two of his lieutenants were charged with the jailhouse murder.

Like the government and the rest of the establishment, the criminal justice system was, as far as Brother Minister Aziz was concerned, run by the same "white devils" who had massacred his Brothers in Orangeburg, South Carolina. Consequently, the last thing he wanted was a white man representing him in court. When he asked for black representation, the judge denied his request so he, in turn, refused to participate in his own defense. Whether it was the white attorney or the abundance of evidence they had against him, Brother Minister Aziz was convicted on both counts of murder. The judge gave him life for the street homicide and ten to twenty years for the jailhouse murder.

By the time he arrived at Riverview Penitentiary, Champ was a seasoned leader of men who were born to follow. He loved his fellow Muslims, but he loved even more the brothers he had grown up with on Oxford Street. Blue Light. Omar Ali. Gus. Disco Bob. Big Jake. Shotgun. Cheese. Percy. Soul Train. And even crazy ass Fat Daddy. These were his homeboys and they were all there, doing time together.

What some people considered his only vice, Champ considered reparations: The Native-American and the arsonist who lived in the cells on either side of him had both been feminized long before Champ laid on their backs. On alternating days these pretty boys pulled Champ's curtain shut and struck a salacious pose, angling the hips just so, poking out their narrow behinds. He grudge-fucked them and took care of their material needs. The ambience they created gave Champ's life a new semblance of domesticity.

1989

chapter thirteen

THREE HUNDRED AND SIXTY-TWO prisoners poured into the dining hall to attend an emergency meeting of the Pennsylvania Lifers Association. Those who called themselves the walking dead—baby, cop and serial killers, murderers by arson and the one who strangled a nun with her own rosary beads—were the first to arrive. Though the walking dead didn't have a hope or prayer of ever receiving a pardon due to their heinous crimes, they nevertheless participated in life. They filed grievances, pressed license plates, fed the birds, watched movies, jerked off, demanded sheets without blood stains, completed Bible correspondence courses and showed up at every function of the only organization left in the world they could rightly call their own. To show his appreciation for their solidarity, Champ had given these men the title of official custodians of the association shortly after becoming their new president. No matter what the occasion was, the walking dead showed up ahead of time to clean the restroom, mop the floors, wipe the tables and set up the refreshments.

The hall was noisier than a train station before Champ called the meeting to order. Some men were calling out numbers. A Christian at one table shouted 6-6-6 to a Christian two tables over. A bookie hollered the daily number 3-6-9 up and down the aisle. A drug dealer called out his prices, three for ten, seven for twenty. And one man who had been crossed by another told him he had his number.

The rookie guard thought he was sitting on a powder keg the way those black, white and red faces smiled and frowned at one another while they drank mugs of black coffee and ate sugar cookies by the handful. When he saw two stamping and pawing at the ground, he called for backup.

The roly-poly guard, Sergeant Mervis Dewey, entered the hall. "What's the problem? We got a problem here?"

"Sir, I believe there may be too many men in this room for one officer to handle."

"You do? Well, let me school you about these lifers, officer. You let them be. They are the best-behaved men we have. Let them have their meeting. Can we do that?"

"Sir, yes, sir."

"Good. You need a break? You want me to stay?"

"Sir, no sir."

"OK. Call me at 2-9-5 if you need me."

Champ's fist was as good as a gavel and when he brought it down, the hall hushed like a congregation. He pointed to Bell who was sitting in the front row wearing a burgundy and grey custom jacket embroidered with the words 3rd Battalion, 187th Infantry, Phong Dien Vietnam, 1969-1970, across the front. "That's a fly-ass jacket you're wearing, Bell," Champ said in earnest. "It's a shame they're going to take it from you any day now."

Bell looked confused.

Champ held up a sheet of paper and said, "Yo! Listen up! We just got this memo, Brothers! The same one that'll be posted on the bulletin boards next week. The administration is taking all our personal clothes from us! Starting next month every man in this joint will be wearing prison browns 24-7. Brown pants, brown shirts and brown sweat clothes."

"Get outta here!" one man said. "They can't do that!"

"Yeah! I just bought a new Philadelphia 76ers warm-up suit. Cost me seventy-five dollars! They gonna reimburse me?" asked a second man.

"This is unconstitutional!" said the first man.

"What are we supposed to do with the clothes we got?" asked a third man.

Champ made his voice empathetic. "Ain't nobody more heated about this than I am, Brothers! I got a whole cell full of clothes. They say we got to mail this stuff home or donate it to Goodwill or have it destroyed—"

"Mr. President! Champ! I've got something to say about that!" Oyster Bey interrupted.

"Come on up," Champ said. Oyster had bounded halfway up the aisle before Champ said come.

When Oyster leaned toward the microphone, his voice was loud and defiant. "We heard this was coming! Nobody wanted to believe the sons a bitches would do it. Now that they are, I got one thing to say. I don't have many personal clothes. A couple of polo shirts, some jeans, a few sweaters and a wool jacket my Aunt Mercy got me a couple Christmases ago. If we have to give up our personal clothes, it doesn't take a genius to figure out where they're going to end up. It won't be the Goodwill Store, that's for sure. These guards will be like goddamned vultures picking through the piles and taking what they want. Bell's jacket and that man's warm-up suit will end up on the backs of their kids. You can bet your ass on that. If you guys are smart, those of you who don't have anywhere to mail your clothes to, you'll do what I'm going to do. Take a razor blade and shred the hell out of them before you turn them in. That's what I'm going to do. Fuck a Goodwill! That's all I got to say and thanks, Big Champ."

As Oyster walked back to his seat, someone shouted, "Good idea, old head! I'm doing the same thing!"

Another man chimed in, "Me, too!"

Champ's voice grew louder as his words tumbled out. "Christian family gatherings. Cut! Varsity sports travel. Cut! Annual picnics. Cut to three hours! Then there's that noon count that's robbing us of a half hour, sometimes a whole hour, of yard every day. Last month they changed the rules for outside picnic visits. Now a lifer has to have ten years in instead of just five." A moment of silence, and he added, "They fucking us every way they can. And they ain't done. Listen to this: Quote, 'Due to the continuing increase in the prison population across the Commonwealth, it has become necessary to place double bunk beds in every cell. The double bunks are currently being built by our corrections industries and installation will begin within ninety days of the date of this memo. Any inmate who refuses to double up will be placed in the behavioral adjustment unit until he agrees to comply.'"

A cacophony of curses rose in the room.

"Oh, hell no!"

"They crazy?"

"Put somebody in my cell, I'm fucking him!"

"You ain't the only one, buddy!"

"Brothers!" Secretary Anwar said. "These six by nine cells designed to hold one man are about to hold two! According to the new deputy warden, only out-of-the-closet homosexuals and the criminally insane will be exempt from this policy. So you can either put a limp in your wrist, go crazy or just plain refuse to live in a cell with another man."

Champ waited until the members settled down and Anwar took his seat before he shook his head in disgust and then forced a smile. "This memo says the double celling may only be temporary because they're planning on building two new cell blocks in the middle of the yard."

"Say that again?" two men shouted simultaneously.

"They're building two cell blocks in the middle of the yard," Champ repeated evenly.

Half the men in the room gasped while the other half said that can't be right.

Everyone knew that building two cellblocks in the middle of the yard would mean an end to summer softball games and Sunday after-noon football games in the fall. The boxing program would have to go, too. To make way for the new buildings, the ball diamond, boxing gym, law library, prison chapel and the redbrick Home Block would all have to be demolished.

"This whole prison's nothing but a fucking cage!" Key-su, a Black Panther from Chicago stood and shouted. "Now they want to make the cage smaller! Brother Champ! May I address the membership?"

Champ motioned for Key-su to come forward. It was prudent, he thought, to let the members hear from someone whose physical presence itself was a warning sign. This black man with braids that glittered and clanged like machetes on his head might portend the future for them and wake them up.

Key-su hustled to the microphone and snarled without preamble. "Brothers, let me put you down with something! The prison system is fast finding its way into corporate Amerika! You see, if you follow the yellow brick road of cause and effect, you will see that the reason they need more cell blocks is because they are locking up our young black brothers faster than you can say there's no place like home.

"Just look what's going on in our cities. The crack cocaine infiltration is nothing but a mass conspiracy by the United Snakes of Amerika to up its racial oppression. Where are these drugs coming from? The last time I checked there weren't any cocoa fields in downtown Philly or Chicago or Baltimore or D.C. I'll tell you where they're coming from! South America via the CIA, my Brothers! And look who the victims are! Some of them are in this room! You young brothers—babies—coming to jail for life! The politicians are knee-deep in this shit, too. They're creating new laws so that a brother who gets arrested with a little crack cocaine gets three times as much time as a white man who gets arrested with three times the amount of the pure shit. It ain't no mystery why they want more cell blocks, Brothers!"

Key-su paused while the members clapped and cheered. Champ smiled to himself and thought how this brother from Chicago reminded him of another brother he had heard speak years ago in Orangeburg, South Carolina. Somewhere in the room, standing in the corners or against the back wall, Champ saw the bright golden eyes of his first cousin Joanne and her college classmates half-circling a freedom fighter who was doing his best to educate them about the racist world in which they were trapped. He saw, too, the mothers of three dead college students crying from grief so sheer you knew they'd been condemned to die from it. And the men they now referred to as white devils, the pink-faced men who caused their grief, who produced it, built hi-rise projects to contain it, designed ways to study it, and then

175

treated those who were sick to death of it so they could be well enough to endure more struggle and pain. Grief was the white man's tool for wearing away his people, Champ was sure.

Key-su went on. "And what about all the other shit that's going on around here? The recent deaths in the hospital! Three this month, two last month! And the mentally deranged Brothers they keep dumping into the population from the state hospital! They be shuffling around this joint day and night picking up cigarette butts off the sidewalk and chasing bogeymen. And what about the Klan beatings going on down in that Home Block? Brothers, there's a war going on right under our noses. You all better wake the fuck up!"

Key-su pumped a Black Power sign in the air and walked to his seat, his bright, angry brown eyes burning like two torches.

Every member in the hall stood up, stamped his feet and cheered wildly. While they went on, old man Willie Dew raised his hand and Champ waved him up to the podium. Arthritis and thirty-six years of penitentiary life had twisted Willie's lean six foot five inch frame into a pretzel, so it took him a minute to get there. His wide wet eyes blinked proudly as he smiled at the Brother who had just inspired and inflamed his heart.

Willie cleared his throat and smacked his lips together several times. "Now you know what …. You know what troubles me? Well, I'll tell you. All these damn pigeons fucking and flying all over this joint." Laughter broke like a dam in the hall and Willie had to wait until it subsided before he went on.

"Everywhere you look around here, there's pigeon shit. Early Greer, listen, brother! I loves you, but you got to stop feeding them damn things." More laughter, and then, "It's getting so it ain't safe to look up in the sky no more. The pigeons fly over the yard dropping bombs of shit all over a man's head and back. You can't hardly walk anywhere without stepping in pigeon shit. Then you walk in your cell with shit on the bottom of your shoe and now you got shit on your rugs and floor. Then later in the night you walk around your cell in your bare feet and now the shit's on the bottom of your feet. Then you crawl in bed and now you got pigeon shit in the bed with you."

The laughter reached a riotous level before Willie raised his hands head high and brought his palms together, touching gracefully. "We had this problem back in '59, and what they did was they put poison in some day-old bread and fed it to 'em. It worked like a damn charm, too. But you have to be careful if they do that cause you know how they like to fly up on the big St. Regis roof and roost right on the edge? Well, when they die roosting up there they more often than not fall five stories down. I saw with my own eyes what it did to one ma'fucker that was standing too close to the building and got clocked. It wasn't a pretty sight, I'll tell you." This time the laughter sounded like thunder. Willie stood there, hat in hand and drop-lipped, until the excitement died down, and then he shuffled to his seat.

Champ smiled compassionately at the old man. "Thank you, Willie. We'll address the pigeon problem with the rest of these issues the next time we meet with the administration. Now I want Omar Ali to come up here and tell you about a new bill the legislators just passed."

"Thank you, Brother Minister. Good evening, Brothers. For those of you who don't know, the state legislators just signed a bill that could make every lifer in this state a walking dead man!"

"Say what?"

"I ain't heard about no new bill!"

"Yeah! What's it's all about?"

Omar Ali and Champ exchanged looks. The sign of rumble in their eyes was clear. "According to this new law, three out of five votes from the Pardons Board is no longer enough to get your sentence commuted. Now all five members of the Board have to agree. This might not be so bad if it wasn't for that crime victims advocate who now sits on the Board. That crazy woman votes no on every application they put in front of her."

"So what you're saying is we're fucked!" shouted a man from the back corner of the room.

"Yeah! The whole thing's a bridge going nowhere now!" Another shouted from the opposite corner.

"Oh, no, Brothers!" Omar Ali protested. "They can't make something like this retroactive! They say it is, but we're planning to file a class action suit on they ass! This thing violates *ex post facto* protection in the United States Constitution! We going to fight this all the way to the United States Supreme Court! Don't lose hope!"

"Hope? I hope those lawmakers die of cancer!"

"Yeah! Those no-good cocksuckers!"

At that moment, Sergeant Dewey walked through the side door, raised his hand and whirled his finger around. Omar Ali walked away from the podium while the conversations swelled in the room. After Champ gestured with his own hand and announced they were out of time, Deacon Bob stood and said, "Brothers, losing all these amenities and rights is a difficult thing. But with the help of the Creator, we shall overcome. No doubt about it."

Outside the dining hall Oliver and Early and the others stood around listening to a group of insurrectionists wielding conversations about ice picks, fire, and blood.

"I know what'll make 'em stop this shit!"

"Yeah! Tear this motherfucker down!"

"Hit 'em where it hurts!"

Another man was singing "Fire!" by the Ohio Players. The one beside him was chanting, "Attica!" over and over. Others mentioned a hunger strike. "Do I look like I'm ready to give up a meal, niggah?" Chinaman asked, squeezing one of the folds of fat around his waist. "How bout a work strike? Now I could go for that."

Oliver cringed as he pictured the routine of his daily life going up in smoke—hostages, fires, torn bodies, bleeding rectums, blood on the sidewalks. Who needed it?

Who needed it? Here he was learning advanced calculus, the laws of metaphysics and theories of information processing, a year away from becoming the first member of his family and the first prisoner in the world to earn a PhD, and they wanted to burn down his classroom. It just didn't make sense. And even worse than the thought of losing his classroom was the thought of losing his lover, friend, mother, sister, and world class mentor. There was no way he could afford to lose her. Not her.

He cocked his head when he saw Champ approaching, and then separated himself from the others to talk to him. They cleared their sinuses at the same time, and Oliver said, "I got something for you, Champ. Meet me at my hut."

Five minutes later they were having a conversation that was better than Oliver imagined a conversation could be. In the middle of it, he removed the poster of Otis Redding at the Monterey Pop Festival from the back wall of his cell and peeled off the hundred dollar bill he had taped to the back of it. "Here's a brand new C-note Champ." Champ smiled and looked at Oliver while he folded the bill five different ways and then stuck it down inside his sock.

Oliver continued, "Goddamn, I wish there was a way to make that bastard disappear." What he meant was, name your price and make it happen! Champ said, "If you're serious that'll cost you five hundred."

Oliver's voice was hollow with wonder. "Five hundred? Just to get him transferred?"

"You fucking right! That kind of move don't come cheap! What you think, I'm going to chop him up and flush him down the toilet for you? There's another man got to take care of this. And he don't come cheap."

Oliver was startled into a smile. "How long would it take?"

"I don't know. I'll have to get back to you on that."

"All right, let's do it. Put the order in, man."

Phlegm and impatience mingled in Champ's voice. "Hold up. You talk to her first. Make sure she's down with it. Not unless you got five-hundred of your own money to spend."

"Look, she wants him gone as much as I do, Champ. She'll pay the money as long as there's no violence. Five hundred's nothing to her. She's brought this thing up a hundred times, how she wished he would just disappear. If I tell her it's going to cost five hundred dollars to get him transferred, she'll bring five brand new C-notes in the next time she comes. I guarantee it. You want the money up front?"

"Nah. I trust you. You know better than to play with my money."

Oliver hesitated and then said, "She won't even let me hold her with this fucking guy around. He's got to go, man."

"All right. I heard you." Champ looked curiously at the calligraphy writing on the wall over Oliver's bed before he said, "I want to ask you something."

"What?"

"That meeting tonight. What'd you think?"

"Man, I don't know. I don't think they can make that law retroactive."

"I'm not talking about that. I'm talking about how hyped up everybody got when we told them about all these changes that are coming down."

"Hell, everybody's frustrated, Champ, including me. But what can we do about it?"

"Lot of people talking about making some noise."

"You can't blame them. They're making changes so fast, it's like they're asking for trouble. I don't know what good it's going to do to start a riot, though, if that's what you're talking about."

"Hey, don't put words in my mouth, Jack. I didn't say nothing about no riot. What would you do if they had one anyway, hide under the bed?" Champ giggled and Oliver smiled.

"No. But I'd get the hell out of the way."

"You wouldn't get involved?"

"For what? They wouldn't need me to help tear shit up, that's for sure."

"You're right. Keep your ass up in that school. Speaking of school, I saw you doing your homework tonight at that meeting."

"Nah, man, I was taking notes for a piece of satire I'm writing. About all this shit that's going on. I'm going to enter it in a literary contest over at the University. It might even get published."

"Satire? What the fuck's that?"

"A literary technique. When you draw attention to a serious problem by suggesting some crazy ass solutions. And the beauty of it all is that the solutions aren't meant to be taken literally, so you can more or less say whatever you want to say."

"That's good. That's what we need."

"Yeah. I'll probably put it in the newsletter too. I'll let you read it when I'm finished. You want to catch a buzz while you're here?"

"Yeah."

"Here. Light it up."

chapter fourteen

MONDAY MORNING, pleased with his plans and armed with a four-page draft of parodies and diatribes, Oliver decided to check out the bakeshop before going to work. He turned right instead of left at the intersection of Tom's Way and Turk's Street and strolled past the chapel, the Young Guns Boxing Gym and the Free Yourself Law Library. Three yardworkers were cleaning up ice cream and candy wrappers along the sidewalks and between the buildings, while a chapel worker stood on a ladder washing the stained glass windows. Oliver watched a blood-red bird hop from limb to limb in the pear tree behind the chapel. When it flew away he looked up and saw a cloud ribbon swirling all the way across a pastel blue sky. It was a sight to behold, he thought. As were the clapboard buildings, the sidewalks that zigged and zagged, the shrubs and manicured flower beds, and the early morning silhouette of five boxers jogging around the courtyard. Why would anyone want to disturb this view? Except for a crack here, a chink there, everything in the prison was intact. There was no need to wonder if taking a wrecking ball to the joint would be a mistake.

As he drew closer to the end of the street, he could smell the aroma of freshly baked bread and sweet sticky rolls in the breeze. When he arrived at the back door of the bakery, he called for Hambone whose albinism caused him to squint and blink perpetually as he opened the screen door and stared at Oliver in the bright morning sunlight. Hambone handed Oliver a warm bag of pastries, and Oliver dropped a fat joint into the palm of Hambone's hand.

The rolls, smelling wonderfully, attracted the cat that lived under the steps. The cat jumped onto the landing, curled around Hambone's ankle and purred, though her eyes remained alert to predators—human and otherwise.

"That's some good shit, Hambone," Oliver said, eyeing the tufts of white hair above Hambone's red eyes. "A few tokes are all you need. See you around, my man."

He walked back up the street with no name and passed two store-room workers who were unloading bags of potatoes from a beat-up Ford delivery truck parked beside the chapel. He always thought the chapel basement was a peculiar place for a potato cellar, though he imagined it was cool and dry down there. Over the years he had seen many shady characters coming and going from the cellar whenever he passed by. He had heard many loose stories about what went on down there, too—war stories; fist fights and who was triumphant; talks of trysts, interrogations and bondage. He pictured Fat Daddy pummeling some white boy on a stack of potato sacks while the born-agains were upstairs practicing "What A Friend We Have In Jesus" in flatted thirds and sevenths. And how those brothers could sing. Now that he thought about it, the born-agains could have been the source of inspiration for all the nefarious activities that went on down there.

As he crossed Tom's Way, it and the side streets seemed to him as busy and noisy as ever for a Monday morning. Three of one-eyed Melvin's boys, five of Champ's, a couple of Homewood old heads, and three MOVE members dawdled on the corners, whispering among themselves. Oliver reassured himself with more force than confidence that all was well. Nothing he could put his fingernail under, just a gnawing sense of conspiracy. He had seen violence, been a part of it, had watched it up close when it was visited on others and felt it firsthand when it was visited on him. Meaning, if it came down to a riot, he knew that bodies would not just fall down, unmoving; they would be ripped apart, burned and pierced by men who took pride in that kind of work.

Oliver saw Donnie Blossom waving at him as he was coming up the walkway. "Hi, Oliver. Mind if I walk with you?"

"Nope, I don't mind. Where are you headed?"

"The Arts and Crafts shop. I'm glad I ran into you. Those word problems are giving me a headache. I need some more one-on-one tutoring."

"I'd like to help you, Donnie, but today's out of the question. I've got an essay to finish this morning and a three-hour class this afternoon with Dr. Ray Garris, my psych professor. If you want, you can stop by my hut after supper." Oliver liked Donnie, not because he was as beautiful and feminine as it was possible for a young man to be, but because he was smart and inquisitive; moreover, he wasn't obnoxious like the other queens in the prison.

"I'll be there," Donnie said. "You know, I never did like math, Oliver."

"That surprises me, as smart as you are."

"Yeah, right. I'm doing twenty to forty for two arsons. How smart is that?"

"I've always wondered what you did to end up in here."

"Now you know."

"Never met an arsonist before."

"I set my father's haberdashery on fire."

"Are you serious?"

"Serious as a heart attack, Oliver."

"He must have pissed you off something terrible," Oliver said.

"Not really. I just got tired of the way he treated me. His store was the only thing he ever cared about. His tweeds and cashmeres and fifty dollar ties. One night I just got fed up. I went in the place and doused the carpets with gasoline from one end of the store to the other. Then I hid in the alley across the street and watched it burn. It was the most exciting thing I had ever done in my life. It really was." They stopped in the middle of Turk's Street and waited for a small red delivery truck to come to a stop alongside the food storeroom. "I don't suppose you've ever seen a mannequin catch fire and melt right down to the floor. Well, there was this one in the front window modeling a pair of red plaid pants and a ruby-red cardigan sweater. It looked just like my father until the head melted. When I realized it wasn't him, I got angry all over again. That's when I decided to drive to my parents' house and set it on fire too. They got out. I knew they would. Smoke detectors were everywhere in that house."

Dumbfounded, Oliver stared into Donnie's face and was certain he saw orange and red flames engulfing the bluest irises he had ever seen. "You're not joking, are you?" Oliver asked.

"I wouldn't joke about something like that."

"Sounds to me like you really like fire."

"I like the smell of gasoline even better. Hi octane. That's why I cut grass in this stupid prison all summer, Oliver. I love smelling gasoline."

Oliver stopped in front of the school door and noticed a woman in a long loose tie-dye skirt standing outside the library at the far end of Turk's Street where it intersected with C.I. Lane. She was writing in a spiral notebook while Mr. Mastros, the librarian, stood beside her talking. Each time the woman looked down, she cocked her head to the side to keep her shoulder length champagne blond hair from falling over her eyes. Oliver was sure he had never seen this woman before; yet she looked familiar.

A movement over his shoulder took his attention, and as he turned, he glimpsed the backs of seven Muslims as they turned into Stickup Alley. Before he pulled open the school door, he turned to Donnie and said, "We've known each other for ten years, and I didn't know anything about you until now. We've got to talk more often, Donnie Boy."

Fifteen minutes later, after he took two sticky rolls for himself and distributed the rest among the staff, Oliver sucked his teeth and pushed aside the books and papers on his desk. He picked up his blue ceramic mug of steaming hot coffee and took a sip before opening his loose-leaf notebook. Without hesitation he scribbled in the margin of the first page: "Capitalize and repeat key words often." Then he wrote down the title of his satirical essay at the top of the page:

HOPE FOR THE HOPELESS:
A MODEST PROPOSAL TO THE LIFE
PRISONERS OF PENNSYLVANIA ON THE
PRACTICALITIES OF SELF-DELIVERANCE

He shuffled through the loose pages of his draft and then reread the opening paragraph. After placing quotation marks around two similes by two of his favorite poets, Langston Hughes and Gwendolyn Brooks, he started writing the final draft of his essay:

"Surely by now all of you know that our well of HOPE dried up 'like a raisin in the sun' last week when Governor Tom Rigid signed House Bill 1725 into law. In sixty days the Board of Pardons will be renamed the Board of Crime Victims' Advocates, and any HOPE for future commutations or acts of clemency for LIFERS will be long gone. The victims advocacy board will still hold hearings for any LIFER who is gullible enough to pay the twenty dollar application fee that guarantees the applicant fifteen minutes of public humiliation, of being forced to sit and listen while his crime is sensationalized again and again; of being reminded that, despite the long passing of time, compassion and mercy are no longer a part of this state's lexicon.

"So many Young Bucks have brought up the question, then what is left but to grow old and die a burden to our families and friends and ourselves? My reply to you, Brothers, is that we must face our demise like dignified human beings. If we must die here, let it not be like helpless, decrepit old men, unless that is the way you choose to die.

"Based on a recent survey conducted by the Pennsylvania Lifers Association, all but 107 of the 403 lifers here at Riverview Penitentiary concede that we are going to die in prison. Of those, 42 are still grasping at appellate court straws, despite the fact that the Chief Justice of the State Supreme Court has publicly proclaimed that due process has become too subjective of a term to allow for any more reversible errors. Still, we want to wish you Brothers well, all of you. The remaining sixty-five, all of whom are Young Bucks under the age of twenty-one, angry and strong, like 'sores in the city that do not want to heal'——still believe the laws can be reversed and amenities regained through acts of INSURRECTION and ANARCHY, by, in the words of one gang of Young Bucks, the RANDOM SLAUGHTERING of prison officials on a daily basis. While we do not encourage such action, we wish you God's speed in your endeavors."

Oliver underscored the words insurrection and anarchy, then wrote empowerment and hope in the margin, drew a line under them, and continued:

"For many hours I have turned my thoughts upon this dilemma of living without HOPE that we all share. For those of us who have come to realize we are going to spend the rest of our lives behind these walls and do not wish to continue day after day, month after month, year after year, in a perpetual state of living without hope, I wish to offer this proposal of HOPE and EMPOWERMENT to you.

"I have been assured by a very high ranking member of the PSPCP (Pennsylvania Society for the Prevention of Cruelty to Prisoners) that SELF-DELIVERANCE is a viable and acceptable option for situations and circumstances where HOPE has 'spoiled like rotten meat.' Although obvious and many, the most important advantages of instituting a SELF-DELIVERANCE program are as follows:

"First, our family and friends who have unselfishly and lovingly endured years of humiliation coming behind these walls to visit us, often to be patted down and fondled by the Jackboots who resent their coming in the first place, would certainly view our SELF-DELIVERANCE as an act of love. Our unselfishness could finally place them in a position where they could live out their lives without having to worry every day they wake up whether we are safe and well.

"Second, creating an acceptable EUTHANASIA program would eliminate the horrifying failed attempts at SELF-DELIVERANCE we so frequently see, such as, slashing one's wrists across the arm as opposed to down the arm and through the veins; overdosing on all-too-mild sedatives only to wind up in a self-induced coma; jumping from the fifth tier of the cell block only to survive as a quadriplegic.

"Third, providing a permanent way out for those without HOPE would greatly lessen the burden on this Commonwealth. In view of the fact that at present, it costs the state about eighteen thousand dollars a year to incarcerate one of us, and considering that the average age of our LIFER population is forty and the LIFE expectancy is seventy, even if only a fourth of our current LIFER population takes advantage of the SELF-DELIVERANCE program, the state would save two million, five hundred dollars in the first year, and a total of seventy-five million, six hundred thousand dollars during the remaining thirty years that these LIFERS would be expected to LIVE. These conservative estimates do not include what the state would save in medical costs as we LIFERS age and become ill."

Oliver stopped, put down his pen and, covering his eyes with his hand, rearranged the details in his head before he went on.

"With the PSPCP's support, I have taken the initiative to study the feasibility of providing EUTHANASIA kits for sale in the prison commissary. A very respectable entrepreneur I know, who also happens to be sympathetic to our plight, recently provided me with a description of four dignified EUTHANASIA kits he has designed and packaged for demonstration purposes. This gentleman, who is a lawyer and member in good standing of the American Hemlock Society, has agreed to meet with a powerful member of the state senate in the near future to discuss the practicalities and feasibility of instituting a SELF-DELIVERANCE program for LIFERS across the state. This distinguished senator is, I have been assured, most supportive of the idea of EUTHANASIA for those of us without HOPE. I will keep you informed of the outcome of that meeting. Meanwhile, I wish to describe here the four EUTHANASIA kits our sympathetic entrepreneur has already designed and packaged for us:

"DEATH HOLLYWOOD-STYLE KIT: This kit comes with a syringe filled with 150 ml of air to be injected directly into the vein causing an embolism and rapid death. This kit would be most suitable for drug addicts and former addicts. It would not be recommended for someone with little or no knowledge of how to inject a needle directly into one's vein. This kit includes a sealed syringe filled with air, an instruction manual, and a Last Will and Testament. It would sell for $10.95.

"HANGMAN'S KIT: This kit consists of a heavy-duty ten foot rope tied in an efficient, professional noose, an instruction manual, and a Last Will and Testament. The kit would sell for $9.95.

"SUPPOSITORY KIT: This kit consists of three rectal suppositories containing 1 g of sodium Phenobarbital in each suppository, an instruction manual, and a Last Will and Testament. This kit would sell for $29.95.

"GAY PRISONER'S KIT: For you homosexual prisoners who wish to die with a good feeling, this kit comes with a nine-inch vibrator that time-releases a lethal dose of barbiturates deep inside the rectum, like warm semen. The kit includes the vibrator loaded with a lethal barbiturate drip, an instruction annual, and a Last Will and Testament. This kit would sell for $39.99. Batteries are not included.

"Other kits are currently being tested for their efficacy, including a self-asphyxiation kit, which I have been assured shows great promise.

"While many among us continue to argue that condemning a man to LIFE WITHOUT HOPE is just as cruel and unusual as condemning him to death by lethal injection, our legal representatives have warned us that the issue is a moral one, not a constitutional one. And therein lies our dilemma. Since a moral appeal is out of the question, our only recourse is to appeal to the logic of practicality. With the shrinking of the state treasury due to the enormous costs incurred in building five new prisons, there is but little doubt that the legislators will agree to draft and unanimously pass the necessary legislation to make legal a EUTHANASIA Program for LIFERS who have otherwise lost all HOPE.

"In conclusion, I ask you all, LIFERS everywhere, to exercise patience and whatever iota of HOPE you have left. EMPOWERMENT is on the way.

"'Or does it explode?'"

Oliver stopped and rubbed the blister on his middle finger. His elbow and shoulder were numb, too, from gripping the pen so hard. He gulped down the last of his coffee, sat back in the chair and, feeling he had crafted a provocative essay, carefully read the final draft.

THE NEXT EVENING B.J. Dallet's high-heels clicked along the main corridor and when the clicking stopped, the high lilt in her laughter echoed throughout the building as she stood talking to a group of students. The prisoners were enjoying the crease in her behind, which was so clearly defined in the bright fluorescent lights.

They looked at her body with outright admiration as she told them about her recent travels, one offering, "I was in D.C. once," and another, "My aunt, she stay in Atlanta." They did not ask her what they really wanted to know: What did she do to stay so beautiful and how much did her perfume cost? B.J. smiled, drank from the water fountain, and the worshipful stares of these men made her long to be in Oliver's presence.

She excused herself and clicked her high-heels all the way into Oliver's classroom. He was sitting at the table looking more beautiful than when he had stood in front of her the first time and she saw genius and mischief commingling in his face, more beautiful than that day in the classroom when his calf kissed hers for the first time, than when he had almost cried telling her about his mother June and how he had protected her. She wanted to sit in his lap and wrap her arms around him, but Chuckie Redshaw and Jimmy Rawls, two of Oliver's students, followed her into the room and sat down at the table, too, so she just walked over and shook Oliver's hand in a friendly, professional manner. He beamed at her with the same adoration as they did, but he did not compete. Chuckie and Jimmy sat back and enjoyed her presence. They looked at Oliver with awe and appraised her like she was a Corvette he had stolen.

Oliver stood up to leave and B.J. picked up her bags to follow him. When Oliver said, "You fellows are going to have to excuse us. I have an essay I need Dr. Dallet to read," Chuckie said, "Yeah, we were leaving anyway. We just wanted to say hello. Nice seeing you again, Dr. Dallet." Chuckie and Jimmy breathed in her scent one last time before walking out the door.

B.J. Dallet followed Oliver into his office and said, "Why didn't you tell me about what's going on with the lifers, Oliver?"

"What do you mean?"

"Mr. Sommers said they've changed the entire pardons process making it almost impossible to get you out of here."

"That law they just passed isn't even legal. They can't make something like that retroactive. We've got lawyers from the ACLU on the case already. It's going to get overturned. Watch."

They were quiet for a moment, thinking about it. Then Oliver walked around the desk and pulled open the center drawer. She stood beside him and rubbed the nape of his neck. "Here's my essay," Oliver said. "I'm dying for you to read it."

She sat at his desk reading his satire while he gazed out the window. After tweaking a sentence here, a phrase there, she said, "This is excellent, baby. I'm very proud of you, Oliver. I'll enter this in the literary contest and I also want a journalist I know to read it. Before I forget, put this away." She unzipped a hidden pocket in her tote bag and pulled out a wad of bills and, curling them into his hand, asked if there was any word yet on you-know-who. He stroked her hand and, soaking in joy, folded the five C-notes she handed him into an envelope, then stashed it in the baseboard behind his desk. "Soon, baby. Real soon I've been told," he said. She crossed her legs, swinging the top one, being girlish. She was being girlish for him.

Across the hall, through the half open door, they could hear Victor LeJeune's high-pitched laugh. For the moment Oliver wished him happiness—something to assuage the unhappiness he would reap in the days to come, exchanging the prosperous ten year run he had had at Riverview for a whole new environment somewhere upstate. If revenge was a dish best served cold, Victor was about to be served up a frozen entrée. Oliver had never waited this long in his life to get even.

1990

chapter fifteen

BOLTS OF LIGHTNING LIT UP a purple and black sky and the rain fell like buckshot as residents poured out of the St. Regises, heading for the auditorium or the gymnasium or the second floor school building. Each time the thunder clapped and exploded, the prisoners picked up their pace, jumping over or dodging around the puddles and potholes in the pitch-black darkness. Interspersed among these pedestrians were Champ and six other men who were on their way to a clandestine meeting in the hospital basement. One by one they entered the lobby where Early Greer stood holding a mop in his hands. To the first man and the six who followed, Early nodded and said, "Down the stairwell. Last door on the right."

The air in the last room on the right was chilly and smelled like fresh rain and formaldehyde. The light bulbs overhead dimmed and flicked in sync with the thunderstorm outside. Each time the lights went off, the men could see dust particles dancing in the thin gray light that seeped through the opaque window overhead.

Champ, who was the last of the secret seven to enter, closed the door behind him and settled himself in a chair in front of the white porcelain autopsy table. He looked around at the others: Luis "Suave" Rodriguez; James "LaMumba" Hutch; E.J. "Queenie" Jackson; Alex "Doza" Love; Jackie "Sonny Corleone" Boyd; and Leroy "Key-su" Hopkins.

"We all know why we're here, brothers," Key-su said. "After everything's said and done, I believe there's only one real solution to this situation." He paused and looked around the room at each man, and then said, "Whatever we decide to do, I hope we'll be in one accord. Now who wants to go first?"

Suave, the undisputed leader of the Latino community, said, "Yo, every time one of my peoples steps on the sidewalk the po-leece is snatching us up, shaking us down, and confiscating our bandannas. We want to give them a reason to leave us the fuck alone." Broad shouldered with short wavy black hair and a puffy, thick-lipped face plagued by fresh wet acne, Suave waved his pudgy hands in front of him. "We ready to tear the roof off this bitch, you hear me?"

Doza went next. "Dig, man, I can relate to that. We asked that little security captain a hundred times to move all of my squad on one tier so we can be out of everyone's way, but he keeps splitting us up. He's got us spread out all over the block in cells next to niggahs they know we got issues with. Those punks just want to see something happen. They eggin' it on. Let's create some drama for they asses. We're tired of this shit." The tall, lanky leader of the Bloods looked like a choir boy when he smiled at Key-su and said, "I'm through."

"What I have to say will be brief," said the one they called Sonny Corleone. "Everybody's frustrated. Some of the white guys want to organize a demonstration. Whether it's a work stoppage or a food strike, I don't know. Some of them want to tear the place apart, too. They all agree we need to do something about all these changes they're making."

Key-su pulled on the sleeves of his orange and black windbreaker and then pointed to Queenie.

At fifty-seven, Queenie was the oldest man in the room. He took out an index card from his inside jacket pocket, and said, "Key-su, you asked for some figures. I got most of them for you. Let's see. Last year thirteen men died in the hospital. Five from cancer, three from heart attacks, four from stab wounds and one died after a gall bladder operation. There were seven suicides in the prison and we've had two this year. The beatings in the Home Block, because they don't keep those kinds of records on paper, I couldn't get. What I can tell you is that medical responded to one hundred twenty-one incidents in the Home Block last year."

Queenie turned the card over and read silently until he found what he was looking for. "I almost forgot. Working in the major's office I'm always hearing something new. Well, I just heard when the clocks get moved ahead in the spring, visiting hours are going to be cut back from all day to three hours a day. Um-hm. It's true, baby," he said to Doza, who twisted his face in disgust at the news.

LaMumba played with a plait on the side of his head. When he spoke, his rich baritone reverberated in the room. "Evening, Brothers. I've been sitting here listening to your articulations, and I'm reminded of something a philosopher by the name of Aristotle once said about democracy. He said when you have a small number of very rich people, the poor people will use their democratic rights to take property away from the rich. This analogy is very fitting to the situation we presently find ourselves in, my brothers. You see, the guards and this administration are rich in power, but small in number. We prisoners are poor, but large in number. It's high time we exercise our democratic rights, Brothers! Now the fourth president of these United States, a man by the name of James Madison, once said that when a large part of the population suffers, it will sigh secretly for a more equal distribution of life's blessings. Suffering as we are from the oppressive boots on our necks, we must do more than talk and secretly sigh about our conditions. There is power in numbers, and we have them. We, being the majority, need to use our powers to bring about reform."

LaMumba paused before he said, "All we need is a plan, Brothers. First, we need an approximation of how many young bucks, Puerto Rican, white, black and otherwise, we can depend on when the time comes. Then we need to decide when and how and what our demands will be. Do we kick it off on a weekday or weekend? Morning, afternoon or night? Do we take hostages and how many? And what about a leader? We need a strong leader and we need captains and—"

"Whoa, whoa! Hold up!" Queenie said, looking stunned and animated. "Are you talking about what I think you're talking about?" He lowered his voice almost to a whisper. "Are you talking about a riot?"

LaMumba rolled his eyes, displaying incredulity.

Key-su said, "Let the brother finish."

"Yeah, but...all right. Go ahead."

LaMumba's voice was low and polite without any hint of impatience. "That's exactly what I'm talking about, Brother. And if it will ease your mind, I have read everything that's ever been written on the Attica riot. I know exactly what those brothers did wrong and what they did right. We will not repeat their mistakes."

LaMumba looked at Key-su who gave him a sign.

"We already have a thorough plan to make them meet some of our demands without any of us getting killed," he said at last. "Now what's on you mind, Queenie?"

Clean-cut and black as polished ebony, Queenie touched his throat. "Okay. Whatever happened to diplomacy?" he asked with a mock frown. "I mean, a riot's rather extreme, wouldn't you say? I was thinking more on the lines of a work strike or a sit-in or something. Maybe we could get the workers in the license plate factory to shut the place down. That in itself would get the public's attention, not to mention the people in the state capitol. Look at all the bonuses and overtime those guys are getting. That should tell you something! License plates are in demand, honey!"

Key-su looked at LaMumba, gave him another sign and said, "Let me respond to that. The bonuses and overtime are the very reasons those bootlickin' niggahs, 'scuse me, those brothers, will never go on strike, Queenie. The reality of the situation is that eighty percent of them have fifteen to twenty years or more in, and they're not thinking of rocking no boat that's going to leave them without a job. All they want is a motherfuckin' bag of commissary every week and their evening sit-coms. Now I agree with you, if it could be done, it could be effective. But I guarantee you that the minute one of us, or anyone else, approaches one of those workers in an effort to tally up the yeas and nays, that person's going to wind up in the Home Block and on the next transfer bus. Now who here would like to head up that census taking?"

For several seconds the room was as quiet as sleep. Then the thunder crashed and boomed and the room went dark again. When the lights came back on a minute later, four of the seven had their backs to the wall.

Suave shuffled to the center of the room. "Ain't every Latino nig-gah thorough, but I got forty who are."

"And I got a good thirty-five raw and ready young niggahs I can count on in a heartbeat," said Doza.

"The problem with so many of the white guys," Sonny Corleone said, "is a lot of them aren't doing much time and don't want to get caught up in a full scale brawl. They're not going to mess up their chances at parole. That's not saying I don't know some men who'll get down, because I do. But I got to know what the deal is before I go approaching any of them about something like this."

Champ said, "There's a good four or five hundred soldiers from Philly and Pittsburgh in this joint who'll go off in a second."

"We need to make some decisions and fast," Key-su said. "First, we need to appoint a leader. Then we need to decide if that leader is also going to serve as our spokesman when the time comes. Will he have full say on tactical procedures? On the timeline? Designating captains? Assigning duties, etcetera?"

Key-su was so overwhelmed with conviction that he could not speak calmly of these things until the matter was official. He paced the middle of the floor while the others sat in silence letting the minutes tick by. Long before Early knocked on the door and said they had ten minutes before the guard would be making his rounds and locking the stairwell, Champ urged Key-su to say what he could not: that not only had the leader been selected. He was the one.

But he knew. He had to know.

THE NEXT MORNING at breakfast—grapefruit sections, scram-bled eggs, toast, jelly, apple juice—Champ walked down the right aisle instead of the left and sat at a table with two white men, one hollering, "Dude, you were awesome in your last fight! Thought you were going to kill that guy." The other saying, "What do you mean, Larry? You bet on the Italian Stallion."

"Phil, don't belittle me in front of the Champ," Larry said.

Champ buttered his toast and said, "You two heard the news?"

"What news?"

Champ lowered his voice. "Something about a work strike? Everybody's talking about it."

"We're pushing for a sit-in, Champ."

"At least you're not talking about a full scale riot. Don't need something like that."

"Nah. Things aren't that bad around here."

Champ raked his scrambled eggs with his fork and said, "Not yet anyway. What you guys think about them freezing our pay?"

"Come on, man! Where'd you hear that?"

"Got it from a good source."

"I'm stuck at twenty-two cents an hour," Dubois Phil said. "What about you, Champ?"

"Thirty-two." Champ drank the last of his apple juice. "Hey, listen, I don't know who's in charge of organizing this little sit-in of yours, but I want you to know I support you guys."

Two weeks later Champ's propaganda proved to be a half-truth. The administration wasn't freezing pay raises; they were merely slashing pay hours from eight a day to six.

"See! They knew better than to freeze our pay!" one man said.

"We ain't never worked eight hours a day anyway," said another.

When the same rumor mill whipped up details about a full-scale riot going down, panic and bravado festered like a boil all over the prison. Weeks of conversations and debates on the yard, in the gym, at the dinner table, and in the classrooms and church pews, turned into signs of ill omen.

Someone said to a friend, "Whatever happens, we're sticking together."

And the friend answered, "I've got your back and you've got mine."

A sugar daddy said to his trick, "Let's do it in broad day light while they're busy protesting, 'stead of at night."

And his trick said, "Okay but make sure you got something sweet for me afterwards. I ain't 'bout to miss a good protest and go hungry too."

Then the born-agains took it up, saying the same people who had insisted it was a no-win situation were now the ones advocating fire and brimstone. "May as well go with the flow and save Jesus the trouble," said Deacon Bob.

In the end, Dubois Phil, a hillbilly with a loud and distinct voice, agreed to be their spokesman. The first thing he did was shave his shaggy beard down and cut four inches off his ponytail so he would look presentable when the time came. Barely literate, he struggled to recite their list of demands. When a black scholar from Lancaster named Cold Duck offered to be Phil's partner, Phil said, "Gawd, yeah! How bout you read the demands to me and I'll say them out loud."

Cold Duck spent the next three days clarifying and organizing their list of demands while Dubois Phil spread the word about the date, time and location of the event.

On the morning it was to go down, the sun popped in and out of the clouds like a warning sign. After breakfast, the prisoners returned to their cells and arranged their belongings until the work-line bell sounded. Then, three hundred strong crammed themselves into the canteen yard. They brought books, magazines, radios, guitars, breakfast rolls, coffee, chessboards, toilet paper, pinochle decks, crossword puzzles, writing tablets and rugs to sit on. Two brought signs: One read "Woodstock!," the other, "Attica!"

Cold Duck saw the Attica sign and pointed to the owner. "Are you crazy? You trying to start a riot? Get that thing down!" Several in the crowd thought the sign was right on time. Those who had to be talked into coming were about to leave until they saw the sign disappear.

Kitchen and laundry workers, gym rats, barbers, students and a handful from the maintenance shops came in enough abundance to effectively shut down their respective job sites. The secret seven, who had spread encouragement like a farmer spreading seeds, stayed away.

Cold Duck and Dubois Phil distributed copies of their list of demands to the demonstrators who were sitting peacefully, enjoying the vibes, listening to music, waiting.

Someone in the middle of the crowd yelled, "What do we want!" The crowd answered, "Change!"

Then: "When do we want it!"

"Now!"

The first question was repeated from a chorus and answered by the masses:

"What do we want?"

"Change!"

"When do we want it?"

"Now!"

After that novelty wore off the demonstrators went back to entertaining themselves. At half past nine a dozen guards gathered around the perimeter of the canteen yard fence, smoking cigarettes, squinting, and talking quietly among themselves. When a crapshooter pulled a knife in the corner of the yard, then stood and shouted, "You cheatin' ass niggah!" the guards turned away as though they hadn't seen the glint of the blade.

Five minutes later the guards and all three hundred protestors looked up in the dirty gray sky at the whirly bird hovering above them. The prisoners cheered and waved. Some wondered aloud if they would be back in their cells in time to see themselves on the noon news.

After the chopper got its footage and disappeared, Deputy Superintendent Jack Offen appeared at the corner gate near the canteen entranceway. He rested the bullhorn on his beach ball stomach and with his other hand he pulled at the skin of his red iguana neck before removing his sunglasses. His close-set pig eyes scanned the crowd before he placed the bullhorn near his mouth, pressed the trigger and demanded, "What's this all about?"

Radios faded, the dice stopped clicking, the crowd hushed. Everyone who had been sitting in the yoga position sat as straight as a soldier. The sun disappeared behind a cloud. Dubois Phil and Cold Duck were sitting right in front of the man. Phil held up a sheet of paper.

"What in the hell is that?" Deputy Jack Offen asked.

"A list of our demands!" said Phil.

"Demands! Demands for what?"

From the back of the yard a voice shouted, "Read them! You ignorant jackoff!"

Cold Duck carried the paper to the fence, curled it up and slid it through. The deputy squeezed his bulbous red nose and reached for the sheet of paper. When he finished reading it, he looked at Phil and Cold Duck as they stood side by side. "I see. Well, we need to talk about this. Some of your demands may be legitimate. Who's in charge here?"

From the crowd: "We're all in this together!"

"Yeah, yeah! I understand that! But I can't talk to all four hundred of you! Now who's your damn spokesman? Would that be you?" He pointed to Phil who wiped his sweating hands on the front of his trousers.

"We they spokesman!" Dubois Phil said. He said it with force.

"Is that a fact? Well, now we're getting somewhere. You two come with me." He raised the bullhorn. "All right, that's it! It's over! You men return to your cells immediately and prepare for lunch! Your representatives are coming with me, and we'll see what we can do for you!"

Only part of that was true.

LATER THAT DAY, long after Dubois Phil and Cold Duck were seen shackled and handcuffed and on their way to the redbrick Home Block, the workers back to work, the dust blowing in the yard, two blood brothers known as the Lynch twins, serving as spotters, turned their backs for a split second at the same time Victor LeJeune lost his grip on the two hundred and fifty-pound barbell he was attempting to bench press. Without support, the weight fell full force onto Victor's neck as he tried to scramble from under the bar. Startled by the metallic clang of the weights hitting the cement floor, followed by Victor's limp body, the others stood around drop-lipped and as helpless as weeds leaning in a field. The Lynch twins leaned over Victor's body and stared through eyes raked with wonder. Victor's windbreaking broke the profound silence and caused two body builders to talk to each other and to themselves. In the midst of someone calling out "Phew! Goddamn! What happened?", they heard Biggie Lynch's "What the fuck did you do, Victor?", but not the "Help me, somebody,

I can't move!" that Victor whispered. Then somebody remembered to go and get help. They found the guard outside smoking a cigarette. By the time the nurses arrived, stabilized Victor's neck in a brace, and directed the two orderlies to lift him onto the stretcher, Biggie and Richard Lynch were standing near the exit doors whispering one to the other, "Let's get the fuck out of here!

On his way to the ambulance Victor cried out for his mother, "Ma! Ma!" Or so it was said. In any case, he had already begun to show signs of complete helplessness. On the way to the Allegheny General Hospital, one of the EMTs held his hand, but Victor didn't know it. When the second EMT pinched his calf and said do you feel that, Victor looked dumbfounded. Three hours later the doctor told him his neck was broken in two places and the prognosis was grim.

Lying in the trauma ward of the prison hospital a week later, which was a screened corner of a larger ward, and grieving over his condition, Victor remembered the admonition of the weightlifter working out next to him not to go too heavy and recalled that sudden warnings were always foreboding. He remembered something else, too, and try as he might to ignore it, he knew that when the Lynch twins had let go of their respective ends of the barbell and he was completely in control of the two hundred and fifty pounds on the bar, he had seen the two of them simultaneously turn their backs. When he mentioned what he thought and what he'd seen to Early Greer and another orderly who had come to give him a sponge bath, they both sympathized with him. Early said, "It's truly a shame what happened to you, Vic. Twins are a strange phenomenon. I read a great deal about how they behave when I was in college. Did you know that twins like the Lynches can have telepathic powers?"

"Yeah," said the other orderly. "These guys are always finishing each other's sentences. Just last week I heard Biggie tell a man, You think I'm playing with you niggah—and no sooner did he say niggah than Richard said try me."

"That's just what I'm talking about," said Early. "Hell, one of them probably got distracted by something or someone and the other one sensed it and turned around to look too."

Early uncovered Victor's legs and began to wipe around the calf.

"Pinch me!" Victor cried. "Pinch my leg till I can feel it!"

Early felt nothing but genuine pity for Victor and said, "Can you feel that?"

"Harder! Pinch me harder, Mr. Early!" Victor was crying. Early pinched the meat of Victor's calf until his skin turned blue. "How 'bout now?"

"No! Nothing, man!"

The other orderly shook his head while he rinsed the sponge out in the basin of warm water.

Early stared into Victor's eyes as solemnly as a preacher delivering a eulogy. "They're transferring you to Farview next week, Vic. You'll be better off there. That hospital has state-of-the-art physical therapy equipment and highly trained therapists. You're going to get the best rehabilitation program you could hope for on all of God's green earth."

chapter sixteen

OLIVER WAS DRINKING coffee and reading a research report on short-term memory when Champ knocked and then pulled open Oliver's cell door. "What's up, Champ? You're just in time for coffee."

"Nah. I just drank two quarts of water. Guess who leaves tomorrow?"

"Yeah, I know. It's about time. I guess it's true what they say about misfortune."

"What do they say?"

"One man's misfortune is another man's gain." Oliver smiled.

"I don't get it. What the fuck are you saying?" Champ asked, chewing on a toothpick fashioned from a Popsicle stick.

"Well, we were about to pay you five hundred to do what the Lynch twins did for nothing."

"Whoa, wait a minute. Dig this, Oliver. That man's transfer was already in motion long before he had that little accident."

"Some are saying that wasn't an accident. What do you think?"

"Don't matter what I think. You still got to pay. My man wants his money and I want mines."

"Okay. I got it up in my office. I'll bring it to you tomorrow."

"Hold on. I don't want it in cash."

"What are you talking about?"

"I need her to do something for me, Oliver."

"Like what?"

"Pick up a package."

"What kind of package."

"Eighty tiny balloons no bigger than a half ounce of weed."

"Come on, Champ. She's not going to want to bring drugs inside—"

Champ cut him off. "What about that good-ass weed she brought you? She didn't mind bringing that in. Two or three times that I know of. Probably more than that."

"Yeah, but reefer's one thing, dope's another story. Where would she get dope from? She wouldn't have a clue where to look for that stuff."

"Up in the Hill District. There's a little restaurant called Lena's right off of Wylie at the top of the Hill. I got the directions and everything right here. All she has to do is call and ask for Chicken Wing. When he comes to the phone tell her to say she's calling for Champ."

"Holy shit. I don't know, man."

"Listen, Oliver. She goes up there in broad daylight, pulls in the alley, knocks on the back door of the joint, gives him the five hundred and he'll give her the dope. That's all there is to it."

"Champ, you realize what I'm asking her to do?" Oliver said it urgently.

"Yeah. And I know she'll do any motherfuckin' thing you ask her to do."

Oliver lit a cigarette. His lower jaw jutted like a bullfrog's, rotated as if he was chewing gristle. "I don't know, man. I just don't know."

Champ blinked at him. "You wouldn't go 'gainst me, would you, Oliver?"

"You know better than that, Champ."

"All right then," Champ said meekly. Too meekly, Oliver thought. A moment of silence, and Champ added, "I got to go now. Get that done for me, Oliver."

Handshakes were cursory. Champ's fingers were long and icy cold.

The next morning Oliver was surprised by how well he had slept. The meeting with Champ the previous night had left him confused and when he went to bed, he laid there wondering if he'd been duped once or twice. He wondered if Champ had hired the Lynch twins to let that barbell drop on Victor's neck. It was quite possible he had,

Oliver thought. Though the Lynches weren't members of Champ's crew, Oliver knew Champ had done business with them before. And everyone knew the Lynches would have gladly carried out the deed for a mere couple bags of dope. As badly as he wanted Victor gone, Oliver would have never agreed to getting rid of him this way, not just because B.J. didn't believe in violence of any kind, but he wouldn't have wanted this on his own conscience. Then there was the matter of payment. He would have never agreed to any deal that called for B.J. driving into the ghetto to exchange cash money for balloons of heroin. When Champ had named his price for getting rid of Victor, Oliver never thought for a split second he needed to specify the method of payment. It was implied. Champ had duped him twice.

Such nagging thoughts, he believed, would keep him awake most of the night, but in the morning, he awoke as if from the soundest sleep.

"HE'S GONE!"

B.J. Dallet dropped her tote bag on Oliver's desk and pulled him to her. She kissed and touched him aggressively, running her hands up and down his hard, perfect body as he fought with her clothes.

"Damn, I missed this!" he said into her mouth. "You're so beautiful." A barrage of her scents wafted to him.

"I've been going crazy without you," B.J. said.

He tore off a button and bent hooks. He gathered her breasts into his hands. She wanted it hard and raw and without limits. She controlled him. She dominated. He helped himself to her until they were exhausted and slippery with sweat.

After she pulled her panties on and tucked her silk blouse into her skirt, she said, "So was that Champ happy when you gave him his money, love?"

"That's what I have to talk to you about, BJ. He wouldn't take the money. Said he never told me when we first made the deal that he wanted to be paid in cash."

Her head snapped back as if struck. "What kind of payment, then?"

"Some drugs. A small package of tiny balloons."

She gasped then sighed long and hard as if she had feared something worse. "Thank God it's not what I was thinking," she said.

"What were you thinking?"

"Sex. Isn't that what every man in prison wants? A woman to have sex with?"

"Not every man. Champ has two pretty boys he calls women."

She closed her eyes and sighed again before saying, "What have I gotten myself into, Oliver?" She paused, turned to him with her arms folded across her body, her fingernails raking her ribs. "I know I'm taking a great risk, I know that clearly. I'm willing to do it if that's all there is to it. I bring in these tiny balloons this one and only time and the slate with Champ is clean?"

"That's all there is to it. Here's the money you left for him, and here's the directions to the place. It's a little restaurant up in the Hill District called Lena's. He said you should go there on a weekday morning. Pull into the alley beside the place and knock on the back door. You have to call ahead of time and ask for Chicken Wing. His family owns the place. Tell him you're calling for Champ and that you have the money. That's all you have to say."

"Should I be afraid?"

"Not if you have to ask."

"I'm serious."

"So am I."

"Who is he, this Chicken Wing?"

"He was here. He went home last summer. He's a drug dealer. He's a straight up fellow. All about business."

She stood up, untangling herself gracefully and, making no attempt to disguise her pride, said, "I'll do this once and that's it."

Oliver's voice was soft, a little sad, and he gazed out the window as he spoke. "Can we change the subject for a minute?"

"What is it, Oliver?"

He was looking around when their eyes touched. "Three lifers were just denied a hearing by the pardons board. All three of them have served over fifteen years. I don't stand a chance, B.J."

She touched her throat. "Oliver, don't get discouraged. This governor may only last one term. If history holds true, a Democrat will replace him whether he gets another term or not. When that happens the new governor will appoint his own people on the pardons board. Isn't that the way it works?"

"Yeah, but I just don't see them ever getting five members to ever agree unanimously. I really don't."

"We'll just have to wait and see, Oliver. Meanwhile you've got plenty of work to keep you busy. How are you coming along in Dr. Garris's class?"

"Fine. We're analyzing theories of learning right now."

They were both silent for a few moments and then B.J. said, "You were a juvenile, Oliver. They're going to let you out eventually. It's only a matter of time. You'll go up there and stand humbly before that board one day, we'll get up and speak about all your accomplishments and your bright future. Of course, you'll need to tell them what happened, why you did what you did."

He knew this was her way of asking him for the hundredth time why he had taken Jimmy Six's life. He decided right then to tell her. He went to the window and looked out. "It was either defend myself or be attacked again, B.J. He was a beast, that boy I killed. A big brutal monster. I'd never met a boy so mean and vicious in all my life. He got me first. He got me real good." Oliver paused for several seconds and when he went on, his countenance waxed with regret. "He broke my body, B.J. I couldn't let him break my spirit. I couldn't take a chance that he would attack me again. I didn't mean to kill him, I really didn't." He exhaled loudly, relieved that he had finally told the woman he loved what had happened.

"That's very sad, Oliver. I'm deeply sorry." She turned, blinked at him several times and then smiled outright. "I know you're not a killer. I knew the moment I met you. I knew it had to be something like this. Thank you for telling me."

It took a long time before he fell asleep that night. She was right. It was sad. Walking through it all again for the first time in so many years, a wave of grief soaked through him so thoroughly he wanted to cry. What stopped him, what restored his dignity, was the hope and assurance she had given him when she told him she knew from day one he was no killer.

But it was not there when she returned a week later. "Can we go into your office?" she asked. "I'm going to be sick."

"You all right?"

She nodded and swallowed visibly, holding down the vomit. Oliver opened the office door, and she stepped over the threshold, bolted right to the trash can beside his desk and threw up three times. Oliver stood over her, watching, his eyebrows pulled together into waves of compassion.

"Something you ate?" he asked, leaning forward to rub her head.

"God, I wish. Would you get me a glass of water?"

He grabbed a large cup from his desk and hurried to the water fountain. When he returned she was sitting behind his desk with the trash can between her knees. "Thanks." She drank slowly and then leaned back into the chair. "I thought it was coke, Oliver."

He didn't understand. "You thought what was coke?"

"In those balloons. I thought they contained coke."

One of his eyebrows rose just enough to signify his anger. "Don't tell me you opened them, B.J.!"

"Two. I opened two." Oliver punched the wall, leaned against it and folded his arms, waiting for her to continue. "I met with Chicken Wing yesterday morning. He was very nice. He only gave me half the package. I have to meet him next week for the other half." She leaned her head back and closed her eyes, sighed. "When I got home from work last night, I was so exhausted. I still had three hours of reading to do. And I was really hurting. So. I thought a little coke would be just what I needed. To keep myself awake awhile. I thought it was coke, Oliv—"

"That's heroin, for Christ sake, B.J.! You said you opened two?"

"I did. I hurt my lower back two days ago. It bothered me all day yesterday. After I tried that stuff last night the pain went away completely. I felt so good. Late this afternoon the pain returned so... I

opened another balloon. Right now there's no pain at all in my back
or anywhere else. If only that stuff didn't make me throw up every
fifteen minutes."

Slowly, she stood, gathered her equilibrium, and went to him. She
sat on his lap, collapsed her head on his shoulder. She wrapped her
arms around him while he unbuttoned her blouse and ran his hand
inside. He pinched her swollen nipple and she said, "Just hold me
tonight, would you please, Oliver? I'm still feeling queasy. Let's just
sit here together in the quiet."

"Listen, B.J., that's it. No more. That stuff's highly addictive."

"I know, Oliver. I know. I'm fine. Don't worry about me."

But worry was all he did until she returned the following Tuesday
night fifteen balloons short but quick to say, "I'll have the rest next
week for sure."

Oliver sat at his new computer staring at her, wondering what the
hell she thought she was doing. Her voice was deep and sultry now,
and the inflections and tone of her words had changed so drastically he
thought he was talking to a phone sex operator. The more she assured
him she was fine, the more his worries gave way to his needs-below-
the-belt. Why cast a pall now? Why diminish the scent of Chanel No.
19 that was wafting at him? Blunt the taste of her thighs awaiting his
lips? Earlier that morning he had planned five or six ways to ease her
mind in case Mr. Sommers happened to mention to her what had really
happened to Victor. He didn't need to say a word. She was oblivious.

"I have a lot to tell you," she said. "Would you put some coffee
on? My mouth is so dry. Would you get me another glass of water?"

When he returned with the water, he poured her a cup and used the
rest to make a half pot of coffee. He sat across from her and watched
her. She faced him but Oliver couldn't tell where she was looking. She
was wearing sunglasses. "Thank you." She drank the water and then
said, "Your essay is getting rave reviews. It really is. I've shared it
with several colleagues in my department. And I sent copies to people
I know in the English and criminal justice departments. Everyone
I've talked to said they were shocked and appalled when they read
your piece. I also shared it with a local journalist who is a very good

friend of mine. Hope Best. You may have read some of her work in the *Pittsburgher Magazine*. Not long ago she did a story called "Libraries in the City." The piece included part of an interview Hope did with your prison librarian. Did you happen to read her article?"

"I may have. I don't remember."

"Well, I had lunch with Hope last week, and she told me she's just been assigned to do a full-length story on the University's program here at the prison. After I spent an hour telling her more about you, she now wants to focus the story around you. Isn't that wonderful?"

"Yeah. As long as she doesn't twist the facts. You know how reporters are."

"No, no, no. It's not that kind of story, Oliver. Her slant's inspirational."

For the first time that night, Oliver noticed she was wiping her nose every two or three minutes. "Do you have a cold?" Oliver asked.

"Why?"

"You keep wiping your nose."

"It's the medication."

"What medication?"

"For my back. When I met with Chicken Wing again, he still didn't have all of Champ's package together yet, but he sold me a few balloons for myself. They really do the trick."

"You're kidding me!"

"Don't worry. I only take one every couple of days. I'm not going to depend on them every day."

"I don't believe what I'm hearing, for Christ sake! Do you know how easy it is to get hooked on that stuff?" Oliver's voice was loud and incredulous.

"Yes, and that's why I only do one every couple of days. I've had lower back pain off and on for several years now, and nothing I've tried has worked as well as this. I'd appreciate it if you'd give me credit for being adult and responsible enough not to do harm to myself, Oliver, for goodness sake."

"Okay. You're right. Just be careful, man."

"I know you're disappointed we didn't make love again tonight. Next time. I promise. Aren't you even a little excited about the news I brought you? You're going to be in the *Pittsburgher*, Oliver."

"Yeah. I'm excited."

"A story like this can give us the exposure we need to bring attention to your case and get you out of here."

"You really think so?"

"Of course. Don't you?"

"I suppose it couldn't hurt."

B.J. finished the water. The coffee aroma was now apparent and she was raking her nails back and forth over her forearms in anticipation. "I can't wait for you to meet Hope. She's a lovely person. Did I mention she was a social activist during the sixties? She was at Woodstock, Oliver."

He poured coffee into her personal cup and handed it to her. She set the cup down and he wrapped a strand of her hair around his fingers. "How lovely is she?" He was teasing her now.

WHEN SHE DIDN'T SHOW at all the following week, Oliver was as humble as a monk. He opened the windows and breathed in the cool evening air. There was so much to do, papers to finish, books to read, lecture notes to decipher. She had gotten him a computer on loan from her department and he was anxious to master the statistical analysis software that came with it, but as hard as he tried, he couldn't concentrate. When he didn't hear from her by the end of the second week, he was disturbed and feeling totally abandoned, like an orphan. She could have called. She had to call Mr. Sommers sooner or later, didn't she? He imagined her getting hooked on H and humping that faculty member who had been trying to get inside her panties for years, or worse, doing it with Chicken Wing. Oliver pictured her completely uninhibited now, spreading her pussy department wide, and blaming him for turning her out.

When another week rolled by and still no B.J., he thought maybe she had come to her senses and was getting help. He asked

Dr. Garris if he had seen her in the halls, and sure enough, he had. She was fine. He thought of talking to Mr. Sommers, but he feared his full-blown angst would give him away. Now he was fuming. At her carelessness, her indifference, her total abandonment. Then he got desperate. In his heart, he knew she would come, sometime, and that she would have a lame excuse or no excuse at all; but she would come. The desperation came from the sense he had of her ruining everything, the love affair they had carved out of a city of stone walls and razor wire. And sheer boldness. What the world knew about what went on between the sheets in prison could be summed up in one breath: Bubbas and pretty Michaels. What went on between their sheets she had summed up as a Greek tragedy. His office, a niche in the city of Troy; she was Helen and he was Paris. The guards were the Greek soldiers turned loose from the great wooden horse in search of any and all Helens—teachers, guards, counselors, nurses, or college professors—who had the temerity to spread their wings for a low-life prisoner whose name could be Troy or Buckwheat for all they cared.

Suddenly, the open windows were not enough. He began to perspire in the new blue and yellow Pitt Panthers tee shirt she had smuggled in for him in the bottom of her tote bag. Anger ricocheted through him like a hollow point .22. He wanted it over——one way or the other. Over and done with so he could grieve once and for all, so he could flush this bitch out of his life completely. His longing, his craving for her had rendered him stupid.

On Tuesday morning of the fourth week, he found respite from his grief when Mr. Sommers escorted that journalist into his office. He recognized her the minute he looked up at her. "Hi, Mr. Priddy!" She didn't say the words, she sang them. Oliver smiled outright for the first time in three weeks. B.J. was right. Hope Best was lovely. She was wearing a sleeveless white linen blouse, an orange paisley peasant skirt and bright blue sandals. Her bare legs were tanned to the nines all the way to her coral-painted toenails. Her champagne colored hair was cut in a bob that shimmered each time she moved her head.

"Aren't you the same lady I saw a few months ago standing outside the library talking with our librarian?" Oliver asked, grinning as if he already knew the answer.

"I probably am," she said.

"Yeah. I remember you. You were wearing a tie-dyed dress. But your hair was longer."

She looked surprised. "It's only shorter now because of a little mishap involving Hubba-Bubba bubble gum." She smiled widely. She had perfect teeth. "One of my nephews was giving me a hug when he decided to blow a bubble." She held a layer of her hair in her hand. "I had to cut it to get all the gum out."

"I see. Well, how are you, Miss Hope Best?"

"I'm fine, thank you, Mr. Oliver Priddy." They both laughed like old friends. He battled his stare and lost every time.

For two hours they talked, laughed and traded anecdotes and by the time Mr. Sommers came to escort her back to the front gate, Oliver had taken a ton of mental notes. She's the nicest person, he thought. Attractive. Intelligent. At ease. She didn't look around the halls at the other prisoners, or jump at the shouting match two were having outside his classroom. She didn't seem to come with any agenda either, other than conversation. She knew more about Sly and the Family Stone than he did, and he thought he knew everything there was to know about his favorite group. It was her favorite group too, she said. They had been the first group to give her an interview at Woodstock. Every word Hope Best uttered was animated and full of wonder. He counted eleven different ways she tilted her head when she smiled, nine rings on her fingers, and not a wedding band among them, and two very thin blue veins showing on the side of her bare calf. "When I return in a couple of weeks," she said, "you'll have to give me all the meat and potatoes for my story, Oliver. I can't wait."

"I'll give you whatever you need," Oliver said. And he meant it.

But as soon as she was gone, he buckled over with loneliness again. He was usually very good at hiding his emotions, even from himself, but this time was different. This time he made no attempt to disguise his pain. He slashed out at the ceramic knick-knack of

Emmett Kelly that B.J. had brought him, hitting it with his closed fist and sending the famous clown flying across the room to smash against the wall. He sat back in his chair, stunned. He was a survivor, he knew that. He was as resilient as they came. He would not play the blame game. If it was over, it was over.

The night she finally brought him the closure he needed, she was wearing sunglasses again, and he asked her to take them off. When she did, he opened his mouth, his eyes were wide and blank, and a red river rose up his neck and into his cheeks. She looked like she hadn't slept in six months. "Here, Oliver. There are twenty balloons there."

"You were only fifteen short."

"Tell him the extras are interest he earned for waiting." He searched her face for a sign, trying to feel, smell her mood. Did she have her panties on? That was the sign. If he knew that he would know whether she was planning to have sex, but he couldn't find out without touching her.

"We need to talk, Oliver," she said. Though serious, she sounded maternal. She put on her sunglasses again, and now he couldn't tell whether she was looking at him or out the window.

"We can talk all you want, B.J.," he said, "but we've got something to take care of first, don't we? Remember? Remember what you said the last time you were here?"

"I know what I promised you. I won't go back on my word, but a lot has happened and we need to talk."

"We can talk." He walked over to where she was standing and came up behind her. "But I've got to have you first." He slid his arms around her waist and squeezed her, kissing and nibbling her neck until she responded with a slow writhing of her pelvis. After a few minutes, he broke away and she stood there swaying her shoulders to the Sam Cooke song playing on his cassette player. Oliver rolled out two rugs on the floor. Then he maneuvered her to her hands and knees. He pressed her head and shoulders gently downward. Her face was turned sideways onto a pillow he made out of his sweatshirt. Her hair flung out in all directions. He positioned himself behind her and watched her hips and buttocks rise to him. Sleek and round. She swayed to the music. As her body quickened, she never stopped crooning and swaying to the music. Not until he entered her, holding her hips so she couldn't get away, did she buck and moan with urgency. Afterwards, they sat together in silence, one grateful as could be for their physical reunion and hopeful it wasn't the last, the other scratching and nodding in a drug-induced stupor. "You said we need to talk," Oliver said at last. "Okay. Let's talk. What's on your mind, B.J.? You cutting me loose?"

1991

chapter seventeen

AT 11 A.M. ON A dismal Friday morning in October, Hambone stood underneath the number one guard tower waiting to feed the old guard Mills who was lowering a galvanized bucket down to him. As the bucket reached eye-level, Hambone dropped two hot roast beef sandwiches, a banana and a carton of milk inside the bucket, then rapped his knuckles on the side to signal he was through. When the bucket didn't move, Hambone looked up just as Mills keeled over on the catwalk, violently clutching at his chest. Crazy Bell, who had been sitting alone in the bleachers, saw Mills, too, and sprung like a jack-in-the-box from the top bleacher. After shoving Hambone to the side, Bell grabbed the rope that was attached to the bucket and tugged on it to make sure it was secured tightly to the catwalk railing. Then he shimmied up the wall with the agility of an alley cat. When he reached the top, he ducked between the railing and snatched Mill's sidearm .38, then tossed it down to a young buck in the courtyard who caught it like a baseball and then ran off with his gang. With one horrendous kick, Bell sent the dead guard over the side. He didn't waste another second before he grabbed the automatic rifle that was leaning against the tower, aimed and shot the guard in the number-two tower right between the eyes. "VC that, motherfucker!" Bell cried. Then he shot the guard who was inspecting a delivery van at the rear gate. The bullet traveled right through the man's Adam's apple and exited the back of his neck. Bell finally barricaded himself inside the tower where he would stay for two more days taking pot shots at anything that moved in a uniform.

Only a few minutes after Bell declared war, Officer Wayne St. Pierre was leaving the hospital with a brand-new first-aid kit in his hand when an urgent cry came over the airways of every walkie-talkie in the prison: "Officer down in front of the dining hall! We need help over here!" Wayne St. Pierre rushed to the scene and almost instantly became the next officer down. As he fell to the ground, he saw the blur of a pipe, a chair leg, and five angry faces—black ones, brown ones, white ones.

The rioters snatched Wayne St. Pierre's ring of keys from his fingertips as they dragged his body down the street with no name and through the sweet peas and clover that grew around the forsythia bushes on the side of the prison chapel. When they reached the sports equipment shed behind the chapel, the enraged prisoners hauled him inside and tore off his clothes. "Break this stick off in his ass!" shouted one man. "Let's kill the cockroach!" added another. One prisoner pushed his knee into the back of Wayne St. Pierre's neck, another held down his legs, and a third one sodomized him with a broom stick until he finally passed out. Before the prisoners left, they kicked him in the face and beat his body thoroughly with a lead pipe and a chair leg. Wayne St. Pierre lay on the floor twitching lightly among the smashed bags of lime, his face a mask of meat and agony so fierce that for months afterwards the people who rescued him would shake their heads in disbelief at the memory of what he had looked like.

Inside the cellblocks the riot spread down the tiers like a brush fire. Prisoners, armed and unarmed, bit their lips, snarled their teeth and turned on their keepers like dogs that had been kicked once too many times. Some prisoners were armed with knives, cans of lye soap and shards of glass slicing through the riotous mob, picking out the uniformed culprits and choosing the spot to abuse their flesh. Two of the most sadistic guards on duty were hung by their wrists side by side, in the shower pit of the big St. Regis. Two others were chased all the way up to the fifth tier and given a choice of jumping off or being torn apart by the pack of salivating young dogs. One leaped, the other was beaten senseless.

The riot continued for three days and three nights and so many guards, pedophiles and snitches were maimed that the authorities could not keep the numbers straight. On the morning of the fourth day, after the rioters had lost their muse, had done all they could to show their keepers what it felt like to lose all hope, they surrendered to the national guardsmen who were standing in wait at the front gate.

Within hours, the worst of the militant rioters were handcuffed, shackled and loaded on a bus headed to an underground prison in Illinois. Another six were carried through the rear gate, stacked three high in the back of a coroner's van.

A SATIRICAL ESSAY in the lifers' newsletter was, according to the authorities, what had incited the prisoners to riot. Five days before they had marched through the joint advertising their rage over the loss of their last rights and amenities, Oliver's essay, HOPE FOR THE HOPELESS, had appeared on the front page of the October issue of *The Wire*. By noon of the same day, Superintendent I.M. White had read it and turned three shades darker than mud before he instructed his secretary to find out who in his administration was responsible for approving the publication and distribution of the newsletter. What made I.M. White's skin itch so deep below the surface that he couldn't scratch it was something he thought he had read between the lines of Oliver's essay: *Listen to me, Brothers! We may as well tear the entrails right out of the belly of this prison because every lifer in this state is a walking dead man anyway!* Late that afternoon, after his assistant reported that she couldn't determine who, if anyone, had approved publication of the offending newsletter, I.M. White ordered his security lieutenant to immediately escort Oliver to the redbrick Home Block.

This wasn't the first time Oliver had given I.M. White that deep-down-worse-than-poison-ivy itch. Six months after he had taken over as warden at Riverview and begun to strip away one amenity after another, I.M. White had become the target of Oliver's diatribe against

African-American professionals who say and do whatever they need to say and do in order to gain the white man's graces. Oliver's biting satire, "Uncle Tom's Cabin of Step-And-Fetch-It Politicians", had ultimately blamed the new snoop-doggie-gangsta-rap culture not on white racism, but on black conservatives like I.M. White himself. On that occasion I.M. White had refused to address the notion that he was indeed a bojangles, ass-kissing negro, a race traitor, and that the term Black Republican should be deemed an oxymoron. I.M. White was far too dignified to respond to the bombastic rants of a white man who didn't have a clue what it was like to be a black man struggling to get ahead in racist America. This time was different, though. This time it wasn't personal, it was business—a matter of dealing with what he perceived to be a major threat to the safety and orderly running of his well-oiled maximum security prison.

When Oliver's friends and professors inquired about him two days after the riot had ended, I.M. White informed them that Oliver was under investigation for publishing and distributing an unauthorized document, and for possibly instigating the riot.

"You don't go around telling a bunch of ignorant-ass ghetto niggahs that they may as well be dead because they're never going to see the streets again. Not in my prison you don't. That's what Priddy did. He poured gasoline on the fire.

"I'm not new at this. Priddy's not the first slick white man I've come across in my career, either. I've been dealing with them ever since affirmative action came about. Don't get me wrong, I'm not a racist by any means, and it make my skin crawl when these white boys call me one. Hell, I'm married to a white woman. This isn't about racism. This is about what happens when you educate one of these prisoners. They get a little knowledge and think they can be slick. I'm educated, too, I can read between the lines. I know what Priddy was doing when he capitalized and underlined those fifty-cent words. INSURRECTION, RANDOM SLAUGHTERING, ANARCHY. Instigating, that's what he was doing.

"Now he has all these reporters and liberal educators sticking their noses in official business, and that's where I have to draw the line. I don't care how many phone calls they make or how many letters they write demanding to see this man, no one but his attorney will see him until this investigation is concluded.

"I've got five dead officers and six dead prisoners on my hands and on top of that a prison to rebuild. This place is on lockdown and will stay that way until we get to the bottom of all this mess. And mark my words. If my hearing examiner finds Priddy guilty of instigating that riot, he can forget all about his little PhD pursuit, which, if you ask me, is a waste of everyone's time anyway in light of the fact that the pardon's door to freedom has been closed once and for all on these lifers. They have about as much chance of getting out of prison now as I do of becoming the next commissioner of corrections."

THAT PLACE IN THE PRISON where men's minds easily disconnected from their spirits did a flourishing business in the days following the riot. And although the riot was over, everyone knew the violence wasn't. The guards would have the final say. On the south side of the Home Block, fifth cell, second tier, Oliver looked up each time a triangle of guards swept past his cell carrying one of the rioters, shackled and hogtied. And each time he turned away, nauseated by the sounds of the guards' heavy boots and arrogant camaraderie and the metallic clanging of keys. When he heard a cell door open or close, he listened for the blows, the pounding of flesh, the wincing in pain. After he heard a tap on the wall late one morning, he thought he recognized the voice that called his name. "Oliver, you awake?"

"Yeah. Who's that?"

"Oyster Bey."

"Oyster? Man, I didn't see them bring you in."

"I came in early this morning. You were still asleep."

The moment he heard Oyster's voice, Oliver's spirits lifted. He hadn't spoken to a single soul in three days and he was thankful and relieved to hear a friend's voice. "What did they lock you up for, Oyster?"

"Two rookies shook my cell down yesterday. One of 'em said the nail I pounded in my wall to hang my coat on fifteen damn years ago was a weapon. I'll be out of here as soon as I go to my hearing. What's the latest with you, Oliver?"

"They charged me with instigating that riot. My hearing's in the morning."

Oyster's laugh was an explosion. "Those rotten crackers! We heard that but we didn't believe it was true. They were going around confiscating all the copies of your newsletter they could find. That was some funny shit you wrote, Ollie. Where'd you come up with that stuff?" Oyster's laugh was contagious.

"In my head. What the hell happened out there, man?"

"During the riot?"

"Yeah."

"These young bucks tore the roof off the place, that's what happened. I guess you didn't hear. Bell's dead."

"Dead? How?"

"He started the whole thing, Oliver. You know how little he was. He climbed the wall right underneath the number-one gun tower. That screw Mills had a heart attack while Hambone was feeding him. Bell grabbed the rope and shimmied up the wall. In less than twenty-four hours he killed three guards and wounded four others before one of them sharpshooters blew his head off two days ago."

"We could hear the gunfire, but we didn't know what was going on," Oliver said. "So that was Bell, huh? My God."

During the pause in conversation they heard a prisoner screaming obscenities and then the responding blows followed by more obscenities. After a long lull, Oliver asked, "Early okay?"

"Early's been in the hospital, Oliver. Gallstones. He was all right the last I knew."

"What about Peabo?"

"Peabo's fine. Another long pause and Oyster continued. "I didn't leave my cell for three days, not until the fourth morning when Donnie Blossom brought me some coffee and told me the young bucks were about to throw in the towel. You shoulda seen what those boys did to Sergeant Dewey. They didn't hurt him too bad, mainly his pride. Made him piss his pants when they smacked him upside the head with that pistol they had. They told him to listen and remember everything they was saying. 'We ain't taking this shit no more. We ain't going back in time. You tell Uncle Tom that, Nigger Ned,' they said. 'You tell him we ain't never tucking our shirttails in, we ain't wearing our hats straight and we ain't never gonna be part of no standing counts. And as long as we ain't got nothin' more to lose, we gonna keep tearin' shit up every chance we get, even if we die doin it. You tell em that, Nigger Dewey.' Poor old Dewey just sat there shaking his head and stuttering like an idiot. Oliver, these young niggahs are a new breed. They ain't got the sense God gave a turnip. They don't care if they live or die. I guess they figure they going to die in here anyway. Sooner or later. Just like you and my sorry ass is."

"Yeah, that's the way it looks, Oyster. What about Champ and one-eyed Melvin? Are they all right?"

"Oh, man. Listen, Oliver. Champ, just about his whole North Philly crew, Melvin, the Lynch twins, the Solomon brothers, LaMumba, Anwar Dukes, Charlie Redshaw, Milky Way, Popalou, Duck, Major Tillery, L'l Ali, Chief, that white boy they call Sonny Corleone, and a couple hundred more are either already shipped out or on their way out. They got so many locked up they using the bottom two tiers on both sides of the little St. Regis as the hole. Hell, they need cells over here in this Home Block so bad they let Fat Daddy out two months early."

"He was in the cell you're in," said Oliver.

"Who?"

"Fat Daddy. He talked my head off for three days. I couldn't believe how civilized he was. Hey, how well do you know him, anyway?"

"Oh, I've known Fat Daddy for about twenty years now. Why?"

"Because I told him I needed to get an extremely important message out to my boss. He said he'd get it to him for me. So I wrote it down and fished it over to him to take out. I was just wondering how thorough he is."

"Oliver, he may be a crazy-ass pervert, but he's as thorough as they get when it comes to something like that. If he told you he would take care of something for you, you can bet he did it before he unpacked his belongings."

"I hope you're right, Oyster. Otherwise, my ass is up shit's creek tomorrow."

"No way in the world they can hold you responsible, Oliver. Stop worrying."

There was another long procession of silence between them before Oliver said, "Worrying's all I got right now, man."

WHEN OLIVER WALKED into the hearing room the next morning, he nodded to the stone-faced security captain before sitting in the chair directly in front of the hearing examiner. "Good morning, Mr. Priddy. My name is Arnold Jerry, and I'll be the decider-of-facts for these proceedings. Let the record reflect that Mr. Priddy is present, along with Captain Twyman and Ms. Jan Christopher, our in-house stenographer. Mr. Priddy, you have been charged with misconduct number 39987, inciting a riot and being in possession of an unauthorized document, namely the October newsletter containing an essay bearing your name as the author. I take it you acknowledge being the author of this essay, 'HOPE FOR THE HOPELESS'?"

"Yes, sir."

And you were the editor of this newsletter, *The Wire*? Is that correct?"

"Yes, sir."

"Pertaining to these two charges, Mr. Priddy, how do you wish to plead?"

"Not guilty. I need my witness present. My boss, Mr. Sommers."

"You indicated that on the hearing form. I called Mr. Sommers' office this morning at eight-thirty. His secretary informed me he would not be in the institution today. I take it you wanted your boss here as a character witness?"

"There's more to it than that."

"I've read your jacket thoroughly, and I'm more than willing to stipulate into the record that you have made remarkable academic achievements over these past ten years, that you've been an asset to the prison's education department and have been a model prisoner as well. Other than attesting to these things, I can see no other reason why we would need to hear from Mr. Sommers."

Oliver's face went red with laughter, and then he turned to look at the Captain. "Hey, there's more to it than that. My boss can clear this whole thing up."

"And how's that?" the Captain asked, raising his thick black eyebrows.

Oliver was almost compelled to tell them, but he didn't. He recalled Fat Daddy's admonition two days ago to keep his mouth shut unless he wanted to be the victim of a cover-up. "All I can say is that Mr. Sommers can clear this up," Oliver repeated.

The examiner looked intensely curious as he took a sip of black coffee from a tin cup before he stood and walked to a corner table to retrieve more documents. He was short, almost a dwarf. His Afro was neat, not ragged, and he wore silver around his neck, one matching stud in his ear. He sat down again and said, "Mr. Priddy, you have already acknowledged being the author of this essay, and there is nothing your supervisor or anyone else can say to negate that fact. So we are going to proceed with this hearing at this time."

"All right," said Oliver, going red again. "What about Deputy Maroney? Call him in here."

"Deputy Maroney has been working in Central Office for the past two and a half weeks. I'm afraid he can't help you."

"A fucking kangaroo court," Oliver muttered.

The security captain stiffened. "What did you say, Priddy?"

"You heard me, Captain. I said kangaroo court. That's all this is!"

"Keep your opinions to yourself, Priddy," the captain admonished. "Let that be a warning."

The examiner shifted his eyes from the Captain to Oliver while he took another swig of coffee. Then he said, "I'm going to begin by asking you what you meant in the very last words of your essay, when you wrote '*or does it explode?*'"

"That line is an allusion, man."

"An illusion? You mean like a large mirror giving the illusion of more space in a small room?"

"No. An *allusion.* That line came from a famous poem by Mr. Langston Hughes, called 'A Dream Deferred.'"

"I see. That's real clever," the hearing examiner said. "This situation reminds me of a legal case I read about in my second year of college in which the famous U.S. Supreme Court Justice Oliver Wendell Holmes said you cannot go around falsely shouting 'Fire!' in a crowded theatre because it causes panic. One could make a good argument that your essay amounts to shouting 'Fire!' in a crowded theatre."

Oliver sighed and shook his head from side to side. "Come on, man. You can't be serious."

The captain gestured with his hand and cut in before the examiner could go on. "I have just two questions for you, Priddy. Why did you emphasize words like *insurrection* and *anarchy* in big bold letters, and why did you wish the young bucks God's speed in their endeavors?"

The captain leaned back in the chair with his hands clasped together and slowly rolled his thumbs in circles, obviously pleased with his questions.

"The whole thing's a satire, man. It's not meant to be taken literally."

The hearing examiner said, "Well, do you agree, Mr. Priddy, that what you wrote was tantamount to telling your fellow lifers that their conditions are hopeless?"

Oliver didn't hesitate. "No, I don't. If you're going to take what I said literally, my essay was about offering hope for the hopeless."

"But you don't believe that telling a man his life is doomed could be enough to incite that man to riot? You don't believe your modest proposal set these men off?"

"That's a laugh."

"No one's laughing, Mr. Priddy, and I would advise you to take these proceedings a little more seriously. You're obviously a talented writer, but what you've written is highly offensive and highly inflammatory. Being a writer carries a certain responsibility with it. And as long as you are a prisoner of the Commonwealth of Pennsylvania, you do not have the same First Amendment rights as people in free society

228

have. Mr. Priddy, do you have anything else you'd like to say on your own behalf?"

"I'm innocent, man."

The examiner scoured through Oliver's essay one last time, wrinkling his forehead and eyebrows each time he read something that offended him. When he was finished writing, he flicked his pen back and forth several times before dropping it on the table.

"This is not a court of law, Mr. Priddy, but if it were, I would still find beyond a reasonable doubt—we call it a preponderance of evidence—that your essay inflamed the hearts and minds of those men who participated in the riot. I therefore find you guilty of this Class 1, Category A misconduct. Your punitive sanction will be eighteen months in the Disciplinary Housing Unit. You have thirty days to appeal this decision to the Superintendent. Good luck to you, Mr. Priddy."

A MONTH TO THE DAY of his hearing, Oliver and the rest of the prisoners confined inside the Home Block were moved to the bottom tiers of the little St. Regis. During the riot the prisoners had broken every windowpane in the cellblock. Now the cold December days were not warmed much by the installation of new panes. There was no notable difference between the thin, noisy air inside the cellblock and the air outside. Oliver stood by the door of his cell watching the prisoners who were being escorted from the lockup tiers and those being led towards them. Not one seemed interested in departure or arrival since the entire prison was a Home Block anyway.

When he discovered on that first day that the St. Regises had not been reopened since the riot, that every man in the joint was locked in a cell somewhere, he stopped feeling betrayed by Fat Daddy. Thinking of his predicament and Fat Daddy's efforts to help him, he sighed heavily, but there was no point in just sitting there moping. First, he sent an official request to his boss letting him know he'd been moved to the little St. Regis and needed to see him as soon as possible. Then while he waited and prayed his request would reach its destination, he turned his thoughts to how he would spend, and not just deposit, his time in solitary confinement. What to do for the next hour, then the next. It took forty-five minutes to clean the floor and all four walls with a wet rag. Writing letters, two hours. Ninety minutes of reading, another hour taking notes.

Contrary to popular belief, planning was everything. Gauge the hours. Recognize yourself. You're all you have.

But after a week of trying that routine, his thoughts failed him—he couldn't write a sentence that made sense, he couldn't comprehend what he read and he lost his drive to exercise.

As the days passed, he could hear the swelling and straining of a yellow diesel caterpillar that had come to make way for two new high-rise cell blocks in the middle of the yard. He listened as it demolished the Young Guns Boxing Gym, the Free-Yourself Law Library, the hundred-year-old chapel and the redbrick Home Block. In all that destruction he knew that the magnificent old oak tree had been torn from its roots, too, along with Early's flowerbeds and shrubs. Hearing all the devastation going on outside only added to his suffering. All he could tell himself was that his stretch of good fortune was over. His self-created world of hope was gone. The prison he had for ten years called his university had finally been ruined and in the process had capsized his world and broken him. He found little consolation in knowing that, in this oppressive place ruled by men whose power to control was out of control, he had at least felt and heard about the esprit de corps of his fellow prisoners.

More and more he did not know how he was going to get from one minute to the next. He felt as though his mind was slipping away, he was terrified. One morning he called out to Oyster, but Oyster was gone. Alone, without witness, he let go of his logic, his reason, and soon all the voices in his mind were rehearsing to themselves every pathological theme of literature he had ever come across: betrayal, cruelty, injustice, loss, vengeance, dishonor and grief. All hope had abandoned him. *What's the use? Your life is over! You're going to die in this prison cell, hopeless and alone,* he told himself.

Every day he fought these voices in his head while the prisoners around him immersed themselves in conversations about murder and suicide. One morning the man on his left called out his name and Oliver shrieked for all the prisoners to hear, like a child might if his mother had been snatched away from him forever.

"Priddy, I know you can hear me," his neighbor said. "That essay you wrote was pretty tough. I ain't ashamed to tell you I almost took my own life once. Went so far as to dump four bags of the most potent smack in the city into a spoon and cook it up." The neighbor on the other side said, "Well, you obviously didn't go through with it. What happened? You chicken out?"

"Yes, I did, brother man."

A prisoner two doors down said, "Having a change of mind don't mean he chickened out. Some people might call following through with it chickening out on life. Some might say it took a lot of courage not to follow through. This may be prison, but we're still alive."

They continued on tediously in this vein more or less for the rest of the day and others within hearing distance of the conversation joined in. An intellectual named Minarik said, "The whole act of taking your own life is the one sole thing a man can control in his life. He writes the play, he inhabits it and he enacts it. He stages everything—just the way he'll be found and how."

Believing that the nightmare he was living was the only reality there was, Oliver laid down on his side with his face on his hands, closed his eyes and pictured a parade of prisoners returning to their cells from the commissary and tearing open their newly purchased Euthanasia kits.

"Slide this deep inside my vagina, Oliver." He imagined Donnie Blossom speaking those words as he took off his clothes and picked up the deadly nine-inch vibrator. He imagined Donnie lying on his stomach and posing salaciously as he cried out, "Do me, Oliver. Do me. I want you before I die."

"Why me?"

"Don't you know, Oliver? I have always loved you. Don't you know that by now?"

He imagined himself saying, "You know I don't swing that way."

"Then put this inside me," he imagined Donnie replying. "I want to die happy, Oliver."

"Don't we all?" Short of breath and dry-mouthed, Oliver blinked that image and conversation away for another one: Geppy, a vicious dope addict, squatting in the corner, a shoelace tied tightly around his bicep. "Get your own, Priddy! Ain't enough here for you!" He imagined Geppy saying this while injecting the massive air bubble into his thin blue vein. And after he pictured a schizophrenic prisoner he knew hanging from the ceiling light fixture with a designer noose around his neck, he cried out, "Fellows, this was all supposed to be humorous! A joke! I never meant for you all to take me serious! It was satire, a stupid literary technique. I learned it in school, for Christsake! I was just trying to be witty, man!"

Two hours later, when the lights went out for the evening, an idea came to him that he thought might ease his suffering. He immediately picked up his pen and tablet and sat on the floor near the cell door, where a shaft of moonlight slanted through the bottom bars. There, he began to write the names of every song he had ever heard and loved, beginning with the stacks of 45s his mother played for him over and over on her phonograph when he was a child. The pen, gripped tightly between his long fingers, circled and swirled across the page with the intensity of a man who knew something about self-soothing. Heartbreak Hotel. The Great Pretender. Smoke Gets In Your Eyes. Fools Rush In. Please Don't Ask Me to Be Lonely. There were hundreds of them. And each title he wrote down was accompanied by one image or another: his mother in the living room showing off a new dance step to him; Ernie Boy the Second storming through the house leaving a trail of blue smoke from the half-chewed cigar he kept in his mouth; Oliver with his ear pressed against the phonograph speaker, his collie Laddie curled up on the rug beside him. Some of these images triggered his olfactory memory also, and he could, at that very moment, smell his mother's perfume, Ernie Boy's pungent cigar smoke and a pot of fresh kale wafting from the kitchen. When he had exhausted these earliest memories, he moved on to his teenage years and his mind was flooded with song titles from his own record collection. Motown, Stax, Decca and Atlantic records. He had owned just about every 45 hit those labels had ever produced. The list went on for more than four pages, front and back, and when his memory began to strain, he started a new page with a different topic that at once spurred him on. He wrote the names of every girl he had ever kissed, held hands with or loved. The list was long and inspiring. In this solitary contemplation of his former life, he stopped from time to time to recall the details of one girl's eyes, the texture and color of another's hair and the unrestrained passion of some of the older girls. He went through each year of his life starting at the age of twelve, and with each year, the list of girls grew as his need for love and physical intimacy became like a bottomless pit. By the time he was finished writing down the last two names, he was, at once, overcome with such happiness that his confidence was restored, his grief displaced. His self-inflicted torment had subsided. The gratitude he felt for having discovered a way to ward off the most terrifying part of solitary confinement—having nothing good to say to one's self and losing all hope—was second only to the sheer joy he felt from reliving those beautiful vivid memories again.

FOOTSTEPS, THEN A RAP, interrupted his high-end reverie. Oliver looked up and thought he saw Mr. Sommers peering through the bars on the cell door.

"Oliver."

"Mr. Sommers?"

"How're you holding up, Oliver?" Mr. Sommers asked. He had a gentle face altogether and a paternal demeanor. "Well, you seem all right physically, at least. Except for that look of desperation on your face, you don't look bad at all."

"And you—all dressed up in a suit," Oliver said, having himself neither changed the jumpsuit they gave him to wear two months ago nor shaved for two weeks. "Man, am I glad to see you, Mr. Sommers."

"Just so you know, I tried three times to get in the Home Block to see you. They wouldn't let me in. I'm afraid the Superintendent has it in for you, Oliver."

"That's okay. You're here now. Thanks for coming." Oliver gestured for his boss to come closer. He lowered his voice. "In the very back of the bottom drawer of my file cabinet, there's a large, frayed manila envelope with Deputy Maroney's signatures on the back. One for each month of this year. He may not have read my essay, but he sure as hell approved it. I need you to get that envelope and show it to the hearing examiner."

Mr. Sommers looked shocked, then sympathetic. "I will if it's still there, Oliver."

"What do you mean? Why wouldn't it be? The riot didn't cause any fire or water damage to the school, did it?"

"No. But security searched your desk and file cabinet thoroughly the day after they locked you up."

"Ah, Christ, Mr. Sommers. Did you see them take anything away?"

"No, I didn't, Oliver. But then again, I wasn't in the room when they were making their search."

"What were they looking for, do you know?"

"No idea. I don't think they knew either." They each paused in thought and then Mr. Sommers said, "You know, I wondered about that. Didn't I drop that envelope off at the Deputy's office for you several times?"

"Just about every month. And that's another thing. On the day of my hearing, I asked that hearing examiner to call you as one of my witnesses, but you weren't in the institution that day. Then I asked for Deputy Maroney to be present and they said he was gone, too."

"He *is* gone. They called him to Central Office a couple of days before you were locked up. He's being groomed for a Superintendent's post. Listen, I'll go right now and try to find that envelope. If it's still there, I'll make copies of it before I turn it over to the hearing examiner. And I'll deliver them to the security captain and the Superintendent himself. Why didn't you write to me about this before now, Oliver? Maybe you wouldn't still be in here."

"I did. I wrote a note and gave it to a fellow who got released from the Home Block a couple days before my hearing. Neither of us knew then that the joint was still locked down. I couldn't take the chance of sending you a note through normal channels because I knew they were screening all my outgoing mail."

"I understand, now. I never thought of that. Is there anything else I can do for you?"

"I was wondering if you've heard from anyone on my behalf?"

"Yes, as a matter of fact, I have. Dr. Dallet called a couple of times and the dean phoned me last week. I've also heard from several of your other professors. And that journalist called three times wanting to know when she can resume her interview. Lots of people care about you, Oliver."

Mr. Sommers' words embarrassed Oliver a little, but at that moment, nothing had ever been nicer to hear. "That's sure soothing to know," Oliver said, shaking his head in the affirmative.

After his boss was gone, Oliver turned his thoughts to B.J. Dallet. There was no danger of tears this time, for his mind welcomed the diversion from his own self-inflicted torment. He thought about the way she had looked the last time he saw her. Scrutinizing her swollen eyes and sunken cheeks, watching her scratch herself like a flea-bitten dog, had made him feel helpless and responsible at the same time. He still didn't understand what had driven her there. Was it simply her curiosity? Or years of chronic physical pain? Or pent-up longing for something more out of life? A combination of all three? He didn't know but he wished with all his heart that she would hit rock bottom and get the help she needed to make a full recovery.

Then, two weeks after Mr. Sommers had come to see him, and on the same afternoon he heard a prisoner three doors down singing, she wrote me a letter, said she couldn't live without me no more, the guard stopped in front of his door. "Mail on the bars!" Oliver jumped up and counted three pieces before he had them in his hand. He dropped the tuition bill and magazine subscription on the bed and ripped open the cream-colored envelope, his face suddenly flushed, his heart pounding in his chest. Dear Oliver: Questions about his well-being, answers about her own; sincere regrets for the way things had turned out. Hang in there. Very sincerely. And then the signer identified herself using her official name, Dr. B.J. Dallet, University of Pittsburgh. He slumped down on his bed on the verge of tears. He fingered the letter, smelled her scent over and over and thought, he could no more figure out now how to console the young lover abandoned by his older mistress than he'd been able to figure out how to reconcile being a convict guilty of starting a riot. But he tried. He told himself, Why have regrets? Why stain the memories now that would only make for more boils on the heart later? She had helped make him a star, a celebrity in this prison and across the university. She had told everyone she knew he was one special fellow, that he had what it takes to make it. And he had! Thanks to her, he had accomplished the impossible—a master's degree and a dissertation away from a Ph.D.—and she had helped make it all happen. He reminded himself now that hope had always run deep in his veins. I've been through worse than this before, he told himself. I'll find it again. I'll find a way. I'll find it—This will pass.

But it did not pass.

One cold morning he was startled by the sound of an envelope falling off the bars of his cell door and onto the cement floor. In-house mail, they called it. Inside the envelope was a note from Mr. Sommers. Oliver's hope swirled and eddied through him before he read the words: "Sorry, Oliver. No envelope to be found. Will keep searching. May have another idea."

Instead of believing that Mr. Sommers would find a way for him to thrive again, Oliver knew it was over. His failures were his, as was the bewildering injustice on which he was impaled.

1992

chapter eighteen

WHEN MARGE HURLEY FIRST met Wayne St. Pierre back in the tenth grade, she knew he was the one for her. From the first day when he had teased her about her golden hair that was softer than corn silk to his fingers, she knew they would be together for a lifetime.

I'll bet that's one of those wigs, he'd said.

Wrong, smart guy. It's the real deal, she'd answered.

After they started dating, fell in love and all but said they would stay together forever, he had teased her about her tiny feet that always got cold even on the warmest summer nights. Later he laughed at how funny her toes looked separated by the white cotton she put between them when she painted her nails.

She had been the perfect wife, the best mother to their two boys, Spencer and Harold. She kept their domestic affairs in order, paid the bills on time, got the boys to scouts each week. And two or three times a month she hired a babysitter to watch the boys while she and Wayne went out to dinner or to see a movie. She had even overlooked the condoms she found hidden in his wallet, and the pink lipstick on his work shirt collar.

She recalled now what they had said to each other that night the storm knocked the maple tree in their front yard right out of its roots as they lay cuddled in a patchwork quilt on the brass bed they had bought in the Amish countryside, that no matter what hardships they endured, no matter how rough the road got, they would stick it out, would always be together.

Marge knew they were anything but together now. Every day since he had come home from the hospital a year ago, he had been relying on one drug after another to maintain the delicate balance of a man vacillating between suicidal despair and homicidal rage. Weekly trips to the psychiatrist's office and daily doses of prescription drugs to fight the pain and insomnia couldn't hide his aggression or calm his nerves. Every day things had gotten a little worse:

"It was barbaric what those prisoners did to my Wayne. He was such a gentle and loving man before all this. He never lost his temper. He never beat me or yelled at the kids. He never used to swear. All he talks about now is the prison, the riot, and those animals who assaulted him. It's been over a year and you would think it would get a little easier, but it's only gotten worse. I'd do anything to have the man I married back.

"It's the rage, you know? He's consumed by it. I know it isn't his fault. The pain is so paralyzing at times that he can't keep it to himself. But Wayne's obsession with what happened doesn't just end with a lot of talk. He's as paranoid as all outdoors. Every night he takes out his guns and cleans them in the living room. He sleeps with a shotgun beside the bed, too, and everywhere he goes he carries a pistol in his waistband. It scares me to death. At first, I thought, Oh, it's okay. The guns make him feel better. He'll never use them. Then one day last week we were coming home from his weekly appointment with the psychiatrist when we passed a van carrying prisoners on the highway. Wayne pulled out his pistol, rolled down the window and came within a squeeze of the trigger of shooting at the van. I was forced to pull the car over to the side until he calmed down.

"He can't even hold a simple conversation anymore without blowing up. He sees a young black man in the most innocuous situation, a television commercial, say, or walking in the mall, and he loses it. He curses and uses the N word over and over. He even uses it in front of the children. The boys have stopped having their friends over because they're afraid and ashamed. Wayne yells at them sometimes for just being boys. They've learned to stay away from him when the rage becomes more than they can handle. Our younger boy went through a terrible period of nightmares. He'd seen his father in the hospital. He'd seen what those prisoners had done to him. Then he started waking up in the middle of the night screaming and crying his little eyes out. The older boy hasn't spoken to his father since he killed their parakeet, Blue-Boy. Wayne strangled the poor little bird in a fit of rage one evening after it landed on his shoulder.

"Yesterday, I came home from work, hung my coat up and walked into the living room. Wayne was sitting in his chair crying. When he saw me he stood up all of a sudden and slapped me down again. All because I had bought a little battery-operated vibrator for myself. At first, I didn't care that he was impotent. It would go away eventually, I told myself. But it hasn't and it's been a year. He hasn't touched me, except for that one night when he was drunk; he thought he could keep it going long enough to make me feel good. It didn't happen. To make matters worse, he was so angry that he squeezed my breasts until they turned black and blue.

"I'm still young and pretty and I have needs, too. My body's still alive. One day I saw a mail order advertisement in one of Wayne's magazines. There was absolutely nothing dirty about buying a vibrator. I once heard Dr. Ruth talking about it on *Oprah*. She said it was healthy for a man or woman to pleasure themselves when their spouse was unable to perform sexually. Wasn't it better than having an affair? I thought so. Well, a week ago Wayne was snooping through my things when he found my green vibrator in the bottom drawer of my dresser. He came into the kitchen, threw it in a paper bag and smashed it to smithereens with a ball peen hammer. Here's your goddam sex toy, Marge! You're so disgusting! he screamed, and right in front of the boys. Then he slapped me so hard blood squirted out my nose.

"You'd think it would get a little easier with each day. But it only gets harder and lonelier. I cry all the time now. I've had two nervous breakdowns, and now I'm taking three kinds of pills a day myself. Probably will be for a long time. I never had to be strong before. I just never had to be strong."

WHEN WAYNE ST. PIERRE TRIES to remember the way it was when he and Marge and their two boys were a family, almost nothing comes to mind. He recalls dates and events and activities, but he can't for the life of him catch what it felt like. He can say, "I loved them so much," but he cannot retrieve that love. In his mind he can replay the scenes of intimacy, fatherly tenderness, and family devotion, but they are drained of everything but the words to say them in. All he can do is sit in his chair remembering every detail of his ordeal again and again, not just because the wounds won't scab over, but because the memory is all there is to feel:

"I don't know what started that riot, or why it started. The fellows I work with said it started because those animals didn't have anything better to do. That's just what they are, too, a bunch of animals. There was a time when I didn't think this way, but I know better now.

"That Friday morning, I went to work just like any other morning. I knew it was going to be a busy day. Fridays always were. Visitors coming and going all day, off-duty officers stopping by to pick up their paychecks or to get a dollar haircut. Fridays were downright hectic. Anyway, somewhere around ten o'clock that morning, I went on my lunch break but instead of eating, I went over to the hospital to see a friend of mine who happens to be the head nurse. While I was there, Betty, that's her name, she gave me a new first-aid kit for the front gate area after massaging a kink out of my neck. All I remember right after that was coming out of the hospital and hearing the call over my walkie-talkie that an officer was down and needed help. I immediately rushed to the scene to render assistance. That's about the last thing I remember.

"Don't talk to me about being fair. I was more than fair. But you know what? You can't be fair to wild animals. You know why? Because they don't have any conscience, that's why. Think how it is, if you can manage it. Your nose crushed and kicked upside down. Your teeth busted off at the gums from the boot of a white trash nigger. Seven ribs cracked. Your testicles crushed. Splinters all through your rectum and intestines from a broken broomstick. That's what they did to me, those low-life animals. I got two goddamn steel plates in my face! An artificial nose! Pulverized cheekbones!

"That young white-trash nigger, the one who kicked my face in? He's going to get his one day. That son-of-a-bitch maxed out his sentence last month! Can you believe that! But I know where he lives. I got his address and one day I might just find that white nigger and see how bad he is without his other nigger friends. That black nigger who broke that stick off in me? His days are numbered, too, just as sure as I'm sitting here. There ain't a prison in this state where he's safe.

"Nobody knows how something like this affects your whole life. Some of my fellow officers were beaten and tortured, too, and they're already back to work. I'm not one of them. With all the metal in my face, I get these god-awful headaches when it gets cold. I don't leave the house much anymore, either. It ain't safe out there. My wife Marge wanted me to go out to dinner on her birthday last week, and I finally gave in after she cried like a goddamn baby for two days. When we got to the restaurant I had to sit with my back against the wall so I could see the front door. I can't stand to have anyone behind me.

"Lately my doctor's been dropping little hints that I might soon be ready to go back to work. He's off his rocker. Tell me how somebody in my condition's supposed to work. Long as I got insurance and my paycheck coming every two weeks, I ain't never going back in that den of niggers. No, sirree.

"Marge keeps bugging me too, about going back to work. One day last week, she left a note for me on the kitchen table. I read it and laughed like a goddamn maniac before I broke every piece of china we owned:

Dear Wayne,

You know that I love you very much. But I can't go on like this much longer. Please, for the sake of our marriage and the kids, please consider going back to work. Or maybe you could find a new job. I don't know how much longer I can go on working two jobs and taking care of you and the boys when I get home. I love you, Wayne, and I just want things to be the way they used to be, that's all. Please don't be mad.

Love, Marge

"That's what her note said. 'Please don't be mad.' Well, next week that psychiatrist will be turning in his recommendation as to whether

I'm healthy enough to return to work. If he says I got to go back, I might just drive down to the city ghetto and turn vigilante. I might just kill me a nigger. Black. White. It wouldn't matter to me.

"As for Marge, I'm not worried about her. She'd never leave me. We made a pact a long time ago. Besides, she knows I'd probably go off the deep end if she ever did."

1993

chapter nineteen

THE DAY THE PRISON REOPENED, Fat Daddy reclaimed Donnie Blossom and then proceeded to give him a vicious ass-whipping for reasons Fat Daddy called general principle. Donnie reciprocated with a homecoming present of his own—a needle and syringe and two fat balloons of heroin. Fat Daddy kissed him for it, then got his last nod on.

In his mind, Donnie still watches Fat Daddy careening backwards onto his bunk, his limbs flopping spasmodically, as if a giant sledgehammer had hit him. Donnie backs out of the cell sloshing the jar's last drops of liquid over the bed sheets, the polyester rugs, and the two cardboard boxes containing everything Fat Daddy owns. He thumbs back the lighter's starter, touches the flame to a red bandanna and tosses it with a deft casualness. The loud whump! blows his hair back as a ball of flame shoots up within the cell. He stares at the ink-black smoke freight-training from the doorway as he closes the cell door, drops the bolt and attaches the lock. He takes the back steps two at a time, savoring the faintly sweet smell of gasoline that trails behind him.

DR. B.J. DALLET TRADED in her marriage and luxurious home on a tree-lined street in the suburbs for a young sculptor named Fiorenzo and a cozy studio apartment in the city. Resilient and reclaimed, she is on the move again, healthy and transformed. She still sees her star pupil, though only once a month now. Each time, she brings him an armful of books and new friends. Now she thinks of her simple needs: silk scarves, French manicures, a steady lover. Now her fountain of youth is in the living, all things in moderation.

OLIVER'S VINDICATION TOOK months but it came. He would return to his old cell around the corner from Oyster, and two tiers below Early. It was a glorious morning the day they released him. For the first time in fifteen months he was able to go outside, but the blessing was mixed. So violet was the sky that he couldn't help contrasting its ultra beauty with the catastrophic sight of a gutted courtyard. Gone was the little clapboard chapel, demolished by the same yellow caterpillar that had dug up the flowers and shrubs and sidewalks, that tore up the hundred-year-old oak tree from its roots; that leveled the redbrick Home Block and sliced through the sheet rock and two-by-fours of the Young Guns Boxing Gym and the Free Yourself Law Library. The chapel steps where the born-agains had sat on summer evenings praying and gossiping were now lying upside down on a heap of broken walls in the corner of the courtyard. Oliver was devastated by the demolition of what was once a street with clean little whitewashed buildings and a lovely church steeple for a skyline. Now the place was nothing but a barren lot of packed dirt.

He walked down Turk's Street and stopped in the education building to see Mr. Sommers and the others. Rhoda Cherry welcomed him back and shocked him when she told him the news about Mr. Sommers. Oliver's good friend and former boss had recently accepted a position as an assistant professor at a local college. "Mr. Sommers said he'd be in touch with you, Oliver. I'm your new boss now. Other than that, nothing else has changed."

At lunchtime he found Early, Oyster and Peabo, and the four friends sat on a concrete slab where the third base bleachers used to be. The air was cool. The pizza for lunch was so fine. Four lifers sitting on a cold slab of concrete, marveling over each other's presence, and startled by the gutted landscape that used to be a neighborhood. When Oliver started humming a Peter, Paul and Mary song, Early said, "My flowers may be gone, but we're still here. What I can't figure out is where all the birds have gone. Hasn't been a single blackbird fly over this place all spring."

"Or a pigeon, either," said Oyster, "thank the good Lord. We thought maybe your gallbladder operation had something to do with it, Early."

"That's the stupidest thing I ever heard," said Early, turning to Oyster and frowning.

"Why? You wasn't around for six months. Who else was going to feed them? Hambone couldn't."

"Hambone was in the riot too?"

"No," said Peabo. "He tried to get pussy from that she-cat he was feeding. The cat damn near scratched his eyes out." They all laughed hysterically.

After he took a deep breath, Oliver said, "Maybe the stench of death is keeping the birds away."

"That's as good a guess as any," Early answered.

To their right, manning the number one gun tower, Sergeant Mervis Dewey eyed the glistening swirls of concertina wire circling along the top of the wall, placed there no doubt to discourage any would-be copy-cats. Better late than never, Oliver thought. Standing beneath the tower was blind Milo tapping his red and silver cane back and forth against the concrete. Oliver stood and wiped his hands on a little paper napkin. "Think I'll go say hello to Milo," he said.

"Don't get mad if he calls you Knuckle Head Smith or something worse," warned Oyster.

"What's that supposed to mean?"

"When was the last time you talked to him?"

"I don't know. It's been a good while."

"I thought so. Nurse Blanche say he's got that old-timers' disease." Oyster said, laughing.

"Goddammit, Oyster! How many times do I have to tell you? He's got Alzheimer's disease, Oliver," Early said. "Oyster, that shit isn't funny one bit."

"Who said it was? All I'm saying is he don't know you or me from a can of paint."

"Hey, lighten up, Early," Oliver said. "Sometimes a man has to laugh to keep from crying, doesn't he, Oyster?" They sat in silence for a while, still appraising the landscape, or lack of one. After a few minutes, Oliver said, "Any good news you can give me, Early?"

"Yeah. I.M. White's black ass got canned."

"Yeah, I heard."

HE MOVED BACK AND FORTH in front of the mirror to catch a glimpse of himself. He was grinning. His green eyes were shining and he was as eager and happy as he had ever been.

Fifteen minutes later he was wishing he had a box of bonbons for the attractive journalist who strolled into his classroom, swinging a tote bag at her hip, her canary yellow and electric blue paisley skirt swirling around her legs. "Hello, Oliver Priddy," Hope Best said, setting her bag on the desk and gliding toward him like an ice skater. "Someone we both know asked me to give you a hug. Is it okay?"

Oliver glanced at the prisoners who were on the trail of her scent and curves outside his classroom door. "I'll let you know when it's safe. How's that?" Oliver said. He sat at a desk in the front of the room and watched her tan legs disappear under her long skirt as she sat cross-legged in the comfortable chair he had arranged for her to sit in. She placed her notebook in her lap and opened it to a page of handwritten notes. Oliver lifted the back of his hand to his mouth and squeezed the soft flesh into his teeth. He didn't want to derail her in any way—shake her out of proportion to her naïveté. He smiled and said in a matter of fact tone, "I hate to say this, but if a certain person sees you sitting on their precious furniture like that I'm going to hear about it later, if you know what I mean."

"Oh, my. Really? I'm sorry. I wasn't thinking." She smiled and gracefully placed her feet on the floor and Oliver said, "You were just being yourself."

For the next ten minutes, riot discussion mingled with questions about his ordeal and exoneration, the chitchat of daily life, and a shopping list of questions she had written on her note pad. "You don't seem bitter about the frame-up job they tried to pull on you," she said.

"Well, the fact is, Ms. Best, this place is run by a bunch of ruthless people who lie and oppress and swindle the same way people who run your world do. I learned a long time ago not to take things too personally because when you do, that's when they really slam their foot on your neck. The trick is to keep your eyes open and stay one step ahead of them at all times." Oliver grinned at her until she turned her head to the side and smiled again. He thought it was the sweetest gesture.

"I don't know what's wrong with the world," she said. "You're so right. Many of the people I work with make good money and have great job security, but they still want more. And what they want is power. Thank goodness you kept good records."

"That and the fact that I had a boss who was decent enough to keep looking for them."

"I was hoping you would start off by giving me a clearer sense of what prison life is like, Oliver. None of the movies I've ever seen get beyond what I think are stereotypes. Like how prisoners deal with loneliness and family relationships, when loved ones die, how friendships are formed, and things like that. Then later you can tell me all about your educational experiences. Oh, and I've heard so much about your award-winning poem. You must read it to me later. Let's see, what else is there?" She looked down at her notes. "Also, if you would, tell me what words like rehabilitation and remorse mean to you."

"Okay, I'll start with loneliness. Every prisoner deals with loneliness in his own way. It's been a long time since I've been lonely. I keep extremely busy. Going on thirteen years now I've had the most fantastic love affair with higher learning and it has turned my entire prison experience into a university. I have a few good friends in here who I wouldn't trade for anything in the world. This is the only life we have now, so we try to make the best of it. We've learned to appreciate little things like the steady rhythm of a rubber ball bouncing against the wall or a pair of dice clicking on the sidewalks, the smell of freshly mowed grass, a clear blue sky speckled with birds. And color. Every prisoner I know is crazy about color. Burgundy red blood on the sidewalk, pink chips in the sky, the Kelly-green sleeves of a secretary's blouse, any color you can think of strikes us with awe." He paused and took out two tea bags from his shirt pocket. "A little birdie told me you like to drink herbal tea," he said, grinning at her. "How many sugars you take?"

"Two, please."

"I'll be right back."

Two minutes later he returned with two steaming hot mugs of water. He set his down and moved the tea bag up and down in B.J. Dallet's blue ceramic mug. He handed it to her and said, "As I was saying, the thing about loneliness is that everyone has his own way of dealing with it. Some stay busy and active and that seems to work for them. Some go crazy and do themselves in. And some resort to homosexuality. Men kill over that stuff in here, and get killed too." He paused for a few seconds and then lowered his voice when he went on. "And in case you didn't know it, there are real-life love affairs in this place, too, just like anywhere else. A secretary, a teacher, a nurse, a female guard, or any other willing woman, can ease the pain in a man's groin and at the same time ease the I'm-so-lonesome-I-could-die stuff in his head." Oliver paused again to give her a chance to ask another question and when she didn't, his serious stare turned into a smile as he said, "Now as to your inquiries about rehabilitation and remorse, no offense now. Those are important sounding subjects, but addressing them in generalities won't tell you much about what you want to know. I take it you want to hear more than some old cliché about how every man is a road to himself, or how the most contrite heart can never undo one's gravest wrongs, don't you?"

"You got it," she said, her jaw hanging. She was mesmerized.

"Okay. I don't want anyone to ever think if I died in here tomorrow my life was a waste or in any way absent of worth. I gotta tell you, Ms. Best, the love and support I've been blessed with over these years has been more profound than you can imagine. The care given to me by my family and professors and friends has been unflinching and unconditional, and that love and care has surrounded me so thoroughly that the dreams and experiences I've had, the journeys I've been on in pursuit of my goals, have made my life as fulfilling and abundant as yours or anyone else's. You may not be able to fathom this, Ms. Best, but, all things considered, I've led a pretty normal life these years I've been in here. It's ironic as hell that I ended up in prison and found my calling. I can't even begin to tell you how much I love the art of teaching. And—"

"Let me interrupt you right there, if I may, Oliver. What is it about teaching that you love so much? Would you explain that to me?"

Oliver smiled again and shook his head and said, "Yes, well, it has to do with the feeling you get inside when you present a new slice of knowledge to someone and you see the light come on when they get it. That's one thing. The other has to do with the professional challenge of presenting information that is completely foreign to someone in such a way that he or she gets it, you know? And that's what moves me the most, this challenge. Okay, I'm in prison, but being in prison does not prohibit me from learning these things, and living life to its fullest. I think it's nobody's loss but our own if we go through life failing to discover that life is inside ourselves, not just in the world that surrounds us. We can still discover all of its splendor, even in a place like this filthy, dilapidated prison." He stopped, surprised by what he had said and how. Then, as if he knew her and her philosophy, he spoke intimately to her, his voice soft and animated. "You know, your name says it all. Hope Best. That's just what I do. I hope for the best every day of my life. It's strange. I feel I know a lot about you just from knowing your name. Like you couldn't possibly go through life with that name and see the glass any other way but half full all the time, could you?" He didn't give her a chance to answer. "And if you yourself, as lovely and dainty as you are, if you were a prisoner like me, you'd still be hoping for the best, wouldn't you?"

"I'd like to think so," she said in wonder.

He paused to bask in the sunshine of her smile. "I know you would, and you know how I know? Because I can tell that you know that life is life everywhere, don't you? You get it, don't you?"

"I get it, Oliver Priddy." She was singing her words again.

Once upon a time he had bragged to himself over and over about his good fortune. Couldn't wait each week to find her sitting in his classroom waiting for him to lead her into his office for their private dance. He was thirty-four now and his feet shivered for a two-step like never before. He wondered if this Hope Best was the kind of woman who was free enough to snatch a moment of privacy with him in the middle of a stupid, blind prison. Would she two-step with him? "You know what?" he said. "I'm going on sixteen years in this place, and I still sing and dance every chance I get. Do you dance?"

"All the time," she said.

"Slow or fast?"

"Whatever the occasion calls for."

"Would you like to dance with me?"

"Sure. Any time."

"Come on. I've got music in my office. And after we dance you can sit cross-legged on top of my desk it you want."

INSIDE HIS OFFICE SHE watches him close the door with a skillful backswing of his foot. He moves quickly to the window and pulls down the Venetian blinds, angles the slats so there is just enough natural light and privacy. She glances at the rows of books on the shelves behind his desk and grows excited by the names: Emerson. James. Frankl. Dickinson. Husserl. Frost. Whitehead. Nietzsche. And so many more. Someone has fed his mind well. The sparkling fringes of her electric blue and yellow skirt swish and glide to the music that has already begun to play in her head. He picks up a shoebox of cassette tapes, says, "How about a little Otis Redding?" She answers, "Excellent choice." He inserts the tape, presses fast forward and stops before his favorite song, "Try a Little Tenderness."

The horns begin and she imitates blowing a slide trombone. When her arm is fully extended, she curtsies like a little girl and closes in on him. He embraces her, his footwork is flawless, his hold on her firm and confident. Never mind the tinny tone of the speaker, they are dancing alone. She is floating inwardly, remembering other such joys. Boardwalks and stuffed tigers. Purple asters she left unpicked in her garden so others passing by could enjoy them too. Bicycle rides and spinning bottles. Breathing into the pocket of his shirt, she hears him whisper, "Here we go." Just then the tempo of the song picks up and, hand in hand, they two-step, balance and twirl in perfect timing. A slow jitterbug. "You're fantastic," she says, and winks. They are inward toward the other now, bound and joined by the sheer fun of it all, a knowing glance, a winking eye. This is what is beneath their private dance.

It's more than serendipity when a grown woman who has seen it all, had it all, finds leaf-sigh rapture in a private dance with a prisoner. Her sagacity tells her he is not in that class of shifty-eyed criminals depicted in novels, with cagey hearts and misanthropic motives, bent on assuaging their luckless existences by hook or crook. Nor does he seem to be one of those unfortunate casualties of fate who avoid complete self-annihilation just so they can taunt the memory of a missing father or a neglectful mother. She knows he is cut out for better things than this. He has so much to offer the world. Not merely a prisoner in prisoner's clothing, but a mind-free man in a drab brown uniform. Graceful. Tattooless. Refined. A gentleman in every way. And handsome to boot.

When the dance is over she says to herself what she has no need to say out loud. That I have made friends all over the world. Have touched lepers on a leper colony, bathed with strangers on a Greek island, eaten roots with a tribe of Zulu warriors. And now I have seen the bright promise of hope shining in the eyes of a condemned man. And, oh the way he dances! How close and loose he holds me, his fingers in my hair.

What she says out loud is how enjoyable that was and would he read his prize poem to her now. Goose pimpled, she sits cross-legged on his desk, blowing gently into her mug of hot herbal tea. She sucks at the cup rim, closes her eyes and sighs in pleasure. She can hear him breathing close to her as he begins to read: "And up/ with the sun/ comes/ two four six/ purple irises /swaying/ in the morning breeze./ And there!/ one two three four five/sparrows singing/in the rain gutter/ high above/ the red gun tower."

ACKNOWLEDGMENTS

Thank you to Judith Trustone, my editor for ten years, without whom the mentor-a-prisoner concept would not be the success it is today. Judith, you are so sagacious. I am eternally grateful to have worked so closely with you over the years. And to my typists and early readers, those lovely Swarthmore seniors, Satya, Melanie and Erika, I thoroughly appreciate all you did to make this book a better read.

Thank you to: Cheryl Simo, Donna Stewart, Kim Passione, Albert Benaglio, Theodore "Champ" Brown, Chuckie Redshaw, John Minarik, Robert Faruq Wideman, Billy Boy Murray, John Pace, Dave Myrick, George Halter, Michael Anwar Dukes, Earl Rahman Box, Anthony "Big Jake" Jacobs, Little Charlie Block, Vincent Sharif Boyd, Roger Button, Gary Gunn, John Mayfield, Tony Dunlap, Donnie Wilson, Theodore Anwar Moody, Luis "Suave" Gonzalez, Chris Reddinger, Wayne "Weezy" Kightlinger, Van, Doza, B.J. Withall and the entire Withall family.

Thank you to everyone at the University of Pittsburgh—Dr. Jean Winsand, without whom this book would not exist; Dr. Fiore Pugliano, Dr. Harry Sartain, Dr. Bob Marshall, Dr. Robert Sattler, Dr. Louis Pingel, Dr. Don McBurney, Dr. Alice Scales, Dr. Shirley Biggs, Dr. Ray Garris, Dr. Ogle Duff, Dr. Anthony Nitko, Dr. Maxine Roberts, Dr. Norman Graves, Dr. Janet Gibson, and Professor John Manear. I also owe a special debt of gratitude to Dr. Stanley Jacobs, my former boss at Villanova University, and that awesome red-headed professor, Kathy Blood, my "supervisor", as well as to Mr. Rob Bender, my former DOC supervisor.

Thank you to everyone at Acer Hill Publishing and Amazon for their enthusiasm and dedication to this project. And many special thanks to the truly brilliant Swarthmore student, Christine Song, who created a spectacular website for this book and my other works:
www.authorpatmiddleton.com

Finally, my deepest passion and thanks to my Marta, for *everything.*

READER'S GUIDE FOR
EUREKA MAN

By Patrick Middleton

DISCUSSION QUESTIONS

1. Who was you favorite character? Why?

2. Why do you think Oliver killed Jimmy Six? Did he lose his temper or was there more to it than that?

3. Oliver's mother is a prime example of someone deeply flawed yet somewhat sympathetic. After her second marriage fails and her children are living with relatives, she ends up in a sanitarium for alcoholics. Yet she shows great resilience. She stops drinking, she remarries, and her life goes on. Do you think Oliver's mother is a sympathetic or unsympathetic character? Explain your answer.

4. Social scientists generally agree that a person's character is shaped to a large extent by the environment in which he or she is raised. To what extent do you think this is true for Oliver? Also, do you think Oliver's character is altered, or changed, by the environment he found at the training school?

5. Do you believe Champ is justified for his hatred of white people? Do you think racism is inherent or taught?

6. Many of the characters in the book are deeply flawed and at the same time sympathetic. Who is the least sympathetic character of all?

7. There are also strong characters in the story who possess both grace and wisdom. Who do you feel is the strongest character?

8. What do you think motivated Fat Daddy? Though he is a vicious rapist and abuser, he shows genuine loyalty and compassion to Handsome Johnny when Johnny returns to the prison after being locked away in a mental hospital for seven years. Do you think one can be a good friend and at the same time a deeply flawed person? Explain your answer.

9. Discuss the options Oliver may have had in dealing with the threat from Fat Daddy. Do you think he would have been justified in carrying out his preemptive strike? Explain.

10. In her keynote address to the graduates, Professor B.J. Dallet tells them the blues is an integral part of life, and "when it plays, it tests the quality and arrangement of our character." Compare her words with musician Willie Dixon's definition of the blues: "The blues is truth. You can't make up the blues, you have to live it." How does Professor Dallet respond to the blues in her life? And how does that blues reveal her character?

11. When the cell door closes on Oliver the first night he arrives in the training school, he settles his nerves and revives his hope when he remembers he only has nine months and a few days before he turns eighteen and is free again. In the final chapters of the story, he loses hope again when it appears his life as a scholar is over. Yet in the end, hope appears on the horizon and he is "as happy as he's ever been." What do you think is the source of Oliver's resilience?

12. What stereotypes about prisoners does this story tend to support? Are there any the story dispels? When considering your answer, think of any preconceived notions you may have held about prisoners before reading this book.

13. What stereotypes about prison itself—the physical environment, setting, and mores – does the story uphold? Are there any it dispels? Again think of your own preconceived notions.

AUTHOR BIOGRAPHY

Patrick Middleton was born in Washington, D.C., and grew up in La Plata, Maryland. He has been incarcerated in Pennsylvania since 1975.

From 1978 to 1990, Middleton was a full-time student at the University of Pittsburgh and the recipient of several distinguished fellowships and teaching awards. He graduated summa cum laude in 1983 and earned his master's degree in language communications. In 1990, Middleton became the first and only prisoner in America to earn a doctoral degree in a classroom setting.

Middleton was an adjunct faculty member at Villanova University from 2007 to 2010. His nonfiction books include two teaching manuals— *Introduction to Experimental Psychology and Research Methods*, a self-help book, *Healing Our Imprisoned Minds*, and a memoir, *Incorrigible. Eureka Man*, a semi-autobiographical work, is his first novel.

CPSIA information can be obtained at www.ICGtesting.com
Printed in the USA
LVOW10s2000301015

460458LV00019B/535/P